SCORCHED EARTH
Robert Muchamore

Hodder
Children's
Books

A division of Hachette Children's Books

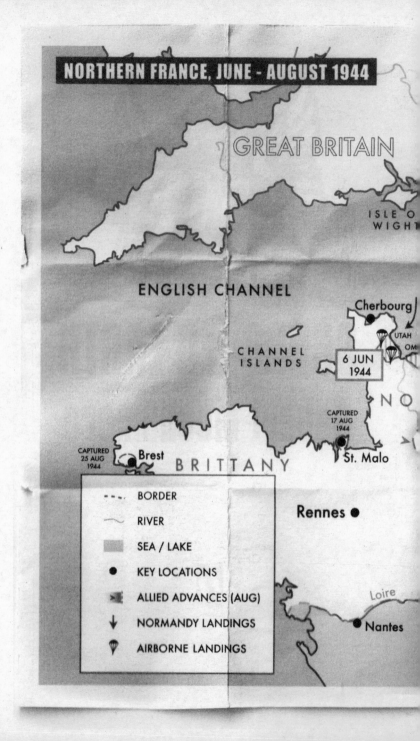

Hitler boasted that his European empire would last 1,000 years, but by June 1944 it was dying. In the east, the Soviet Union had retaken all of the territory he'd invaded three summers earlier and the Red Army now approached German soil. American forces had fought north through Italy to the outskirts of Rome, while in Britain 6,000 ships and half a million men were making final preparations for a cross-Channel invasion.

France remained under German occupation, but Nazi resources were stretched and the population was becoming rebellious. Resistance organisations had infiltrated every aspect of French life and thousands of young men chose to go on the run, rather than submit to deportation and forced labour in German mines and factories.

Many of these runaways formed gangs, known as the

Maquis. Most lived in mountains or woodlands, with limited shelter and no option but to steal to survive. Until Allied boots hit French beaches, these young men were one of the biggest threats to German rule in France, and the Nazis were determined to wipe them out.

Part One

June 5th–June 6th 1944

CHAPTER ONE

Monday 5 June 1944

'Mondays have never liked me,' Paul Clarke said, trying to keep cheerful as his face creased with pain.

The fifteen-year-old had turned his ankle and skidded down an embankment. A khaki backpack cushioned the muddy slide, but he had dark streaks down his trousers and puddle water trickling into his boot.

'Nice slide?' Luc Mayefski asked, offering a hand as rain pelted their waxed jackets.

The teenagers' hands couldn't have been more different. Paul's slender fingers linked with a great ham fist, and even with 30 kilos of explosive in Paul's pack, Luc didn't strain as he tugged his skinny cohort out of the mud.

If it had just been the pair of them Luc would have

taken the piss out of Paul's tumble, but these trained members of Charles Henderson's Espionage Research Unit B (CHERUB) had to show a united front for the benefit of their inexperienced companions, Michel and Daniel.

Michel was an eighteen-year-old Maquis. Nine months' living in the woods had left him stringy, with wild hair and a wire tourniquet holding on the sole of his right boot. His brother Daniel was only eleven. Their father was a prisoner in Germany and their mother had vanished after being arrested by the Gestapo. Daniel had chosen to live on the run with his brother, rather than be dumped at an orphanage.

'Are your explosives OK?' Daniel asked, as Paul joined the brothers on a muddy track at the base of the wooded embankment.

'Plastic explosive is stable,' Paul explained, as he tested his ankle and decided he could walk off the pain. 'You can safely cut it, mould it. It wouldn't blow up if you hit it with a hammer.'

Luc checked his compass and led off, eyes squinting as the early sun shot between tree trunks. Even with the rain Luc was sweating and he liked the earthy forest smell and the little squelch each time his boot landed.

Paul and Michel were suffering after 15 kilometres under heavy packs, but Daniel had done them proud.

He'd walked all night, but refused to stop even when doubled up with a stitch.

Luc had been out this way on a recon trip two days earlier, and he turned off track at a point he'd marked by pushing two sticks into the soft ground.

'There's a good view down from this ridge,' Luc explained, as he led the way. 'But keep quiet. The sound carries across the valley and we're not far from the guard.'

'If there is one,' Paul added.

The undergrowth was dense and Michel lifted his brother over a fast stream carrying the overnight rain. As Daniel got set down, Paul was touched by the way Michel put an arm around his little brother's back and kissed his cheek.

'Proud of you,' Michel whispered.

Daniel smiled, then squirmed away, embarrassed, when he realised Paul was looking.

After a dozen more paces, Luc crouched and pushed branches aside. He'd opened a view over a ledge into a steep-walled valley cut into chalkstone. Water dripped off leaves on to Paul's neck as he peered at two sets of train tracks running along the valley's base. Sixty metres to his right, the tracks entered the mouth of a tunnel blasted through the steep hillside.

'You'd never be able to bomb this from the air,' Luc whispered, as he slid a pair of German Zeiss binoculars from their case. After wiping condensation off the lenses, he raised them to his eyes and looked towards a wooden guard hut near the tunnel mouth. The magnified view showed no sign of life and a padlock on the door.

'We're in luck,' Luc said.

The tunnel formed part of a main line running north from Paris, taking trains to Calais on the Channel coast, or forking east into Belgium and Germany. The Germans had built guard huts at the ends of hundreds of important bridges and tunnels, but only had enough manpower to staff a fraction of them.

'Nice binoculars,' Paul noted, as Luc passed them over. 'Where'd you get them?'

'Drunk Osttruppen[1],' Luc explained. 'They'd swap the uniform on their backs for a bottle of brandy.'

Paul backed away from the ledge as Luc glanced at his pocket watch. 'If there's a guard at the other end, we'll sneak up and take him out from behind. Our target train is due to reach the tunnel at around seven a.m. That gives us half an hour to lay explosives along the tunnel and get in position, but with air raids and sabotage, there's no guarantee that any train will run on time.

---

[1] Osttruppen – German soldiers recruited from occupied countries such as Russia, Ukraine and Poland. Most volunteered to avoid starvation in labour camps. Osttruppen were regarded as poor soldiers and were usually given lowly duties such as emptying latrines, burying bodies and working as servants to senior officers.

Especially one that's come all the way from Hanover.'

As Luc spoke, Paul slid canvas straps off his badly-chafed shoulders and moaned with relief as his pack settled in the undergrowth. An exploratory finger under the shirt collar came out bloody, but there was no time for first aid.

After unbuckling the pack, Paul took out two grubby cloth sacks. They seemed to be half full of potatoes, but the uneven lumps were plastic explosive, linked with detonator cord like a string of giant Christmas lights.

Paul looked at Michel. 'Remember what Henderson said. The weakest part of the tunnel is around the mouth, so pack plenty around there.'

As Luc and Michel each grabbed one of Paul's sacks and slung it over their shoulders alongside their own heavy packs, Paul looked at Daniel and tried to sound upbeat. 'Ready to hike?'

The brothers quickly hugged, then Luc gave Daniel his binoculars before leading Michel along the side of the valley.

'You break those and I'll break you,' Luc warned.

As there was no guard, Luc and Michel faced an easy journey down to the tunnel mouth using uneven steps carved into the chalkstone. When they reached the mouth, their task was to unravel the chains of explosive along the tunnel's 300-metre length and retreat to a safe distance, ready to trigger them.

Meantime, Paul and Daniel had to find a vantage point atop the forested hill through which the tunnel cut. Once in position, they had to identify their target: a 600-metre-long cargo train carrying twenty Tiger II tanks, dozens of 88-mm artillery guns and enough spare parts and ammunition to keep the 108th Heavy Panzer Battalion functioning for several weeks.

Since handing over the explosives, the weight of Paul's pack had dropped from 30 kilos to less than four. The bread, cheese and apples that had spent the night at the bottom were squashed, but the two lads scoffed eagerly and shared a canteen of milk as they followed a track to the top of the hill.

Two trains steamed south through the tunnel as they walked and Paul was glad to be up here in fresh air, rather than laying explosives along the dank, soot-filled tunnel.

'Hope they're OK,' Daniel said warily, as he eyed plumes of smoke billowing from either end of the tunnel.

'You have to keep low and put a wet cloth over your face,' Paul said. 'It's not fun, but they'll survive.'

Daniel stopped worrying when he found a bend in the narrow footpath, and spotted another marker from Luc's recon trip. The dense forest made trainspotting hopeless from ground level, but Luc said he'd climbed to a position where he could see trains approaching along several kilometres of snaking track.

The eleven-year-old wasn't just along for the ride. Growing up in Paris, Daniel had earned a reputation as a daredevil, clambering over rooftops, diving off bridges and breaking both arms when he'd leapt between two balconies for a dare. After joining the Maquis in the woods north of Paris, Daniel made a name for himself as a forest lookout, able to climb branches too slim to hold an adult's weight.

'I'll have to lose all this gear,' Daniel said. 'Put it in your pack in case we need to make a quick getaway.'

Paul didn't like taking orders from an eleven-year-old, but Daniel was a good kid and he watched the youngster pull off his boots and strip down to a stocky frame, clad in grotty vest and undershorts. Regular climbing had toughened Daniel's skin and he looked more ape than human as he launched himself into the branches with Luc's binoculars swinging from his neck.

'Careful,' Paul warned, as Daniel vanished into the leafy canopy, becoming nothing but rustling sounds and occasional shifts in the early sunlight.

Paul burrowed down his pack and found the phosphorous grenade he'd use to warn Luc and Michel when they spotted their target. Twenty metres up, Daniel swung his leg over a fork, clamped the thick branch between his thighs and wiped a palm smeared in bird crap down the front of his vest.

'Slippery, but the view's great,' Daniel said, happy with himself as he stared over the treetops at fields, villages and a clear view of the railway tracks approaching both ends of the tunnel. 'Why don't you hop up and join me?'

CHAPTER TWO

Edith Mercier looked uncomfortable as she lugged a wicker basket along Beauvais' Rue Desgroux. The rain had stopped, but the slim fifteen-year-old trod cautiously because the cobbles were still damp. She'd passed a postman and a few folks heading to work, but this municipal district would stay quiet for another hour.

Allied bombs had demolished shops and houses behind the Rue Desgroux and opened deep cracks in the façade of the town's main administrative office. Behind stacked sandbags and a side wall braced with wooden props, staff inside the offices continued with duties, ranging from civil weddings to issuing bicycle licences.

The upper floor was used by the city's German

administrators, so the building warranted a rain-soaked swastika pennant and a single German guard out front. Edith quickly glanced at this guard before taking a long step and deliberately losing her balance. Her basket spilled, sending onions bobbling in all directions, and she howled to make sure that her 'accident' wasn't missed.

She'd hoped the guard would rush to her aid. But the young soldier had arranged sandbags into a kind of lounger and had the air of someone who'd only get up if a bomb went off, or a senior officer threatened a court martial for lying down on the job.

Edith steamed. She'd practised realistic falls back in the woods and the slippery cobbles should have made her stunt believable.

'Oh, my back,' she moaned. 'Can you give me a hand?'

Edith's summer dress was getting soaked and the young German still wasn't taking the bait. She righted the basket and started crawling around, picking up the onions. She went for the onions nearest the sandbag wall and growled at the guard.

'*What* a gentleman you are!'

The guard raised one eyebrow sarcastically as he rested a small book in his lap. He was handsome, no older than twenty. Edith found this odd because the German army sent young men to fight, and left older ones playing night watchmen in small French towns. But as the man leaned out of shadow, his horribly scarred cheek emerged, followed by a knotted sleeve where his left arm ended in a stump.

The German gave a sly smile, then spoke slow but accurate French. 'What if mademoiselle is a resistance spy sent to distract me?' he asked. 'What if one of your onions explodes when I pick it up?'

'Do I look like someone with explosive onions?' Edith replied, hands on hips as she scowled over the sandbags.

'How should I know what a spy looks like?'

It didn't matter how Edith distracted the German and, while he hadn't offered to help, a night alone on guard duty had bored him enough to crave conversation.

'What happened to your arm?' Edith asked.

'The war happened,' he said grumpily.

'Could have worked that one out,' Edith said. 'Don't you like talking about it?'

'Saw plenty come off worse,' the guard said. 'And I can't hold a rifle, so I can't go anywhere there's bullets flying.'

As he said this, the guard finally stepped out from behind the sandbags. He kicked an onion backwards with his heel, let it roll up the front of his other boot and skilfully flipped it into the air. A clumsy one-handed catch spoiled the stunt, but it still made Edith smile.

'You play football?' she asked.

'I was apprenticed to a factory team, before I ran off to join the army.'

'You volunteered?' Edith asked.

The German shrugged and gestured towards his stump. 'Not my greatest decision, but they would have conscripted me within a year anyway.'

*

As the guard focused on his trick with the onion, CHERUB agent PT Bivott shot out of a doorway 20 metres away. The eighteen-year-old had dark, slicked back hair and a frame that had bulked up in the two years since he'd stopped growing taller.

PT was trailed by a middle-aged teacher named Jean Leclerc. The pair kept low as they ran 10 metres over cobbles, then cut down four stone steps into a passageway where the administrative building adjoined a disused fire station.

After doing their best not to crunch rubble and broken glass, they came to a peeling blue door at the end. Their key was a handmade copy and it took rattling and hand strength to turn, but Edith was still speaking to the one-armed German as they ducked to safety through the low entrance and breathed mildew and rodent piss in the admin building's basement.

Flipping the light switch did nothing, but Jean had a battery-powered torch to guide them over mounds of rubbish and cleaning gear. They turned into a gloomy hallway running beneath a stage, and looked through metal grilles into a 200-seat hall.

'Married my second wife in there,' Jean whispered.

A door took them out beneath a staircase, then past the brass rails and oil paintings into the building's deserted foyer.

PT led the way up two thickly carpeted flights through the gloomy light created by the boarded-up stained glass on the landing. They ignored the German commander's double-doored office and cut into a long corridor with offices off either side.

'She told me it's F, halfway down on our left,' Jean said.

The door of Room F was already ajar and as PT stepped in, a movement made him jolt.

'Shit,' PT blurted, taking a step back and ripping a silenced pistol out of its holster. When there was no further movement, he jumped into the room, sweeping the weapon from side to side.

PT had just about convinced himself that he was imagining things when a vast ginger cat belted out of the gap between two filing cabinets. It brushed PT's trousers and shot out into the hallway.

'Judging by the rat shit downstairs, I'd bet that moggy eats better than we do,' Jean said, shaking his head with relief.

As the cat sloped off, PT holstered his gun and opened

the middle of three desk drawers. He picked out two vellum folders and a pair of keys dropped out from between them.

'Looks like your friend has done us proud,' PT said.

Jean nodded. 'I've known this woman thirty years. Taught all of her sons.'

The cat stared from the top of the grand staircase as they crossed the hallway into Office 2B. This was a larger space, with five desks, a wooden counter and a waiting area lined with unmatched chairs.

A noticeboard above the chairs had the latest German regulations covering curfew times, penalties for spitting in the street and a reminder that anyone failing to report resistance or Maquis activity faced the death penalty.

PT made a dramatic slide over the polished counter, while Jean took the trouble to lift a flap and step through. They both had the same destination, a huge black and gold safe built into a wall at the far side of the room.

The two keys fitted into slots 3 metres apart. They had to be turned simultaneously, which made it impossible for a single key holder to steal its contents. After some fuss over which key went on which side, Jean began a count.

'One, two . . .'

They turned on three. There was a clank as a bolt dropped and the squeal of hinges that needed oiling. The safe was tall and shallow, with shelves designed to hold documents such as blank identity cards, curfew passes and birth certificates. All of these held some value, but for the Maquis the most precious were the small, lime-coloured ration cards which were required to buy any kind of food.

Jean's informant had not only secured copies of the two safe keys, she'd also told them that the fortnightly ration card delivery had arrived the previous afternoon.

'Beautiful,' PT said, kissing one stack of cards before scooping mounds of them into a leather satchel.

As PT picked smaller quantities of less valuable documents, Jean moved between desks stealing the rubber stamps, embossers and wax seals needed to validate their stash of blank documents.

'Nearly there,' Jean said, dropping assorted stamps into his backpack. 'I'm looking for a bottle of the radium ink they use on identity cards.'

PT closed the safe and slid back over the counter. He hadn't buckled his satchel properly and a few purple tobacco-ration cards trailed behind him. As he crouched to pick them up there was a gunshot.

Jean's neck snapped towards the sound. PT leaned cautiously into the hallway and saw the huge cat belting towards him with half its innards hanging out. The jumpy marksman who'd shot it was coming around the top of the stairs, dressed in a navy jacket and dented French soldier's helmet.

'Milice[2],' PT shouted, as the agonised cat tripped over its own intestines. 'I thought you trusted this woman.'

Their planned exit was via a ladder lowered out of a window in the ladies' toilet. But if they'd been betrayed, would the ladder be there?

PT decided that attack was the best form of defence and took aim at the man coming around the stairs. He couldn't tell where his bullet struck, but it knocked the man backwards and grunts and shouts came up as his body fell on to men further down the steps.

Jean now reached the office door. The balding teacher held a service revolver from the last war in hand as he gave PT a bag filled with stamps and ink pads.

'You're younger and faster,' Jean said. 'You run, I'll cover.'

Jean covered with wild shots as PT sprinted down the hallway to the ladies' toilet. He booted the toilet door, half expecting someone to burst out of a stall. But the only sound was a drizzling tap and the long ladder was where he'd been told to expect it.

'We're OK,' PT shouted, as he opened a boarded sash window.

---

[2] Milice – A police organisation set up by the Germans in 1943. Milicens were all Frenchmen. They were notoriously brutal and specialised in operations that regular French police were reluctant to undertake, especially hunting down Jews, communists and members of the resistance.

Edith was down below in the rubble and she'd swapped her basket of onions for a compact STEN machine gun.

'Who's shooting?' she shouted up, as PT went for the ladder.

'Jean, let's go!' PT shouted. 'It's clear out back.'

PT almost threw the ladder out and Edith kicked rubble out of the way to allow it to stand level.

'Jean,' PT shouted again, as he lobbed the satchels and bag out the window and swung a leg on to the ladder.

PT hurried down, half expecting never to see Jean again, but the elderly teacher put his boot on to the window ledge and caught him up by sliding down the outside of the ladder.

'Shot two of the buggers,' Jean said.

Edith knocked the ladder away to stop anyone else getting down, while PT and Jean grabbed the bags of loot and set off across shattered bricks and roof tiles. As Edith turned she noticed a figure taking aim out of a first-floor window and opened up with the STEN. It wasn't an accurate weapon, but the shooter ducked out of the hail of bullets for long enough to let the trio clear the open rubble and get behind the chimney breast of a bombed-out house.

From here they clambered through the roofless shell of a cobbler's shop and began sprinting down a curving road between houses.

'I thought you'd known her for thirty years,' PT said breathlessly.

They'd reached a point where the alleyway met one of the main routes out of town. There was no sign of any Milice following as PT stretched over a low garden wall and lifted the first of three getaway bikes.

'Someone might have betrayed us, but not her,' Jean replied, as he straddled a bike. 'If they'd known about the ladder they'd have ambushed us out back.'

'Well *someone* certainly told them we were coming,' Edith said as PT handed her the second bike. 'And when I find out who, they'll be sorry.'

CHAPTER THREE

'Daniel, I hear a train,' Paul shouted.

Branches rustled, but Paul got nervous when there was no answer.

'Daniel?'

Twenty metres up, Daniel gasped as he grabbed madly to steady himself and realised that he'd dozed off momentarily. The eleven-year-old shuddered, imagining what might have happened as he tightened his thigh grip on the branch between his legs. His throat was dry, his vision blurry and his head weighed down by the loss of a night's sleep.

The youngster had his reputation as a lookout to protect, so he tried not to sound like he'd scared himself to death. 'Don't worry, I'm on it.'

There had been a freight train just after seven that

had caused some confusion, but Daniel had no doubt this time.

'It's the one,' Daniel yelled. 'Send the signal.'

Paul pulled the grenade out of his pocket. 'Are you *completely* sure?'

'Two locomotives pulling. I can see tanks under tarpaulins and an anti-aircraft draisine hooked on the back of the train.'

'Good stuff,' Paul said happily. 'Cover your ears and hang on tight.'

'Kinda hard to do both,' Daniel noted, but not loud enough for Paul to hear.

The grenade had to be thrown carefully, because the forest was dense and the result might be deadly if it bounced off a branch and came back at him. Paul had used some of the hour he'd spent standing at the base of Daniel's tree to find the best aiming point and after pulling the pin he flung the grenade in a high arc between two trees, before taking cover behind the trunk.

'Hold it,' Daniel shouted.

Before Paul could respond a bang echoed down the hillside and clumps of burning white phosphorus shot off in all directions. Paul shielded his eyes as the blast cracked and when he stood up, Daniel's bare feet swung off the branches barely a metre above his head.

'There's another train,' Daniel said anxiously, before

jumping to the ground and gasping as the side of his foot scraped on a tree root.

Paul's ears rang from the blast. 'How can there be two trains?'

'Coming the other way,' Daniel explained.

'Passenger or cargo?'

'Eight passenger coaches.'

'Could it reach the tunnel before the tank train?' Paul asked, horrified at the prospect of accidentally blowing up a train full of passengers. And with Allied bombings wrecking France's railway network and the resistance regularly sabotaging rolling stock, every passenger train ran full.

As Daniel went down on one knee to put his boots back on, Paul thought about the distance to the track and spoke rhetorically.

'Even if we could make it down there in time, how would we signal the train to stop?'

'I don't wanna be anywhere near that tunnel when all that explosive goes off,' Daniel answered, now wide awake from the adrenaline rush. 'What if we could get to Luc and Michel and stop them setting the explosion?'

'Any train you see can't be more than three minutes from the tunnel,' Paul said. 'It took us over ten minutes to get up here from the ridge and we don't know exactly where they're hiding out with the detonators.'

Paul didn't add that his orders were to do everything

necessary to stop the tank train, and that even if they found the others in time, Luc was completely ruthless and would blow the tunnel anyway.

'Gotta be eighty people in each carriage,' Daniel said. 'Eight carriages times eighty people, comes to—'

Paul grabbed his backpack and interrupted as Daniel completed the sum in his head. 'Nothing we can do, and it's dangerous to stick around here any longer than necessary. Let's start walking.'

'What about Michel and Luc?'

'They might catch us up, but there's no point waiting around for them.'

*

'Two for one,' Luc said, smiling at Michel.

They were crouching on a chalkstone ledge, 50 metres from the tunnel mouth, with candlewax plugs in their ears. The clanking military train directly below moved at no more than 20 kilometres per hour, even though it was being pulled by a pair of Germany's most powerful locomotives.

The lads' low-lying position and plugged ears meant they had no clue about the passenger train coming the other way. Luc's 'two for one' comment referred to their plan to incapacitate a tank battalion while simultaneously wrecking a tunnel on a railway line the Germans would desperately need when the Allies invaded.

Trackside explosions could derail a train, but it took

a blast reflecting off tunnel walls and the intense fire that was sure to follow to wreck heavily-armoured Tiger tanks. Luc watched as the twin locomotives entered the tunnel, followed by several cargo wagons.

To detonate he needed to make a circuit by touching two bared wires together. His hands trembled as he thought about the pummelling the fragile detonators had taken during their rainy overnight trek, and the fact that their explosives were stretched out across a puddled tunnel and had been laid hurriedly in the dark as the sooty air choked them. One broken wire in the firing circuit and the whole show would fizzle.

'Take cover,' Luc ordered. 'Keep your mouth open so the shockwave doesn't burst your eardrums.'

Because of the earplugs, Luc accompanied his words with gestures. As he counted a sixteenth tarpaulin-covered tank entering the tunnel, Luc touched the bare wires and felt the crack from a blue spark as he dived behind a tree trunk on top of Michel.

Within a second the ground shook. A shockwave stripped leaves off the trees and filled the sky with fleeing birds. The train made a huge metallic shriek as the explosion filled the length of the tunnel. Luc was scared that the ledge was going to collapse down on to the tracks and he made the mistake of taking a peek around the trunk as the tunnel mouth spat a vast fireball.

The air was unbreathably hot as Michel's anxious

fingers clawed Luc's back. The ground shook again as the part of the train that hadn't entered the tunnel began to concertina. Birds killed by the shockwave rained through the trees as Luc gave Michel a tug.

'I think we should have backed up further!'

But Luc's humour didn't last. The fireball down on the tracks had reached a truck filled with high-explosive tank shells. Two went off in rapid succession and as carriages continued to grind and buckle the remaining shells went off in a deafening chain reaction. White-hot chunks of shell case were flung several hundred metres in the air, slicing through the canopy of leaves and igniting smoky fires in the damp hillside.

Michel looked terrified as Luc led him up the hillside. Less than 20 metres ahead a red-hot train wheel smashed through the canopy, shattering a trunk and forcing the pair to dive and hope for the best.

When Luc looked up, he saw a huge, smouldering chunk of tree balanced precariously in branches overhead.

'Move!'

This time Michel didn't need any pulling and he charged off ahead of Luc. They both had sweat dripping into their eyes as they reached a path that crossed the hill, back to the spot where they'd split from Paul and Daniel ninety minutes earlier.

'We bloody did it,' Michel shouted, grinning as he

picked out a wax plug that had been softened by the intense heat.

Luc could only nod as his heart slammed under his shirt. The rumbling had become more subdued but there were still shells exploding and metal grinding as the carriages that had derailed outside the tunnel continued shedding their cargoes.

'There might be survivors at the back,' Luc said. 'We need to—'

Before Luc could say *keep moving*, the ground shifted again and he looked up, half expecting to see a tree coming down on top of him. But the sounds that played out were like the easy-listening version of what had happened a moment earlier, and they echoed from the other side of the hill.

'Is that another train?' Michel asked.

Rather than answer, Luc started running. At first he thought he was hearing an echo, or perhaps some part of the train that had broken its coupling and rolled clean out of the tunnel, but it was soon clear that the noise was too much for that.

He ran for several minutes, with Michel gradually falling behind. When Luc reached a broader path, he caught a reflection 30 metres further uphill. It was like two little discs of light. Shouting was a risk, but he'd rambled around this area two days earlier without seeing a soul.

'Paul?'

Luc saw the reflections again, this time pointing his way, and he was certain he was seeing the low sun hitting his binoculars. He didn't want to lose his companion, but as soon as Michel came into sight Luc started charging uphill.

'Michel?' Daniel shouted down anxiously.

Luc reached Paul and snatched the binoculars. 'What happened?'

'I sent your signal before Daniel spotted the train coming the other way,' Paul explained, as he noticed that Luc's cheek and forehead had reddened in the blast. 'The driver slammed the brakes on when he saw the explosion, but he didn't have time to stop completely.'

Luc adjusted the focus and looked down into the valley. A locomotive and two passenger coaches had entered the tunnel and been annihilated by the inferno. The two carriages nearest the tunnel mouth were twisted out of recognition and scorched by the blast, but by slowing down, the driver had saved many lives in the rear four coaches. All the coaches had derailed, but remained upright after scraping along the chalkstone embankments leading towards the tunnel mouth.

'I'm seeing mostly Germans down there,' Luc said, looking at a man throwing up on the tracks while others staggered about in shock. Most seemed to be nursing minor injuries, while the more seriously hurt were being brought out of the carriages by survivors.

When Michel arrived, Daniel gave his big brother a hug.

'You did good,' Michel said, rubbing his brother's clammy back.

Daniel shook his head and tried to say something, but he was overwhelmed and only managed to sob.

'Hey,' Michel said softly, as he scooped Daniel off his feet. 'Don't cry.'

Luc lowered his binoculars and shook his head contemptuously as Michel tried to soothe his little brother.

'Daniel, mate, there's nothing you could have done,' Paul said. 'Think of how many soldiers those tanks could have killed.'

'I know,' Daniel said, rubbing his eye. 'But all those poor people . . .'

'If there's a couple of officers and a few fit soldiers down on the tracks, the first thing they'll do is send out search parties,' Luc warned. 'So let's cut all the boo-hoos and get moving.'

Paul scowled at Luc, but didn't say anything.

'Big baby,' Luc sneered as he started walking. 'I'm out of here. Stick around and let the Nazis catch you, *then* you'll have something worth crying about.'

Michel was angry at Luc's attitude, but he was right about not sticking around.

'Come on,' Paul said, tousling Daniel's hair as he set off after Luc. 'You'll be a massive hero when we get back to camp.'

CHAPTER FOUR

A fast fifteen-minute ride took PT, Jean and Edith into the country north-east of Beauvais. There were no tanks or bomb-damaged buildings out here, but the effects of the occupation were just as obvious. Over four years the Germans had forced manpower from rural areas into mines and factories, commandeered hundreds of thousands of French farm horses and diverted minerals needed to make fertiliser into explosives factories.

The trio were lashed by branches from untended hedgerows as the bikes passed poorly-maintained fields. France was surviving on starvation rations and with the farmland continuing to decline, people feared that the next winter would bring famine.

Jean had been caught by a piece of shrapnel in the crossfire back at the town hall. The wound wasn't debilitating, but there was a large bloody patch across the back of his shirt and the wound would clearly benefit from stitching. PT gave Edith all the stolen documents and told her to ride on into the woods, while he accompanied Jean to a nearby boys' orphanage.

'I don't need an escort,' Jean said.

PT shook his head. 'It's hot, you're out of breath and you've lost blood.'

Edith suspected that PT wanted to see the nurse rather than help Jean, but she chose not to tease him.

The orphanage and adjoining monastery felt like an oasis amidst decay. Neat vegetable plots stretched across land that had once been reserved for play and, as the local school had closed down, cross-legged boys were taking their first morning lesson under the sun.

A young nun carrying a bail of damp washing stepped aside, allowing the speeding bikes down the path to a nearby cottage. It had once been the home of the orphanage's director, but the earth-floored house now served as a secret nursing station for the Maquis who lived in the surrounding fields and woodland.

'Anyone home?' PT shouted, thumping the cottage door as Jean hopped off the bike behind him. He smiled when seventeen-year-old Rosie Clarke answered. 'I hoped you'd be here.'

Her attractive figure was disguised by a nun's habit.

She tried to mouth something, but tripped over her words and only managed a *come in* gesture.

PT and Rosie had once been an item, but it had ended after PT pressured her into having sex. Eighteen months on, the pair remained fond of each other, but their interactions were spoiled by jarring memories of nakedness and a bitter break-up.

'You been OK?' PT asked.

'Enough Maquis injuring themselves to keep me busy,' Rosie said, as her lower jaw toyed with the idea of yawning.

'Wanna go for a walk some time, get a break from it all?'

Rosie snorted as Jean stepped through the door. 'Might look weird while I'm disguised as a nun,' she pointed out as she backed away from PT and looked towards Jean. 'Get that bloody shirt off and I'll take a look at you.'

Jean was breathless, but shunned PT's offer of a supporting arm.

The cottage's ground floor was a single room, with a sink, a kitchen range and a dining table softened with blankets for examinations. A grubby teenaged Maquis slept on cushions by the staircase with one foot elevated. He'd been carried in a few hours earlier with a badly gashed leg and his BO hung in the air, even though Rosie had all the windows open.

As Jean sat on the blanketed table, unbuttoning, Rosie scrubbed her hands under the cold tap.

PT whispered in her ear, 'I don't wanna harass you, Rosie, but I still think there's something between us.'

'Maybe there is,' Rosie said, as she dampened a sterile cloth. 'But I told you I need time.'

'How much longer?' PT asked.

But Rosie ignored him and stepped across to the table. Jean's blood had started to clot and the balding teacher winced as Rosie peeled the bloody linen of his shirt away from the cut.

'I'm trying to be gentle,' she said, adopting her best nurse's manner. But her tone stiffened when she threw Jean's shirt at PT. 'Run that under the standpipe outside before the blood sets. Then take it next door to the orphanage and see if one of the nuns can put it in with today's laundry.'

As PT turned on the tap outside, Rosie carefully dabbed clotted blood from the shoulder wound. Bullets and shrapnel travel at such high speed that a small entry wound doesn't guarantee that there isn't serious internal bleeding. Rosie was always conscious of this fact, because a small piece of shrapnel after a bomb blast had killed her father.

'This will sting,' Rosie said, as she picked up tweezers. 'I need to open the wound to see what's going on.'

Jean gripped the edges of the table as Rosie dug

tweezers into his shoulder wound. The metal tips immediately tapped something hard and Jean hissed with pain as his young nurse dug the object out and dropped it into an enamel bowl.

'Hold this cloth in place to stop the bleeding,' Rosie ordered.

As fresh blood streaked down Jean's back, Rosie inspected the bloody lump and saw that it was a piece of thin, curved glass.

'Looks like part of a broken light bulb,' Rosie said, as she held it up with the tweezers so that Jean could see.

'One of the Milice shot a light fitting as I was running away,' Jean said, nodding. 'I didn't feel it, but I guess I had other things on my mind.'

'The cut could do with stitching,' Rosie said. 'But we're out of sterile cord and low on bandages. I'll paint on some iodine to stop an infection, but you'll have to hold that gauze there until it scabs over.'

'Henderson said we were good for medical supplies,' Jean noted.

Rosie nodded. 'We picked quite a bit of stuff up in the last parachute drop, but Sister Honestus used three whole packs stitching up our fragrant friend in the corner.'

'His nickname's Franco,' Jean said. 'He's a good man if you can stand the smell.'

PT came back in holding a tattered man's shirt. 'The

nuns gave me this. Yours should be scrubbed and dried by this evening.'

Jean held up the shirt for inspection, but Rosie swept it away when he moved to pull it on.

'You've lost a fair bit of blood,' Rosie said. 'Stay here and sleep for a couple of hours.'

'I could fetch some medical supplies from the woods,' PT said. 'What else do you need, apart from cord and bandages?'

Rosie looked longingly at the sun before giving PT an awkward smile. 'I need fresh air and a break from this dingy cottage,' she said. 'How about I borrow Jean's bike and ride with you?'

PT smiled, but before he could answer a figure darted past the open window. As she stepped forward to investigate, a man in a navy Milice tunic booted the cottage door open and charged in with a rifle poised, shouting, 'Hands in the air!'

*

The Maquis band in the woodland north of Beauvais was a fluid movement. A hard core of sixty young men and a couple of girls were led by Jean Leclerc. The sixty were supplemented by up to a hundred others, who drifted in and out of the woods depending upon climate, availability of food and the latest gossip on whether a young draft dodger was safer in town, in the woods or hiding in his mother's attic.

The other authority figure in this chaotic group was Captain Charles Henderson. Some of the young runaways admired this tough, broken-toothed British intelligence officer, but many others were communists who resented having an Englishman calling the shots.

While Jean had assumed leadership through a mixture of an old teacher's natural authority, good judgement and his soldiering experience in the Great War, Henderson earned respect because he was connected with the near-legendary Ghost resistance circuit in Paris, and had the power to control Allied parachute drops to Maquis and resistance groups.

These supply drops brought everything from dried oats to plastic explosives. Henderson regularly received lists of sabotage targets via a coded radio link with CHERUB campus, and a hungry, bored Maquis who successfully carried out one of Henderson's operations could earn his own rifle, new boots and, most importantly, a few days with a full belly.

But parachutes could only drop light weapons. Larger Maquis groups in southern France had tried holding territory, but got ripped apart by German tanks and artillery. So Jean ensured that his group was split into half a dozen mobile squads, which regularly switched between farm buildings, cottages and temporary shelters erected in the woods.

Edith hid her bike behind a hedge before heading into the woods and finding Henderson at an abandoned logging camp. She relayed the story of the ambush at the administration building as Henderson squatted on a tree stump.

Four bored-looking Maquis listened in, along with trained CHERUB agents Joel and Sam Voclain. Joel was a good-looking fifteen-year-old who'd let his blond hair grow wild in the woods. At thirteen, Sam was a clone of his older brother and the youngest member of Henderson's team.

'Milice,' Henderson said, before squirting spit through a gap where he'd lost three front teeth the year before. 'Absolute scum.'

Sam and Joel joined the spitting.

In the eighteen months since the organisation had been formed, Milice had become the dirtiest word in the French language. As the war turned against Germany, Nazis had run short of military manpower and French police became reluctant to carry out their most extreme orders. The occupiers solved this problem by forming the Milice.

The first Milice were loyal French Nazis, but after four years of occupation these were thin on the ground. The net was cast wider and Milice were recruited from the dregs of society. Thugs and criminals were given navy tunics and metal helmets. Answerable only to the

Nazis' Gestapo secret police, Milice units enthusiastically infiltrated resistance groups, rounded up homosexuals and Jews and ruthlessly hunted down Maquis.

The Milice terrorised their own countrymen and often used their new authority for criminal ends. In many areas the Milice took control of the black-market food supply, set up brutal extortion rackets and used their search powers to rob homes and shops.

'You must have been betrayed by the informant inside the office,' Joel told Edith.

'If it was her, why was the getaway ladder still in the toilet where she'd promised to leave it?' Edith asked.

Joel shrugged. 'Well, who else could it be?'

'She could have been under duress,' Joel's younger brother Sam pointed out. 'Like, suppose the Gestapo found out somehow and threatened her. But she didn't tell them everything, so you still had a chance of getting away?'

Edith nodded. 'If she's never seen again, we'll know the Gestapo got to her.'

'Too many people knew Jean was going into Beauvais,' Sam said. 'We're not secure here with so many men coming and going. Any one of them could be a Nazi spy.'

'But we keep operational details to a core group, plus anyone going on the operation,' Joel said.

'Someone could easily have followed you into Beauvais.'

'Or—' Edith began, but Henderson had lost patience with the chatter.

'Stop,' Henderson said, as he stood up. 'Why spend all morning speculating when you know it won't get you anywhere? When we have the facts we'll make use of them. For now, we remain vigilant in case someone has ratted us out. We'll station extra lookouts and make sure everyone moves deeper into the woods.'

'You want me to take a message around to the other squads' camps?' Edith asked.

Henderson shook his head. 'You get some rest. Joel and Sam can get word around. The Nazis will be jumpy after a shootout in town and the Milice will be out for blood. Everyone must lie low for a couple of days. Tell every squad to double up on lookouts and make it clear that nobody is allowed to leave until this dies down.'

'A lot of the lads won't take orders from you,' Sam said.

'Tell me something I don't know,' Henderson said, with a shrug. 'But if Jean was here, he'd say exactly the same.'

CHAPTER FIVE

The Milice were ruthless, but poorly trained. Any decent soldier would have kept low and pointed rifles through the cottage's open windows. Booting the door and charging in gave PT a second to spread himself out and launch a rugby tackle.

As Rosie took cover and Jean went for his pistol, the Milice officer shot the ceiling before PT locked an arm around his neck and started choking him.

The shoulder wound meant Jean had to shoot left-handed, but his aim was good when another Milice bobbed up at the window less than 3 metres away. After PT's victim made his last gurgle, things went quiet apart from Rosie thumping upstairs to grab a hidden gun and get a look out of the upper windows.

Franco sat up, looking startled as PT crawled to the

open door. There were two cars on the road in front of the orphanage and some kind of disturbance amongst the kids taking outdoor lessons. Rosie glanced out front from the upper floor and saw the same, but gasped when she got to the rear.

Two Milice crouched behind a low garden fence and one had just lobbed something towards an open window.

'Grenade!' Rosie shouted.

PT thought about scrambling out of the door as the grenade bounced off the table and hit the dirt floor. Jean instinctively flicked it away with his boot before PT bravely intercepted and flipped it backwards over his head out of the rear window.

He'd come within a second of getting his arm blown off. Glass blasted across the room as the grenade exploded and splinters of window frame speared the ceiling.

'Is anybody hurt?' PT yelled, as debris settled and his ears rang.

Upstairs, Rosie pulled a pistol from under a loose floorboard and aimed out of the window. Her three bullets tore through the back fence, halting a second grenade throw and knocking both men back with large stomach wounds.

Miraculously, nobody downstairs got hurt by shrapnel, but a bottle of medical alcohol had shattered and combusted in the heat from the blast. Lines of blue flame shot across the kitchen dresser and into a coal bucket.

Within seconds the coal, dresser and front curtains were ablaze and choking smoke curled up to the ceiling.

'Rosie, we're on fire,' PT shouted.

Rosie charged downstairs, as fast as her billowing nun's habit allowed. 'I hit the two guys out back,' she said. 'Can't see anyone else on that side.'

'What if there's an ambush?' Franco asked, coughing from the smoke as he grabbed hold of his boots and tried standing on his good leg.

'I doubt it,' Rosie said. 'If they had a lot of men they'd have surrounded us rather than sneaking up and bursting in.'

'Gotta get out one way or another,' PT said, trying not to breathe the smoke as he headed for the rear.

There was no back door so they had to straddle through the window. This wasn't hard, but it was impossible not to tread on the gruesome remains of the Milice, who Jean had killed with a headshot before his corpse caught the grenade blast.

As Rosie and Jean covered with their pistols, PT hauled Franco out and supported him as they hobbled to the back gate.

One of the guys Rosie had shot behind the fence looked dead, but the other still writhed. She finished him with a shot through the heart, then reached down, grabbed his MP35 sub-machine gun and tugged off a shoulder-belt fitted with grenades and ammo clips.

Rosie looked comical in her nun's habit, accessorised with ammo belt and machine gun, but nobody was in the mood to laugh. She reached cover 20 metres from the burning cottage and tried to work out what they were up against as Jean arrived, trailed by PT who was still helping Franco.

One Milice officer had escaped from the vicinity of the cottage, but Rosie didn't get a chance to shoot before he vanished into the lines of flapping laundry pegged out behind the orphanage. Their position gave no view over the front of the orphanage, but they could hear Milice officers shouting orders over the wails and shouts of distressed kids.

'There's a car down here and another further up the road,' Rosie said. 'I reckon we're up against eight or ten Milice at most.'

PT nodded in agreement. 'And we took out four of them already.'

Round the front of the orphanage a nun screamed and young boys wailed in a way that made you know something horrible had just happened.

'We need to get out of here,' PT said.

Jean shook his head. 'You'd abandon defenceless nuns and children?'

'They'll probably give the nuns a hard time and slap a few of the older boys around,' PT said. 'If we attack, we'll be shooting towards the kids you're so eager to protect.'

Jean tutted with frustration. 'I suppose.'

A cocky, amplified voice echoed through a megaphone. 'Jean Leclerc.'

Rosie, PT and the others exchanged confused glances before megaphone man spoke again.

'Jean Leclerc, I am Milice Commander Robert. I know you're out there. I've got eighty men surrounding your position. Come out with your hands raised and nobody else will be harmed.'

'Eighty men, my arse,' PT said.

'How does he know we've not scarpered?' Franco asked.

'He doesn't,' Rosie said. 'But what's he got to lose by bluffing?'

'If you don't show yourself, the orphanage will be destroyed and three nuns executed,' Robert continued. 'I will execute the first nun in thirty seconds.'

Jean stepped forward, but PT pulled him back.

'You can't surrender,' PT said firmly. 'They'll torture you for the names of everyone in the woods. Then they'll start going after their families.'

'Twenty seconds.'

Clutching the German machine gun, Rosie handed Franco her pistol. At the same moment part of the cottage roof caved, releasing plumes of trapped smoke.

'Five seconds.'

'He's bluffing,' PT said. 'Come on, let's get out of here.'

A gunshot rang out, closely followed by the sound of kids screaming hysterically and cries of 'No!'.

'One dead nun,' Commander Robert shouted through the megaphone. 'Thirty seconds until the next one gets it.'

Jean moved and this time PT didn't stop him.

'I'm not giving in,' Jean said resolutely. 'But we can't let them behave like this.'

'He's relying on your decency,' PT said. 'Don't fall into their trap.'

Jean scowled back at PT as he started walking towards the orphanage. 'It's home to over a hundred children. Where will they go if it's burned down?'

'I doubt there's more than six Milice left,' Rosie said as she jogged to catch up with Jean.

'You keep out of sight,' PT told Franco. 'We'll come back for you.'

'Twenty seconds,' Commander Robert announced.

Jean kept low and used the thick smoke as cover.

'You two go outside the wall by the road,' Jean ordered. 'I'll surrender to buy time. Do your best to stop them taking me away. If it goes bad you've *got* to kill me rather than let them take me back to Beauvais for torture.'

The crumbling wall ran parallel with the road. The orphanage was slightly uphill, but it gave Rosie and PT decent cover and a clear view of what was happening out front.

'Five seconds.'

'Wait,' Jean shouted, emerging through smoke, bare-chested and with his hands raised.

PT and Rosie made a crouching sprint along the wall with their heads down. The scene in front of the orphanage was horrific, with boys ranging from three to thirteen in hysterics while a nun bled out on the front steps. Another nun was on her knees, praying quietly with Commander Robert's gun at her temple. As Jean got closer, the moustached Milice commander handed his megaphone to a colleague and broke into a smile.

'Well, well, I have a prize,' Robert said, cracking a self-satisfied smile as he took his gun away from the elderly nun's head and sent her sprawling with a muddy boot in the back.

'Where are the other two from the robbery?' Robert asked, as Jean stepped to within a few metres.

'I was injured,' Jean said, turning to show his bloody shoulder. 'They brought me to the cottage to get fixed up, but they didn't stick around.'

A giant Milice officer ordered the balding ex-teacher to kneel, before unhooking a set of handcuffs from his belt. Down by the road, PT knifed the front tyres of the nearest Milice car, before joining Rosie by a crack in the wall.

'You holding up OK?' PT asked.

'Not exactly the fresh air I was after,' Rosie said, as a

breeze blew smoke into her eyes. 'I can only count four Milice, but there could be more inside the orphanage or in the woods.'

'They've caught a big fish and Robert looks twitchy,' PT said. 'He's four men down and this is Maquis turf. They're not gonna want to stick around here a second longer than they have to.'

PT's opinion got confirmed as the nuns were allowed to begin shepherding hysterical kids inside the orphanage. Commander Robert's fear of a Maquis ambush was obvious as he began jogging downhill towards the open-topped Milice car parked across the orphanage gate.

PT would have liked to stab the tyres, but the gate was open so there was no way to approach without being seen and shooting would give their position away.

'When the giant one gets close I'll shoot him,' PT whispered to Rosie. 'Jean's cuffed, but he can still make a run for it. You'll have to be ready to take the others out with the machine gun.'

'Sounds like a plan,' Rosie said, as she double-checked that her unfamiliar German machine gun had the safety off and a full clip of ammo. Then she gave PT a quick peck on the cheek. 'Be careful.'

Before PT could react, he noticed Jean's giant guard losing his footing on the damp ground. It was too good a chance to miss and PT took aim as the Milice's butt hit the soft turf. But another voice sounded behind before he could shoot.

'Drop your weapons.'

When PT spun around he saw a tiny Milice officer standing behind the car with the slashed tyres. Rosie didn't hesitate with the machine gun and ripped the man in half. The blast sent Jean's guard diving for cover, while Jean himself began sprinting towards the wall.

PT leaned over the wall and took two shots, but he only hit the giant in the thigh. At the same moment Rosie opened up on Commander Robert and his two goons as they began a full-on sprint towards the car.

The giant got a couple of wild shots into the air with his rifle and forced PT to duck behind the wall, but Jean had doubled back. The balding ex-teacher jumped on top of the giant and used his cuffed hands to ram home a small dagger that he kept concealed inside his boot.

Down by the gate, Commander Robert braved machine-gun bullets as he jumped into the back of the open-topped car without bothering to open a door. As his two colleagues scrambled in the front and started the engine, Robert dived flat across the back seat.

The crying kids were all back inside the orphanage as Jean rolled off the giant, leaving his dagger sticking out of his neck, and the car began moving.

'Christ,' Jean gasped, keeping low as he searched the giant's pockets for handcuff keys.

'We need to keep an eye out,' PT said, as he stood up and glanced around. 'That commander looked so scared, I wouldn't be surprised if he'd left a man behind.'

Down by the gate, Rosie took aim at the retreating car, but only got an empty click from her machine gun. It would be out of range before she could reload, so she decided to take cover by scrambling over the wall. As she prepared to vault, Commander Robert sat up in the back seat and took two quick pistol shots.

One bullet skimmed PT's arm, close enough for its vortex to ruffle his shirt sleeve. He dived clumsily into weeds growing close to the wall and grazed his knuckles on bricks as the bullet tore up a bush metres behind.

'Too bloody close,' PT gasped, assuming Jean was within earshot. 'That commander's either a very lucky shot, or a very good shot.'

PT didn't want to move until the Milice car was out of sight, but he could hear Jean running on the other side of the wall.

'Rosie!' Jean shouted.

Down by the gate, Rosie lay on her back with her legs sprawled. PT began a sprint towards her as Jean ran through the gate, doubled back and got down on one knee in front of Rosie.

'Is she OK?' PT shouted.

When PT got close enough to see the blood he felt like he'd been smashed across the back of the head with a brick. Commander Robert's pistol shot had hit the base of Rosie's nose as she'd straddled the wall. The bullet had splintered inside her brain and torn a great chunk out of the back of her skull.

'Rosie?'

Gravel and dirt spewed up as PT dived down on his knees in front of her. When he looked up, he saw Jean, with tear-filled eyes and the half-unlocked cuffs swinging off his right wrist.

'You can't be,' PT gasped, tears welling as he snatched Rosie's wrist and felt for a pulse where he knew there couldn't possibly be one. 'It can't . . .'

PT felt like his chest was in a vice as his eyes fixed on Rosie's glazed face and her blood trickling between chunks of gravel.

CHAPTER SIX

Reliable news on the successful tunnel blast reached Henderson just after 10 a.m., via a nineteen-year-old Maquis whose girlfriend worked inside the Beauvais telephone exchange.

Henderson and his squad had retreated from the logging camp, delving a full kilometre into woodland. With the tunnel blast and the raid on the admin building in town, there was a good chance of German retaliation, so he doubled up on lookouts and advised the eight other Maquis squads spread through the woods to do the same.

Henderson was a poor radio operator, so he relied on Edith and Sam for his daily Morse code communication with CHERUB campus. But Sam was out running messages and Edith had cooled off in a stream before taking a nap, so Henderson sat under a tree, grumpily encoding that afternoon's radio transmission using a printed silk square known as a one-time pad.

These highly flammable squares had been devised by British cryptologists. They made encoding messages fairly easy, and once a tissue-thin square was burned – or torn up and swallowed if you got desperate – the message could only be decoded by a radio operator with a codebook containing an identical grid of printed letters.

'Shit, shit, shit!' Henderson muttered, as his fountain pen made a blotch that spoiled several letters on his squared paper.

Whenever Henderson blobbed ink, his mind always wandered back to the rap on the knuckles his schoolmaster had given him when he'd done it as a boy. This flashback to a life of inkwells and wooden desks was shattered by a barefoot teenager named Gilles. He wasn't one of Henderson's trained agents, but he was loyal and had been on several raids.

'Couple of bodies seen walking up the hill,' Gilles said. 'Probably ours, but I thought you'd like to know.'

'Thanks,' Henderson said. 'It's possible one of our boys has been captured, so keep vigilant, even if they give the right password.'

Henderson smiled when Jean and PT reached him, but a quick read of their faces was enough to know something was seriously wrong.

PT rubbed a wet eye as he told the story. Henderson had been extremely fond of Rosie and had a lump in his throat as he turned to Jean.

'What's with your shoulder?' he asked.

'The least of my worries,' Jean said. 'It'll heal.'

'Edith's sleeping and no point waking her up for bad news,' Henderson said. 'There's a chance Milice or army will return to the orphanage in force, either to interrogate the nuns or cause general mayhem.'

'Agreed,' Jean said.

'Should we get the nuns to evacuate?' PT asked.

Henderson thought for a couple of seconds before shaking his head. 'The nuns won't leave the orphans behind, and how would we feed and shelter over a hundred boys? All we can do is send a protection squad down there. I'll make sure they're led by someone with half a brain and if it comes to the worst, they're not to try to stand their ground. Their job is to protect the orphanage for as long as it takes to safely evacuate the nuns and the children.'

'I'll lead the team,' PT said. 'Make sure the kids are ready to evacuate if necessary. Station lookouts on the road. Scout some hiding places and plan out a route so that the kids can be moved to safety at the first sign of trouble.'

In the four months they'd been with the Maquis, PT had proved himself capable. But Henderson wasn't sure about putting him in charge right now.

'Things got frosty after you broke up,' Henderson said. 'But I know Rosie was special to you.'

'It's kinda my fault,' PT said. 'She saved my life, killing a guy who popped up behind us. Then I missed two pistol shots from close range, so she had no back-up covering the commander's car.'

Henderson stood up. 'Don't go there,' he said firmly, as he placed one hand on PT's shoulder. 'Blame games just mess up your head. The only reason *any* of us are here is because there's a war and the only reason there's a war is because of the Nazis. So, hate Adolf Hitler, not yourself.'

As Henderson said this he let out a tiny sob and yanked PT into a tight hug.

'Can't believe she's dead,' PT said weakly.

'I believe in you,' Henderson said decisively. 'Pick seven or eight of the best lads. Make sure they've got weapons, but stay mobile. Don't weigh yourselves down with too much crap.'

'Haven't forgotten my training, sir,' PT said, tapping his head to indicate that the knowledge was all inside.

As PT jogged off to gather a team to protect the orphanage, Henderson stared up into the sunlight over the trees then, after a pause, down at Jean.

'I knew Rosie and Paul's father,' Henderson said, as he glanced at his wristwatch. 'First saw her when she was knee high, playing in the gardens at the British Embassy in Paris. And now I've got to tell her brother that she's gone.'

*

Luc, Paul, Michel and Daniel had walked out to the tunnel in darkness, but the 18-kilometre return trip was in daylight. Once they were 5 kilometres from the tunnel blast and sure nobody was following, they stopped off at a safe house that Luc had organised during his reconnaissance trip.

They washed in cold water and ate a late breakfast of biscuits, cheese and raw eggs. An hour's rest seemed to pass in a flash and they left their guns behind before setting off with new sets of identity papers and a handcart laden with firewood.

As there was no coal ration for civilians in summertime there was nothing unusual about youngsters foraging for wood to cook with. The only checkpoint they encountered was staffed by a bored-looking French policeman. He gave the barest glance at their papers and cracked up laughing when he saw Daniel nestled in the wood pile, snoring his head off with his big brother's shirt draped over his face to stop it getting sunburned.

'He's got a woman who keeps him up all night,' Michel explained.

The friendly cop kept on laughing as they set off. Paul and Luc appreciated the joke too, but they were exhausted and the casualties on the passenger train muted any sense of triumph.

It was two in the afternoon when they reached countryside north-west of Beauvais, which some lads nicknamed the Badlands. The main threat here wasn't from Germans or Milice, but from a thirty-strong band of Maquis bad boys, many of whom either didn't like obeying Jean's rules or had been kicked out for breaking them.

With no resistance contacts and no access to Allied supply drops, these young rebels were forced to steal and frequently made violent raids on farms, or held up shops. Many locals found it impossible to distinguish between different Maquis groups, and feared the gangs of young men living close by.

Luckily the quartet's only problem was that they had to abandon the handcart when they left the road. Daniel moaned like hell when his pleas for a piggyback got turned down and he had to walk the last couple of kilometres.

News of Rosie's death had spread through the young men stationed in the woods when PT had gone round picking his team to defend the orphanage. But if anyone acted strangely around Paul, he was too exhausted to notice.

By the time Henderson caught up, Paul had stripped off his boots and trousers and taken shelter from the sun under a canopy of woven branches. He now lay fast asleep on top of a sleeping bag, bony ribcage rising and falling with each breath.

Luc was officially in charge of the tunnel mission. He admired Henderson, but they rubbed each other up the wrong way and Luc spoke formally. 'Would you like a briefing, sir?'

Henderson waved his hand dismissively. 'You blew the train up and blocked the tunnel. Word from our sources in Beauvais is that the line will be out of action for two weeks. Perhaps more, if the fire buckled the iron trusses holding up the tunnel.'

'Shame about the passenger train,' Luc said coldly.

'It's a busy line,' Henderson said. 'There was always that risk. You did an excellent job. Now try catching some sleep and make sure Paul speaks to me as soon as he wakes up.'

Luc saw the hurt on Henderson's face and could only think of one reason. 'Is Rosie OK?'

Henderson almost said it, but it seemed wrong that Luc should find out first and he sounded annoyed. 'Just do as I say for once.'

CHAPTER SEVEN

A Maquis might spend a few hours a day hunting, fishing, patrolling or collecting firewood. A couple of times per week there might be some extra excitement, like moving camp, a trip into town with a fake ration card or being picked for one of Henderson's sabotage operations. But that still left a typical Maquis with a lot of free time.

Cards, dice and boxing were common, but the number one pastime was spreading and discussing rumours. Only the participants and a couple of Henderson's agents knew about the tunnel raid, but everyone knew about the raid on the admin building, and the carnage at the orphanage was a full-blown sensation.

Henderson had asked the Maquis to stay in the forest to minimise the chances of further trouble, but for hard-core rumour mongers this only spurred a widespread belief that the Milice were now out to get them. By the end of a hot afternoon, the main debate was whether the Milice would stage a revenge attack on the orphanage, or come charging into the forest itself, backed up by German tanks and artillery.

Henderson sat under a woven branch canopy as Gilles asked for his opinion.

'Every day someone tells me we're doomed,' Henderson said. 'If the Germans had the will and resources to flush us out of the woods, why wait until now?'

'Other Maquis groups have been smashed,' Gilles pointed out.

'Mainly in the south and usually when they stopped being mobile,' Henderson said. 'Anything is possible, but don't tie yourself in knots over rumours.'

'What about the orphanage?'

Henderson was less comfortable on this subject. 'They're vulnerable because they can't vanish into the woods like we do. In our favour, people aren't exactly queuing out the doors of Milice recruitment offices.'

Gilles nodded. 'Especially since the communist resistance began killing family members of Milice officers.'

'There're many fewer men in Milice uniforms than the Germans would like us to think, that's for sure,' Henderson said.

Gilles was about to ask another question when Paul

stepped into the shelter, dressed in a vest and ragged undershorts.

'I'll leave you to it,' Gilles said. His mouth gaped and he put a clumsy foot in Henderson's mess tin as he backed out.

'My sister's dead, isn't she?' Paul said.

'Did Luc tell you?' Henderson asked irritably. 'I specifically asked—'

Paul interrupted and pointed back at Gilles. 'Nobody told me, but everyone reacts like Gilles just did when they see me.'

'You want to sit down and talk about it?' Henderson said, standing up as he realised he had the only seat under the canopy.

Paul sounded eerily calm. 'I don't feel . . . I've seen so much shit in the last four years, I almost expected something like this.'

'Shock,' Henderson said.

Paul nodded, then Henderson took some time explaining what had happened at the orphanage.

'Any time you want to talk, I'm here. I thought you might want a few days away from the woods. I'm sure you'd be welcome at Morel's farm.'

'Have they buried her?'

'I told PT to wait,' Henderson said. 'Though it's hot and she's got an open wound, so she can't stay above ground for too long.'

'I know she'll be a mess, but I'd like to see her one last time.'

'You're sure?'

Paul nodded.

'OK,' Henderson said. 'I need to see how PT has set up his defences down at the orphanage. I'll walk down there with you and we can pay our last respects.'

Paul's feet were painful after a 36-kilometre round trip and his sweaty shirt had been taken away to be washed while he slept. By the time Gilles found a clean shirt, Paul had painfully pulled boots over his blisters.

Henderson was also ready to leave, but Edith and Sam came racing back from the hillside where they handled daily communications with CHERUB campus.

'So sorry,' Edith told Paul.

Edith and Paul got along well and he sobbed as the pair hugged. Meantime, Sam urgently presented Henderson with the radio message.

'We ran back as soon as we saw what was in it,' Sam said, as he passed over three sheets of squared paper holding the decoded message. 'It's a big one.'

The daily message from campus rarely filled more than one sheet. For extra security, the messages contained code words that only Henderson understood and he did a double take when he saw that the opening word was BADGER.

'Blast,' Henderson said, as he flicked through the long message, reading a list of three sabotage operations which he'd been ordered to carry out immediately.

The importance of all operations fell into one of four categories. BADGER was the one which meant *Do this even if your entire team gets wiped out* and he'd never seen it in a message until now.

'Something big must be going down, sir,' Sam said.

'Looks like it,' Henderson agreed, backing out of the canopy into a forest clearing as he continued squinting at the long message. 'But keep that to yourself. I'm going to need two teams put together. Sam, you run a team. Edith, go to the next clearing and fetch Luc and Joel to run the other one.'

Paul felt abandoned as Edith ran off and Henderson began briefing Sam. As Sam had worked on decoding the message, he already knew that his task was to travel east and deliver two dozen phosphorous grenades to a train guard. The message didn't say what would happen next, but presumably the guard would pass them on to a resistance group further down the line.

Joel and Luc soon arrived. Henderson ordered them to put a team of four together and cut the phone lines of the Luftwaffe airfield east of Beauvais. When Jean heard what was going on he raced across from his dilapidated French army command tent, in which he'd been working with a team stamping and validating some of their stolen ration cards.

'We agreed to send teams deeper into the woods and lie low,' Jean yelled at Henderson. 'You can only poke your stick into the German hive so many times before the swarm comes out to sting us.'

'The timing's bad and I'd never do this out of choice,' Henderson admitted, as he rattled his decoded message in front of Jean. 'But these are top priority.'

Jean scoffed. 'It's always top priority.'

'Jean, I know you put your life on the line every day to protect the young men out here. But they'll only be truly safe when our side wins the war and that's what *I'm* trying to do.'

'And what's the point winning the war if they're all dead before it's over?' Jean spat. 'I care about these boys. For you they're just a means to achieve British goals.'

Henderson always got riled when someone suggested that British agents were only in France to protect British interests.

'You live in a fantasy land,' Henderson snapped. 'Without Allied food and clothes drops, half of your boys would have starved or frozen last winter.'

Jean couldn't deny this, but was too proud to admit how much his Maquis' survival depended on Allied air drops.

'I don't have time for this fight,' Henderson shouted, as he backed away. 'Go back to your tent and deal with your ration cards.'

'Or what?' Jean hissed. 'Are you threatening me?'

Jean and Henderson regularly fought over how to run the Maquis, but there were a dozen onlookers, none of whom had ever seen the pair in such a violent public disagreement. Awkwardly for Henderson, Jean was well liked and Henderson knew that he'd be the one kicked out of the woods if it came down to a popularity contest.

'Do what you have to,' Henderson told Jean, after a pause. 'I've got orders and I'm sending these teams out.'

Jean glowered then cursed, as he stormed back to his tent.

'Want me to cut Jean's throat in the night, sir?' Luc asked, only half joking.

'Don't *you* start winding me up,' Henderson hissed, as he handed Joel the last sheet of his decoded message. 'Stop gawping and get on with your jobs.'

While everyone else dashed off to prepare for the latest sabotage operations, Edith and Paul were left facing Henderson.

'Shall I walk down to the orphanage with Paul?' Edith asked.

'Yes,' Henderson said, as he absent-mindedly reached back under the canopy. 'You two start walking, I'll catch you up.'

'Aren't you sorting out the operations back here?' Edith asked.

'Joel, Luc and Sam are perfectly capable, and there's another code word in my message. It's a job only I can do.'

CHAPTER EIGHT

Marc Kilgour had spent his first twelve years living in the orphanage where Rosie had died earlier that day. He'd run away when the Germans invaded four summers earlier, met Charles Henderson, escaped to the UK, trained as part of the first group of CHERUB agents, completed several espionage missions, spent a year as a prisoner in Germany, then escaped and completed two more critical missions.

Marc was sixteen now and felt more man than boy after all that he'd been through. He was still part of Henderson's team, but while Paul, Luc, Sam, Joel, PT and Edith slummed it in the woods, Marc lived with his girlfriend Jae Morel in the area's most luxurious farmhouse.

The Morel farm stretched over several hundred acres,

but labour shortages meant that over half the land had gone fallow. Even this level of cultivation relied on groups of Maquis coming out of the woods and working the land in exchange for food. But this was dangerous, because farmers caught using undocumented labourers could be thrown in prison and have their land seized by the requisition authority.

'Paul,' Marc said softly, as he opened a double front door, with a grand staircase directly behind. 'I don't know what to say.'

It was 9 p.m., but being June the sun had barely dropped. Behind Paul stood Edith, and behind her Henderson held the rails of a wooden handcart which bore Rosie's body wrapped in a cotton sheet.

'What about the others?' Marc asked.

'Luc, Joel and Sam are on operations,' Edith explained. 'We asked PT if he wanted to come, but he didn't want to leave his team at the orphanage.'

'What's it like down there?' Marc asked.

'PT's got things well organised and there's no sign of Milice activity,' Henderson said. 'But all the kids saw Sister Magdalene executed. The nuns are doing their best, but you can imagine the state some of the boys are in.'

As Henderson explained this, Marc's girlfriend Jae came down the staircase. She was taller than Marc, but her slender body probably weighed half as much.

'I had to put my father to bed,' Jae said, needing no further explanation because everyone knew that the stress of the war had turned Farmer Morel into an alcoholic.

Jae hugged Paul. He appreciated the gesture, though Paul didn't much like her. Marc and Paul remained good friends, but Marc was madly in love and Paul was jealous that he spent all of his free time with Jae.

'You're welcome to come out of the woods and stay with us for a few days,' Jae said, as she reached behind the open door and grabbed a basket of wild flowers. 'I thought Rosie would have liked these.'

Marc led a solemn walk across fields and between two large barns to the side of a lake. It was a peaceful spot, with thick reed beds and pond-skaters darting across the water. Marc and a couple of farm labourers had prepared a deep grave.

With no coffin, Henderson made the most graceful job he could of lifting Rosie's body off the handcart. She was stiff with rigor mortis and there was no option but to drop her into the hole. Her body rotated, making her toes poke out of the sheet in which she'd been wrapped.

Paul teared up when he saw this, thinking how our fingers and toes are as individual as our faces and how he'd never see these toes again.

'I'm no priest,' Henderson said, once he'd realised

that everyone was expecting him to say something. 'Wherever Rosie is now, I hope it's a better place than this, and that someday I'll have the pleasure of meeting her there.'

'Amen,' Paul said, as he smudged a tear off his cheek and silently mouthed, 'I love you, Rosie.'

Jae threw a handful of wild flowers on the white sheet and held the basket out so that Paul could do the same.

Starting with Paul, each of them took it in turns to gently drop a shovelful of earth into the grave.

'I'll finish filling it in before I go to bed,' Marc said. 'There's food and drink back at the house.'

'I'm afraid I can't stay,' Henderson said. 'Ideally, I need some muscle to help with heavy lifting.'

'I'll come,' Paul said eagerly. 'It's not like I'm going to sleep tonight and I'd rather stay busy.'

'Absolutely not,' Henderson said. 'You're in no state and you've already missed a night's sleep. Go back to the house with Edith and Jae. I'm sure the girls can fill a bath and sort out your blisters.'

Edith nodded to Henderson, then smiled at Paul. 'We'll look after you.'

Marc's location on the farm meant he didn't get a crack at Henderson's operations as often as the others. He liked the idea of an adventure, but Jae looked wary.

'You be careful,' Jae said.

Marc broke into a cheeky smile and pointed a thumb at Henderson. 'All the scrapes we've been through, we're invincible.'

Edith and Paul had begun a stroll back to the house, and Jae gave it a few seconds for them to get out of earshot before pointing at Rosie's grave and hissing, 'I suppose *she* was invincible too.'

Marc tried kissing Jae but she put up her hands and spun around to catch Paul and Edith up.

'Sorry about her,' Marc said.

'She cares for you,' Henderson said. 'There's nothing wrong with that.'

'So what are we up to?'

'We need to get that German truck out of hiding,' Henderson began. 'I've got about eight hundred kilos of plastic explosive stashed in a barn two farms over. It's all got to be taken up to Abbeville by midnight. The message from campus said they need someone who can show the local resistance how to set up detonations, so that's your job.'

'Can't you do it?' Marc asked.

'Looks like they've got something else planned for me in Abbeville, so we'll be travelling up together,' Henderson said. 'It's an hour and a half's drive, but we'll have to pass through or around Amiens, which is a garrison town, so we can add a good hour to that for all the checkpoints.'

It was a full moon and the air was muggy as a stolen German-made truck rolled to the front of a short checkpoint queue. Marc sat in the passenger seat, dressed in a workman's overall. At the wheel, Henderson wore the brown uniform of Organisation Todt (OT), the paramilitary organisation responsible for all major Nazi construction projects.

The soldier carefully inspected Marc and Henderson's false paperwork before speaking in German.

'Don't go north of here without enough fuel to return,' the guard said. 'The resistance have sabotaged two fuel depots and the entire area is dry.'

Marc spoke enough German to understand and Henderson's reply was fluent. 'I should be OK,' he said. 'Thanks for the tip.'

Henderson pressed the gas pedal as the guard opened the gate and they turned on to the road heading north-east to Abbeville. A large yellow sign warned that they were 15 kilometres from the protected coastal zone, which French civilians could only enter with a special pass.

The moonlit road was eerily quiet and Henderson drove slowly to conserve fuel. As they came around a bend he had to brake because a dead horse lay in the road ahead. There was no apparent blast damage to the trees alongside the road and it looked suspiciously like the animal had been positioned to stop a vehicle from passing in either direction.

'Not good,' Henderson said anxiously. 'Jump in the back.'

Henderson threw the gearbox into reverse the instant he stopped, but before he could start rolling back a man leaped on to the running board and held a pistol through the open window.

'Resistance!' the man shouted. 'Stop the engine or I'll blow your head off.'

Henderson left the engine running, but raised his hands and spoke in French. 'I'm one of you.'

The man with the gun laughed, as a much older man opened the passenger side door and clambered into the cab.

'Outside,' he ordered.

Nobody had seen Marc vault over the back of his seat and he lay in a canvas-covered cargo area, sandwiched between sacks.

One of the resistance men dragged Henderson out of the cab and spat in his face before slamming him against the side of the truck. Someone else peeked in the back to see what the truck was carrying, but he didn't spot Marc in the darkness and the sticks of British-made plastic explosive were buried inside sacks filled with powdered chalkstone.

The booze-breathed resister sneered in Henderson's

face. 'The only thing worse than a German is a Frenchman who puts on their uniform.'

'You're making a mistake,' Henderson said, sounding uncharacteristically desperate. 'Look in my bag. You'll find maps and American detonators. If your leaders are connected to anyone, you can easily find out who I am.'

The older of the two men laughed. 'For sure! I'll give you a tour of my headquarters. Let you see the faces of all my bosses before we send you back to your Nazi pals.'

'At least you're OT,' the other man added. 'If you were Milice I'd cut your throat and feed you to my pigs.'

The truck had canvas sides and Marc crawled about in the back, peeking through gaps to work out what was going on. There was no way to tell how many men were hiding out at the side of the road, but as well as the two men interrogating Henderson, there was a man guarding the rear and a pair using metal cans and rubber tubes to siphon fuel out of the tank.

Marc had a gun, but didn't fancy his chances against five men with the possibility of more in hiding. He thought about setting off a ball of explosive as a scare tactic, but Henderson had taken the basic safety precaution of keeping all the detonators in a bag in the cab.

After a glance between the front seats, Marc decided that he could probably get a hand on Henderson's bag without being seen. A panicked shout went up as Marc got the bag. He jumped, but realised that the sound came from way back down the road.

Henderson could hear a column of German army trucks driving at speed towards them. He feared a bullet as the resister who'd dragged him out of the cab raised his gun, but the older man pulled him off.

'There's a village down there,' the older man warned. 'Kill him and they'll go looking for revenge.'

So Henderson got off with a pistol butt slammed in the gut. The resistance gang disappeared quickly, apart from the pair siphoning fuel, who waited for a German headlight beam on their faces before disconnecting their tubes and scooting into the bushes.

The four-truck convoy squealed to a halt. Just like Henderson, their lead driver assumed that the dead horse was an ambush, and rough-looking German infantrymen jumped out of the lead truck with rifles ready.

Henderson soon had guns aimed at him from all directions, but they backed off when they saw his uniform and heard him speak in German. As Marc jumped out and gave Henderson a canteen of water, two German officers debated trying to flush out the resisters.

'It was a large group,' Henderson told them, sticking up for his resistance colleagues even though they'd hardly been friendly. 'Maquis. At least twenty of them, and armed with American weapons. I'll bet they know every ditch and hedgerow in these fields as well.'

After hearing about this vicious-sounding Maquis, the officers decided not to send a team into the fields. Instead, they got men to drag the horse to the side of the road and then set a grenade under it so that the resisters couldn't repeat their ruse.

'Where are you headed?'

'Abbeville,' Henderson said.

The shabby-looking SS officer nodded. 'The roads around here can be dangerous after dark. You must ride with our convoy until you're safely inside the town.'

'I'd be grateful for that,' Henderson said. 'I've had quite a fright.'

As soon as Henderson was back in the cab he looked nervously at the fuel gauge. 'We'll get to Abbeville, but we won't get back,' he told Marc.

Henderson had to drive a couple of kilometres sandwiched between real Germans before his nerves settled enough to give Marc a wary smile.

'No bad thing, really,' Henderson said, 'knowing that Germans are no safer moving around France at night than we are.'

CHAPTER NINE

Tuesday 6 June 1944

It was a quarter past midnight when the convoy pulled up alongside a small hotel, which had locked its main door at curfew an hour earlier. The sight of five German trucks sent half a dozen senior resistance members scrambling out of the hotel bar, down through a basement wine cellar and into a hidden room with an escape hatch leading into the local sewers.

Henderson was in the sights of three resistance machine guns as he jumped down from the cab, walked to the lead truck and thumped on the passenger's side door to thank the officer who'd arranged his escort.

'*Heil Hitler,*' Henderson said.

Instead of saluting back, the shabby-looking officer raised one eyebrow and tutted. Henderson might have expected that attitude from regular German army, but it was unexpected coming from one of Hitler's elite SS officers.

Three storeys up, resistance lookouts on the hotel roof changed from being alarmed to curious as four of the five trucks drove away. They watched Marc jump out as Henderson approached the hotel's front door.

As he rang the bell, Henderson pushed a cigarette-sized detonator through the letterbox and said, 'Delivery from Beauvais.'

Twenty seconds ticked by, before Henderson heard a bolt slide on the other side of the door.

'Henderson?' a smartly suited hotel manager asked warily. 'Can I see your mouth?'

The Abbeville resistance had been told about Henderson's missing front teeth and the tension dissipated when Henderson used his tongue to pop out his lower denture plate.

'A-ha!' the man said. 'Your dentist's name?'

'Dr Helen Murray, of London.'

'That's what I heard,' the man said, smiling slightly. 'I'm told that you are a man of influence.'

As Marc came through the door, Henderson turned into a smoky area that combined the hotel's reception with a small bar. Brandy glasses sat on the tables and a cigar burned in an ashtray, but it took a while for the men and women who'd taken refuge when the German convoy pulled up to start emerging up the steps behind the bar.

'Sorry if I gave you a scare,' Henderson said.

There were four men and two women. Henderson had met two of them before in Paris. Both were leaders of important resistance groups and Henderson guessed that the others were too.

'You certainly know how to make an entrance, Captain Henderson,' a woman named Celine said, as Henderson kissed her on the cheek. 'They made *me* crawl in the back through the sewer.'

Celine was only twenty-two. Her mother had formed an important communist resistance group in eastern Paris. Celine's followers had twice busted her out of prison, but her mother and both sisters had been executed by a Gestapo firing squad.

'Am I the last to arrive?' Henderson asked, as he looked around nervously.

It was extraordinarily risky to bring so many resistance leaders to one place. If anyone was being followed or blackmailed, the Germans would be able to move in and sweep up the whole lot of them.

'Two or three more,' the barman said. 'And of course, Ghost herself.'

Ghost was Maxine Clere, a tall, beautiful, thirty-something with a history of sleeping with Henderson. Her highly successful resistance group had begun in

Paris, but now spanned northern France.

Dozens of Ghost's operatives had been arrested and tortured by the Nazis, but painstaking security meant that the Ghost Circuit survived circumstances that had resulted in other groups being rounded up and executed.

As the hotel manager poured Henderson a complimentary brandy, a bodyguard led Marc to less grand surroundings in the hotel's gas-lit kitchen. The gloomy space had a smell of old cooking fat and a group of boys sitting around a table. Any male aged between seventeen and forty who didn't have a full set of exemption papers could be swept off the street for immediate deportation, so the resistance increasingly relied on women and boys in their early teens.

After a glass of wine and a chunk of gritty black bread, Marc was allowed to reverse the German truck into a courtyard. One bag of explosives was brought inside and once the powdered chalk in which they'd been packed was swept up, Marc stood in front of a gnarled butcher's block and began giving Abbeville's youngest resistance members a crash course in blowing stuff up.

Topics involved were wiring, detonator cords, the merits of various timing devices and the quantity and placement of explosives required for different objectives. These ranged from a simple tripwire used to blow up a motorcycle messenger, to a large multi-stage detonation that would be required to destroy an iron bridge.

When Maxine finally arrived at the back door with two further resistance leaders, it was gone 2 a.m. She'd known Marc for four years, and gave him a hug. When Marc turned back to his pupils, he found the young faces staring in awe.

'Was that Ghost?'

'She's your friend!' an awe-struck girl blurted.

'Can't possibly say,' Marc said teasingly, as he wondered how Maxine had got through town after curfew, accompanied by a dozen bodyguards.

These guards began positioning themselves in spots ranging from the hotel's rear courtyard to the rooftop. The hotel only had twenty rooms and as each resistance leader had brought their own entourage, disputes broke out over the best vantage points.

While the leaders in the bar kept things civil, the atmosphere between guards was tense. All resistance groups were fighting to kick the Germans out of France, but beyond that goal lay huge divides. Communists hated nationalists; resistance groups who believed that extreme violence might provoke a people's revolution were despised by those who'd do anything to avoid provoking Nazi retribution. And besides the big political issues there were local squabbles over territory and equipment drops.

With all the tension and the fact that armed bodyguards were making frequent trips to the hotel's wine cellar, Marc started wondering whether the odds of the resistance groups starting to shoot at each other were greater than the odds of a Gestapo raid.

On the plus side, this meeting showed how powerful the resistance had become. A couple of years earlier it had been tiny and the Nazi security apparatus had such a grip that its leaders would never have dared assemble like this.

Upstairs in the bar, Henderson found himself squashed against the back wall in a haze of cigarette smoke. When Maxine entered, Henderson was surprised to recognise the man alongside her. He was a US Army colonel named Hawk. Henderson had met him three months earlier, during a short and risky return trip to the UK aboard a Lysander aircraft.

'Good evening,' Hawk said, speaking French that was competent, but clearly not his first language. 'I'm sorry to have kept you waiting, but the information I'm about to give was extremely time sensitive. It is exactly 0300 hours. We have a full moon, so by now German spotter planes and coastal lookouts can't have failed to see a massive Allied fleet crossing the English Channel.

'Paratroops have already begun advanced raids to soften up heavily defended beaches. The invasion fleet is the largest in human history. More ships, more men, more planes than any previous operation. Four summers ago, Hitler snatched France, and you've been living under his tyranny ever since. Tonight, the United States and her allies will begin the job of taking France back.'

Henderson drained his second brandy as the room erupted in cheers and wild clapping. A full minute passed before Hawk felt able to resume.

'Now that the invasion has begun, the resistance must act as our eyes and ears behind German lines,' Hawk announced. 'Your groups were assigned multiple operations tonight. By the time the first Allied troops hit the beaches in a couple of hours' time, resistance and Maquis groups all over France will have performed seven hundred separate operations, ranging from the destruction of German radar stations, to cutting railway lines and telephone cables. There are tough times ahead and some of us aren't going to make it. But France will soon be free again!'

*

Henderson didn't have enough fuel to drive the truck back to Beauvais. The local resistance reluctantly offered 20 litres of diesel, but said it was too risky carrying it through the streets during Abbeville's midnight-to-sunrise curfew. They'd have to wait until morning.

After Maxine, Colonel Hawk, the other resistance leaders and the bodyguards left, Marc and Henderson found themselves sharing a small but comfortable twin bedroom on the hotel's second floor.

It was 4.30 a.m. and nearing first light when they

climbed into bed. Henderson was wary about spending time in a location known to ten resistance leaders and their entourages, any one of whom might have been compromised by the Nazis. But a proper bed beat his bunk in the forest and he woke at eight to the echo of Royal Navy artillery blasting the coast 10 kilometres away.

Marc had slept less soundly and stood by the window, already dressed. 'I wonder how it's going,' Marc said. 'The Germans have had four years to fortify the beaches.'

Henderson sat up and rubbed his eyes. 'There's not enough money in the world to make me swap places with some poor infantryman jumping out of a landing craft, that's for sure,' he said. 'The sea will be choppy too, judging by the way that tree out there is swaying.'

'You think they can do it?' Marc asked.

Henderson laughed. 'If they're trying, someone must be confident that they can pull it off.'

'What's in the dossier Colonel Hawk gave you?' Marc asked, pointing at a fat manila wallet on the table between the beds.

'Hawk's got a task for us. Says it's going to be our only focus during the initial phase of the invasion.'

As Henderson spoke he opened the wallet, pulled out a map and spread it over the bed to show Marc.

'I only got a minute with Hawk, because he had dossiers for all the other resistance groups too,' Henderson explained. 'The thing that scares the Allies most is getting their men off heavily defended beaches. Once that's accomplished, the thing that scares them most is the German heavy tanks, in particular the Tiger and King Tiger.'

'Our side will bring tanks though, won't it?' Marc asked.

'Naturally,' Henderson said. 'But Tigers have bigger guns with much greater firing range than any British or American tank. In the east, Tigers have wiped out whole battalions of Soviet T34 tanks before they return one accurate shot.'

'Are our tanks better than Soviet ones?'

Henderson shrugged. 'American Shermans are fast, but they're lightly armoured and none of their crews have battle experience. British tank crews have more experience, but the less said about the quality of British tanks the better.'

'The Tigers can't be indestructible,' Marc said. 'The Soviets have been winning their war for months.'

'Of course not,' Henderson said, as he pointed to the map. 'The turret of a tank has to be light enough to move quickly so that's always lightly armoured, and if you're brave enough to get close, a wodge of plastic or a well-placed grenade will blow the tracks off. There's also a reason why everyone but the Germans prefers light tanks. Tigers are expensive to make and difficult to maintain, so they're only built in small quantities.'

'So what's our job?' Marc asked.

'Hitler has no idea whether the Allies are going to invade via the shortest crossing near Calais, further west in Normandy, or both.'

'So where *are* we going to invade?' Marc asked.

Henderson smiled. 'Colonel Hawk didn't tell us that, probably doesn't even know himself. I expect we'll find out where the first landings have taken place when we next listen to BBC France. The point is, Hitler has merged two tank battalions to create the 108th Heavy Tank Battalion and stationed them exactly halfway between Calais and Normandy.'

'Beauvais,' Marc said, as he worked it out. 'That's why Luc and Paul were sent to blow up the tank train.'

Henderson nodded. 'Our masters in Britain clearly knew the invasion was coming when they asked us to pull that one off.'

The conversation was interrupted by a knock at the door. As Henderson threw his bedcovers over the map, a stooped maid waddled in holding a tray of bread and cheese, a carafe of water and a pot of coffee.

'Your fuel will be here in one hour,' the woman said. 'The sooner you leave the better, because your German truck can be seen from the road.'

Henderson nodded in agreement. 'I'll be gone as soon as I'm fuelled.'

Marc peeled the covers off the map as the maid closed the door.

'So,' Henderson said. 'According to this dossier, the 108th currently has twenty-two Tigers and thirty-four King Tigers – and they'll be low on fuel and spare parts following the tunnel blast. Our job is to keep the 108th in the Beauvais area for as long as possible. And when they set off for the front lines, we've got to try getting ahead of them to make sure they don't go anywhere fast.'

Part Two

June 15th–June 16th 1944

CHAPTER TEN

Thursday 15 June 1944

The Germans who swept through France in 1940 had snappy uniforms and modern equipment that made them seem like men from the future. These first occupying troops had orders to behave correctly towards French people and faced heavy punishment from their own officers if they looted or behaved badly.

Four years on, Captain Henderson found himself among Germans who seemed much more sinister. Sun streamed through the windows as he sat in one of Beauvais' largest bars, dressed in his stolen OT uniform. Beauvais had once been a Luftwaffe town, but German air power had collapsed and the place was crammed with soldiers from the 108th Heavy Tank.

The 108th had been created by merging two depleted

battalions that had fought long campaigns in the east. Six million Germans and fifteen million Soviets had already died in this war. Both sides employed scorched-earth tactics in which retreating armies burned or blew up entire towns and villages.

Civilians who survived the fighting were routinely rounded up and shot, or shipped off to Soviet Gulags or Nazi labour camps, depending on which side won.

This kind of ruthlessness wasn't something men could switch on and off, and Germans who'd fought in the east brought brutal tactics with them when they got reassigned to France. As individuals Henderson found the men of the 108th OK, but as a group there was a casual viciousness about them. It was like stroking a massive dog that might turn on you at any second.

The veteran tank crews had threadbare uniforms with patches sewn over patches. Razor blades were in such short supply that the only men who didn't have beards were teenaged reinforcements too young to grow them.

Henderson had got himself into a poker game. One of his fellow players threatened a waiter with a bullet in the foot when he took too long delivering a round of drinks. It was hard to laugh with them at incidents like these, but people who upset the 108th had a nasty tendency to get strung from lampposts or turn up dead in a ditch.

'Two pair,' Henderson said in German, as he laid his cards on the table in front of him.

The crowd gathered around the poker table jeered as a bearlike tank commander named Otto Scholl screwed up his face.

'Two pair,' he growled. 'Queen and nines, beats your eight and five.'

Henderson acted annoyed as the burly commander scooped two months' wages off the table, but he was actually relieved. The mood in the room was heavy and things might have turned nasty if he'd cleaned Scholl out.

'I'm broke,' Henderson said, as he stood up. 'Good afternoon, gentlemen.'

Nobody minded Henderson leaving the table, but four other losing players wanted a chance to win their money back and didn't like it when Scholl stood up and started stacking his winnings into neat piles.

'Hard luck, OT,' Scholl said, as he slapped Henderson on the back. He made *OT* sound like an insult, because soldiers had a natural resentment for any organisation that didn't fight on the front lines. 'How about I buy you a drink with some of your own money?'

He and Henderson moved to the bar and ordered red wine, because that's all there was.

'You must travel, working for the OT,' Scholl said. 'See much?'

Henderson knew Scholl wanted news about the invasion. 'Only what I hear on the radio, same as everyone. The Allies have their foothold in Normandy, but are going nowhere fast.'

This remark gave Henderson an opportunity to try getting information out of the tank commander. 'I'm surprised your battalion hasn't been moved up to the front.'

'Army command is scared that they'll divert their forces to Normandy, only for the Yanks to stage a second landing in Calais or Dieppe.'

'Bet you can't wait to get at 'em?' Henderson asked.

Scholl shook his head. 'I've done my share of fighting,' he said. 'Happy enough letting some other poor bugger get on with it. And besides, Normandy's a long way.'

Henderson faked surprise. 'From here? Can't be more than two days' drive.'

'Tanks are built to ride long distances on trains,' Scholl explained.

'There's hardly a train line in northern France that's not been cut by the resistance,' Henderson said. 'That much I *do* know.'

'A Tiger needs an overhaul every 750km. And although their top speed is good enough, things start to break if you drive at more than fifteen kph over any distance,' Scholl said. 'Designers kept adding more and more weight to the Tiger, but the engine struggles to shift it. If they send us to Normandy we'll be lucky if half the tanks make it without at least one breakdown.'

'And fuel?' Henderson asked.

Scholl rocked back on his seat. 'Why are you so interested?'

'Those beasts must burn a lot of juice,' Henderson said. 'And it'd be nice to know you're gonna be around long enough for me to win my money back.'

Scholl roared with laughter as he tapped the bundle of francs and reichsmarks inside his jacket. 'If I hang on to this I'll lose it to someone,' Scholl said.

'I'll take care of it for you,' Henderson said.

It wasn't a great line, but Scholl had drunk a skinful and erupted with laughter. 'I bet you would,' he roared. 'Bet you bloody would, but I'll get it sent to my sister before you get your hands on it!'

Henderson wondered how to steer the conversation back towards the fuel situation. 'I guess there's worse things than spending a sunny afternoon in a bar,' he said. 'But I really need to get back to work.'

Scholl snorted. 'I'm not stopping you.'

'No, no!' Henderson said, waving his hands at the misunderstanding. 'I'm supposed to be surveying bridges on the road to Amiens, but my truck is bone dry. I've heard a rumour that there's a fuel train coming into town later this week.'

'*You* won't get a drop – our battalion will have priority,' Scholl said. 'I don't know of anything coming by rail, but they're expecting a dozen road tankers this evening.'

Henderson smiled. 'If I made it worth your while, do you think there's any chance that fifty litres of diesel might find its way into my tank?'

'Why are you so keen to get back to work? Why not stay here and take things easy?' Scholl asked.

'I like to keep my mind occupied,' Henderson said. 'And the poker games get expensive.'

Henderson wanted to press Scholl further, but at that moment a pistol blast ripped across the room and made him spew red wine down his lapel. The joke about shooting the waiter in the foot had turned real and men of the 108th applauded the shooter as the waiter lay on the floor, moaning in agony.

'Bet you wish you'd hurried up now, you lazy French shit!' Scholl shouted.

A woman behind the bar stepped bravely towards her injured colleague and shouted in poor German, 'All of you – get out, we're closing.'

None of the men took any notice until the near-hysterical woman tried dragging the waiter to safety. As she bent forward a soldier grabbed the back of her dress, lifting her into the air as it ripped down the back.

'Forget your boyfriend,' the man barked, slapping the

woman's arse as the crowd made wolf whistles. 'Go fetch our drinks.'

'Unless you want your bar smashed up,' someone added, while another man sadistically kicked the writhing waiter.

'These frogs take our money, but look down their noses at us,' someone shouted. 'Let's smash the place up!'

Henderson ducked as an empty wine bottle flew through the air and shattered against the back of the bar. More glass broke and tables got tipped over as tank crews began vaulting the bar and helping themselves to bottles of wine.

'It's like Poland all over again!' Scholl said happily, moving away from Henderson as a third member of staff got dragged up from the wine cellar and dumped in the middle of the room, with the woman in the torn dress and the man who'd been shot in the foot.

'If you kiss our boots, we might not set your bar on fire,' a man shouted, but over in the corner a mechanic was already holding a lighter to the blackout curtains.

Henderson tried to think of something he could do, but there were at least forty Germans in the bar. His OT uniform meant they might even turn on him, so his only option was to clear out and hope that nothing too awful happened before the men of the 108th finished their latest conquest and staggered back to their camouflaged tanks for an afternoon nap.

*

'Where were you?' Luc shouted aggressively.

The muscular sixteen-year-old booted a three-legged milking stool so hard that it spun out from beneath Paul's arse. Paul went sideways, sending a miniature watercolour set and small sketchbook flying.

'Eighteen bags of onions, forty sacks of potatoes I lugged,' Luc said, making Paul flinch as he threw a punch, but pulled it a centimetre from Paul's nose. 'Dead sister's no excuse to sit on your arse painting all day.'

Sometimes Paul started to think Luc was changing, but then something like this would happen and he'd realise that he was the same bully he'd always been.

'Is there any more to carry?' Paul asked. 'I'd have given you a hand if you'd asked.'

Luc smiled nastily. 'You're so puny. If I hadn't seen your dick with my own eyes, I'd swear that you were a girl.'

Paul wanted to retaliate, but he was out by the lake on Morel's farm and if Luc went psycho there'd be no way to stop him.

'Her majesty sent me out to find you,' Luc said, and Paul knew that this meant Jae. 'Lunch is ready back at the house.'

Luc loomed over Paul as he picked up his paints.

When Luc snatched the pad, he saw that Paul had used the tiny brushes to paint the scene around the lake, except instead of the grave Paul had painted his sister standing amidst the reeds.

'You might be a dick, but you're a talented dick,' Luc said, as he passed the pad back to Paul. 'Looks exactly like her.'

Paul had stayed on the farm since Rosie's death and expected lunch in the Morels' dining room. However, Marc and PT were there and since they stank of manure and hard graft, the Morels' cook didn't let them beyond a staff dining area.

'Nobody starves around here, do they?' Luc said, as he sat at the table and started ladling out a casserole filled with big chunks of lamb.

Paul considered telling PT and Marc what had happened at the lake, but he liked to fight his own battles and tattling would make him feel like a wimp.

'I found something out this morning,' PT said. 'You know Corentin? Not the tall one, the one with the big conk?'

The three other boys around the table nodded. 'Nice guy,' Marc said. 'I don't know him well but he worked hard when he was down here on the farm.'

'Corentin's got a cousin, Gil,' PT said. 'He works as a janitor in an apartment building. Apparently he was moaning about these guys giving him trouble. Turns out, the Milice have been staying on the top floor.'

Paul sounded surprised. 'Milice are so scared of reprisals against their families, I thought they'd drive up from Paris or something.'

'They do,' PT said. 'Corentin reckons they come and go. Sometimes there's fifteen or twenty guys in the apartment, sometimes only a couple.'

'Useful,' Marc said. 'Presumably the extra men come in when there's going to be a big operation, so if we keep the place under watch we'll know when stuff's about to happen.'

'What did Henderson say about this?' Luc asked.

PT shook his head. 'I asked Corentin not to tell Jean or Henderson for a day or two.'

Paul looked confused. 'Why?'

'Because Jean is so scared of reprisals he doesn't want to take any risks,' PT said. 'And Henderson's only interest right now is in sabotaging the 108th.'

'There's been no sign of Milice activity since their guys got killed at the orphanage,' Marc said. 'I wouldn't want to do anything that provoked them.'

'We caught a break there,' PT said.

Marc nodded in agreement. 'The invasion threw everyone off balance for a couple of days.'

'I still don't understand why you're waiting to tell Henderson,' Paul said. 'I know he's mainly interested in the 108th, but there's two hundred Maquis twiddling their thumbs in the woods. Setting up a rota to spy on the Milice's apartment building won't be a problem.'

'I thought it might be better for us to take a look around in there first,' PT explained. 'Corentin's cousin has keys to all the apartments and I'd like to know who Commander Robert is.'

Paul baulked when he heard the name of the man who'd killed Rosie. 'I'd like to see the bastard dead,' he said. 'But the Germans have been wound tight since the invasion. If a Milice commander turns up dead now, they're likely to hang a bunch of people, or set the building on fire.'

'I know,' PT said. 'I'm not saying we kill the commander now, but we know that the Milice don't work close to home; they usually use false identities to stop us locating their families.'

Paul had started to understand. 'So you're saying we go into the apartment, have a rummage and try to find out who Robert is and where he comes from?'

PT nodded. 'He's the commanding officer, so he must have a desk or some papers at the apartment. It might be that I put a bullet through his head next week, or that he faces a tribunal after the war. I couldn't live with myself knowing that the bastard who killed Rosie goes on the run and lives happily ever after.'

Paul nodded solemnly. 'I'd like to come to the apartment with you.'

'You're entitled,' PT said. 'What about you two?'

'Four lads walking around Beauvais will attract attention and I've got a lot to do on the farm,' Marc said.

'I'm with you two,' Luc said.

'Lookout on the ground,' Paul said. 'Lookout upstairs, and one to actually search the apartment.'

'A trio sounds good to me,' PT said. 'We'll go take a look as soon as we've finished eating.'

CHAPTER ELEVEN

Henderson knew most of the Maquis lads in the woods north-east of Beauvais. But they were a trigger-happy bunch, so he entered a barn and switched OT uniform for peasant garb before delving into the countryside.

The Maquis' forest headquarters had moved that morning and Henderson wasted fifteen minutes going down the wrong path. A Maquis with a better sense of direction had made it back from town faster and Jean hurried out of his tent when Henderson finally arrived.

'Have you heard what's happened in Beauvais?' Jean asked.

'I was in the bar where it started,' Henderson said, nodding as he caught his breath. 'Some maniac shot a waiter in the foot. Then they all started wrecking the joint. Set the place on fire and beat the hell out of the staff.'

'I heard it was all along the main drag,' Jean said.

Henderson nodded. 'I cleared out as fast as I could, but once they'd kicked off in one bar the whole street went off. Fights, fires, anyone local was for it. Men beaten up, women mauled.'

'Animals,' Jean hissed, shaking his head. 'I've heard they're leaving soon, at least.'

'Where'd you hear that?' Henderson asked.

'Prostitutes in town,' Jean said.

This news, combined with the riotous mood of the tank crews and the information Scholl had given about the fuel tankers made Henderson certain that the 108th was making final preparations to leave. The only problem was, while Jean and pretty much everyone else in the Beauvais area wanted to see the back of the 108th, Henderson's job was to keep them here.

'Are any of my team around?' Henderson asked.

'Joel and Edith were here a while back,' Jean said. 'They can't have got far.'

Henderson found the pair, along with Sam, at a larger encampment a few hundred metres away. But he blew his top when he discovered that Paul, PT and Luc had gone into town.

'It's bloody dangerous in town right now,' Henderson said. 'Did they say where they were going?'

Edith had heard about the boys' plan to check out the Milice apartment, but didn't want to snitch. She shook her head.

'I need good people on this,' Henderson said anxiously.

'There's plenty of Maquis around,' Sam pointed out.

'Jean won't like any operation that stops the 108th leaving the area,' Henderson said. 'They've always been unruly, but since the invasion they're on edge and they've become downright nasty.'

'What about the communist lads?' Sam asked thoughtfully. 'Their underground newspapers are full of stories about Soviet sacrifice, so they can hardly turn down a fight to rid their country of fascists. Plus, Jean's fair with rations, but he picks favourites when the weapons get dished out and the communists are at the bottom of the pile.'

'Smart thinking,' Henderson said as he drummed his chin with an index finger.

'A lot of the communists are boneheads though,' Edith pointed out. 'We've got rifles and plastic, but we can't make them soldiers by sunset.'

'Agreed,' Henderson said decisively, as he reached his tent. 'But we don't have the luxury of choice, so we'll just have to keep our tactics simple.'

As Joel and Sam hurried off to recruit a posse of young communists without Jean noticing, Edith found herself studying maps under Henderson's small shelter.

The Allies dominated the skies over France, so the 108th had hidden its weapons and vehicles under camouflage netting in dozens of separate locations in the countryside surrounding Beauvais. Since they'd been made Henderson's sole target, Maquis scouts had located fifty out of fifty-six Tiger tanks, along with two dozen motorised artillery pieces and a few more specialised vehicles such as mobile bridges, mine-clearing vehicles and flamethrower tanks.

Henderson had logged each find on a map and now tried to work out the most likely routes for the fuel tankers and the best spots to ambush them.

'They won't risk having a dozen fuel tankers on one stretch of road,' he told Edith. 'One rocket from a Tempest flying overhead would blow up the whole convoy. I'd say we're looking for individual tankers, arriving on different routes over a period of several hours.'

'Small teams?' Edith said.

Henderson nodded. 'Exactly.'

*

Paul, Luc and PT didn't know about the mini-riot staged by the 108th, but picked up the tense vibe in town. There were few people on the streets, and those that were moved quickly.

The apartment building known as Le Grand Americain would have blended into any of Paris' wealthier districts, but its six storeys and marble frontage made it exceptional in a small town like Beauvais.

The war had left the building with a crippled revolving door and lifts that only worked one hour per day when the electricity was on. The three boys scouted the building from a bench across the street and the only movements over thirty minutes were a pair of Luftwaffe officers stepping out of the door into a chauffeured car, and a woman running in.

When Corentin's cousin, Gil, appeared in the lobby with a mop and bucket, Paul and PT left Luc behind as a lookout and crossed the empty street. The double-height lobby had an echo and they kept their voices low.

'We're friends of Corentin,' PT whispered. 'I want to ask you a question about the Milice on the top floor.'

Gil was a bulky man in his twenties, who'd have been shipped to Germany as forced labour but for mild cerebral palsy.

'There's nobody up there,' Gil blurted. 'Do you want to look around?'

'Ssssh!' Paul said anxiously.

Gil leaned his mop against the wall and opened a service door disguised within the lobby's wood panelling. The windowless room they stepped into contained cleaning gear and a table with Gil's half-eaten lunch on it.

'You need this and these,' Gil said, picking a key from a row of hooks and grabbing two blue caretaker's smocks, identical to the one he was wearing. 'Put them on.'

'Why are you so sure nobody's up there?' PT asked, as he buttoned a smock that was too small for him.

'I water the plants when it's empty.'

'Who asks you to do that?' Paul said.

'The commander.'

'Commander Robert?' Paul asked, and Corentin nodded. 'How long before he comes back?'

Gil thought quite hard and stuttered his answer. 'One or two days. Or more. Like, two weeks sometimes.'

PT and Paul hadn't expected it to be as easy as getting a key to an empty apartment. Luc was still keeping watch across the street and PT gave him the thumbs up through the glass of the revolving door before they started up twelve flights to the top floor.

The lower floors had three or four apartments, but the top level was one grand apartment with a full-length balcony. It seemed that the Milice weren't immune to food shortages, because there were vegetables growing out on the balcony and cages with scrawny rabbits inside.

Before the war this had probably been the grandest penthouse in Beauvais, but it now reeked of cigarettes and unwashed bodies. The main living area was squalid, with dozens of empty wine bottles and cigarette butts deliberately stubbed on the antique rugs.

Two bedrooms and the dining room were filled with enough metal bunks for twenty Milice. Most just had skinny mattresses, but a couple had blankets and photos pinned up, indicating regular use by the same person.

Paul checked a bureau and found nothing but a couple of rusty pistols inside it. PT had more luck in the smallest bedroom, which contained a single bed, filing cabinet and desk. He immediately recognised Commander Robert as the chunky man with two daughters in the desktop photo. But there was nothing written on the back and no personal papers on the desktop or in the desk drawers.

As PT started working through the filing cabinet, Paul picked up an overflowing waste-paper basket. After giving it a bang so that most of the cigarette ash dropped to the bottom, Paul delved in for a bunch of screwed-up papers.

The first one was an expired membership card for a Paris shooting club in the name Pierre Robert.

'Looks like the shot that killed Rosie was no fluke,' Paul said, as he showed the card to PT before pushing it into his trouser pocket.

'He only missed me by a few centimetres,' PT said.

The next two papers were tickets from a Beauvais laundry. After that came an envelope addressed to Pierre Robert at a café in an eastern district of Paris.

The paper inside was a final reminder for an unpaid water bill.

'A Parisian café proprietor,' Paul said. 'Hopefully that'll make him easy to track down.'

PT pocketed one of the family photos pinned behind the desk.

'He'll notice that it's gone,' Paul said.

'In this mess? He'll assume it fell down and got thrown out by mistake,' PT said, as he studied the face of a man he'd only previously seen from a distance. 'Pierre Robert, you have *no* idea how much I look forward to catching up with you.'

CHAPTER TWELVE

Henderson had pinpointed three spots where he thought there was a good chance of ambushing fuel trucks and sent a small team to each one. Tanker trucks had no armour and thousands of litres of fuel on board, so could be obliterated by a single grenade, but Henderson doubted they'd have things all their own way. It was high summer, so it would stay light until 10 p.m. and, with fuel desperately short, the tankers were sure to have armed escorts.

Joel led a team of three Maquis, Sam and Edith led another, while Henderson's own group comprised two seventeen-year-old Maquis and eleven-year-old Daniel.

It was 8.30 p.m. when Marc and Paul tracked Henderson down to a stretch of curved road half a kilometre north-east of Beauvais. Marc made a peace offering with slices of chicken pie from the farmhouse. The two Maquis accepted them eagerly, but Henderson kept scowling.

'I don't expect three of my best people to disappear,' he said, keeping his voice low because there was always the chance of a German patrol this close to town. 'I told you we only have *one* objective right now.'

'It's all my fault,' Paul said. 'PT found a lead on Commander Robert and I wanted—'

'I don't give a damn,' Henderson interrupted. 'When we're on operations you follow *my* orders. And since the briefing at Abbeville, has there been any ambiguity about what those orders are?'

Paul and Marc spoke in unison. 'No, sir.'

'Where are PT and Luc?'

'When we got back to the woods and heard what had happened we thought you'd want us spread around,' Paul explained. 'So we all grabbed our equipment. We came here, and PT and Luc went to find Sam and Edith's team.'

This made sense, but Henderson was in too much of a mood to voice approval. 'We all loved Rosie, but she'd have wanted us to respect her memory by continuing to fight the war, not by going off on some wild goose chase tracking down the man who killed her.'

'Yes, sir,' Paul said. 'So shall we stick here with you?'

Henderson nodded. 'I picked this spot for myself

because it's central. The other two teams are all within a kilometre. If we hear any tankers getting blown up we can reinforce them if necessary—'

'Captain, sssh!' one of the Maquis boys said.

He was a small blond lad who looked younger than his seventeen years. Henderson didn't like his tone, but soon realised there were vehicles coming. Daniel was up a tree 20 metres back from the road and gave a shout.

'Eight vehicles, including three tankers. Six hundred metres, moving fast.'

Henderson grinned as he turned towards Marc and Paul. 'Good job you turned up – eight vehicles is a big chunk to bite.' Then he looked around at the two Maquis and addressed them as well. 'There's a lot of them and not many of us. This is strictly blast and run. No heroics. Is that clear?'

As the boys nodded or said, 'Yes, sir,' Henderson grabbed a package of explosives stuck to a wooden bar tray. He planned to throw them into the road a few seconds ahead of the lead vehicle.

Daniel had jumped out of his tree and emerged breathlessly at the roadside as the convoy started getting loud. 'Can I help?'

Henderson shook his head. 'Run now, and don't stop until you get to the woods.'

It was just dark enough for the lead truck in the convoy to have its headlight on. Henderson had to slide his tray of explosives skilfully. Too soon and the driver might swerve, too late and it wouldn't blow until the vehicle passed over.

'Spread out,' Marc told the two Maquis. 'Wait for the first bang, then aim everything you've got at the tankers.'

As Paul grabbed a couple of grenades from a sack, Marc flipped up the scope on his sniper rifle and dropped into a firing position. Springing up from his crouching position at the side of the road, Henderson shoved his tray of explosives in front of the lead vehicle, which was an open-backed truck equipped with a heavy-calibre anti-aircraft gun.

The truck's front wheel hit the tray, spilling plastic explosive across the road. The back wheels cleared before a dozen balls of explosive detonated, but the blast was still enough to lift the truck off the road and shatter the rear axle.

As Henderson ducked chunks of shrapnel big enough to kill him, the blast caught the second vehicle in the convoy – a troop truck. The shockwave instantly killed the driver, while the soldiers behind were forced to bail out through a flaming canvas canopy.

Marc had moved further down the road to attack the tankers sandwiched in the middle of the halting convoy. With two deadly shots, he targeted the drivers of two out of three tankers, then took cover as Paul and the two Maquis lobbed grenades followed by much more powerful balls of plastic explosive.

They'd begun scrambling away when the first fuel tanker exploded. Paul felt scorching heat on his back as he started running. The towers of flame were so bright that he didn't dare look back.

It wasn't clear whether it was plastic or the force of the first truck exploding, but the second and third tankers blew simultaneously. As the noise and heat died off, Paul became aware that someone was charging through the overgrown grass behind him.

He looked back, hoping it was Henderson, but there was an Alsatian dog in the lead, followed by two Germans. Paul was fit after training on CHERUB campus, but he was no athlete and they were all closing fast.

He'd almost reached a hedge at the end of the field when the dog jumped on his back and brought him down. Paul rolled over and reached for the knife in his belt as he tried forcing the animal off with a two-footed kick.

The kick was ineffective, but as the dog sunk its teeth into his thigh Paul drove his knife into the top of the dog's spine, instantly paralysing it. He sat up, reaching for his pistol, but had no serious expectation of getting a shot in before the two chasing Germans were on top of him.

A pistol shot came from behind Paul, hitting one of the men, and when he glanced up he saw a knife rotate through the air and hit the other German in the side of the neck. He knew instantly that Marc was the expert knife thrower, but he was shocked when he glanced behind and saw Daniel crouching in the hedge, holding a smoking revolver and looking rather stunned.

'You OK?' Marc asked, as he grabbed Paul then glanced behind to see if anyone else was following.

'Bastard dog bit me,' Paul gasped, as Marc hauled him up and shoved him through the hedge, before stepping back to pull his favourite throwing knife out of the dead German.

The sky was still lit with flame as Paul started scrambling across the next field. Henderson and the two Maquis lads were running ahead of them.

'Nice shot, Daniel,' Marc said.

'*Please* don't tell Henderson,' Daniel begged. 'He said I didn't need a gun.'

*

It was 22.10 and properly dark as Henderson got back to headquarters in the woods. Marc was right behind, but Paul and Daniel had fallen half a kilometre back during a twenty-five-minute run.

Jean and a couple of his closest aides stormed furiously from a tent and began yelling at Henderson before he'd caught his breath.

'You've gone too far,' Jean screamed. 'Four people were lynched in town this afternoon. Businesses got smashed up, half a dozen women got dragged off. How dare you go behind *my* back and recruit *my* boys to provoke these bastards further?'

Before Henderson could answer, Luc arrived at a run and interrupted breathlessly.

'Sir,' Luc gasped, as Henderson looked his way. 'Me and PT found Edith and Sam's team, but the tankers came in on a different route, so none of us got anywhere. So we snuck up to the German camp to see if we could do some damage before the tanks set off.'

'Those weren't my orders,' Henderson barked.

Luc ignored him, but sounded irritated. 'The point is, the Tiger crews were getting ready to move and some support vehicles had already headed off west. But at least one group of trucks and motorised artillery are preparing to go on the rampage before they leave.'

'How can you possibly know that?' Jean asked.

'Edith speaks a little German and got close enough to hear what was being said,' Luc explained. 'They'd heard about their tankers getting blown up and they were planning to teach the locals a lesson before they ship out.'

'I *knew* something like this would happen,' Jean roared desperately.

Marc looked at Luc. 'Are the others OK?'

'I stole a bike and raced back to let you know,' Luc explained. 'We sneaked some time-delayed bombs under trucks before I left and PT's going to lay explosive traps on the roads.'

Jean furiously jabbed his finger against Henderson's lapel. 'You can't even control a bunch of boys! The Germans are going to be all over us now. What are you going to do, Captain?' he demanded.

Before Henderson could answer, one of Jean's angry sidekicks pulled out a pistol and aimed it point blank at Henderson's chest.

'You're a guest here,' the youth shouted furiously. 'But you've caused us nothing but trouble.'

'No,' Jean said, batting the gun away. 'Where does shooting get us? Do you want a bloodbath?'

'My team and I will be gone soon enough,' Henderson told Jean. 'And you don't have that much to worry about.'

'They have tanks and artillery,' Jean spat.

Henderson took a step back and tried to sound calm. 'The 108th has a vicious reputation, but they're short of everything from fuel to shells, and they have orders to move west.'

Jean seemed to accept some of this, but still looked angry.

'Marc, get my maps,' Henderson ordered.

While Marc dashed 30 metres to Henderson's tent,

Paul, Daniel, Edith and Joel all arrived within moments of each other. Their breathless stories reinforced the picture that they'd had no success in destroying any more fuel tankers and that the 108th's Tiger tanks were making final preparations to move west.

Henderson spread his map of the Beauvais area over the ground so that Jean's crew and his own team could see it.

'Let's assume that the 108th wants to cause mayhem,' Henderson began. 'But their priority is to conserve fuel and move west towards Normandy. Some of their hidden vehicles will have to pass through Beauvais and there could be trouble in the town centre, but I'd say that the real danger of retaliation lies here, in the villages and countryside west of the city.'

Marc felt a tingle as Henderson drew an invisible oval across the map with his fingertip. If he was right, the area most at risk included Morel's farm, the orphanage and two tiny hamlets nearby.

'What can we do?' Jean asked.

Luc snorted. 'What do *you* think rifles and small explosives can do against an entire tank battalion?'

Henderson didn't like agreeing with Luc, but nodded. 'We can't confront the 108th head on,' he said. 'We're powerless to stop them going on the rampage, but we can pick off stragglers and harass them every step of the way to Normandy.'

Edith looked confused. 'You just said it's impossible to stop them.'

Henderson nodded again. 'In a direct confrontation, it is. But we know where they're heading. They'll average fifteen kph at best and route options are compromised, because most rural bridges were built for horse-drawn wagons, not fifty-tonne tanks. On top of all that, they'll need to refuel at least twice a day.'

Luc looked at Jean and sneered. 'So I guess *we'll* be leaving to do some fighting, while you boys keep hiding in the woods.'

Henderson glowered at Luc, before turning to Jean. 'I can't carry all the supplies, so plenty will be left here for your men. My operation will involve two teams, and half a dozen volunteers from your ranks would make things easier.'

Henderson was trying to be conciliatory, but Jean remained bitter.

'I won't try to stop anyone who volunteers,' Jean said. 'Not that you'd take any notice if I did.'

Henderson glanced at his wristwatch, then at his team. 'The tanks are already on the move and we need to stay close,' he said. 'You've got twenty minutes to find your volunteers and pack up.'

CHAPTER THIRTEEN

For every Maquis who was happy hiding in the woods, there seemed to be another bored of the long, hungry days and up for a fight. Six lads lined up for Henderson's briefing, along with Edith and Henderson's six fully-trained agents.

'Two squads,' Henderson announced. 'PT runs Team A. Marc and Luc are his deputies, plus Edith and two Maquis. Your job is to trail the 108th. Harass and destroy broken-down vehicles. If possible try to get ahead and block roads or sabotage bridges.'

As Henderson spoke, Edith and Marc doled out tinned rations, canteens, grenades and ammo clips, while making sure that everyone had a decent backpack to carry them in.

'You'll be living rough, scrounging and stealing food

wherever you can for as long as this takes,' Henderson warned. 'There will be no radios or communication between units, though you have fall-back points here and in Paris. If things get desperate we can try contacting local resistance groups, but be careful when dealing with anyone you can't vouch for.

'I'll lead Team B,' Henderson continued, as he crouched over his map and tapped on the town of Rouen, roughly halfway between Beauvais and the Normandy coastline. 'Rouen is a major German transport hub. There are large fuel depots there and unless the 108th goes on an epic diversion it will pass through or near the city en route to Normandy. I'm going to take the OT truck. My team and I will drive through the night. Tanks can't move quickly, so we'll try to reach Rouen before the 108th and do what we can to stop them from moving on. Questions?'

Nobody spoke, but several sets of eyes looked down at Daniel. Henderson nodded thoughtfully.

'He wants to come and he's already proved his worth,' Henderson announced. 'If there's one thing I've learned in this war, it's that there's not much of a link between a person's age and a person's ability. Daniel and Michel will go with Team A.'

Although Jean didn't approve of Henderson's operation, the elderly ex-teacher cared about the young men. He made sure that everyone who was about to leave was equipped with ration cards, some kind of fake ID and decent boots.

Henderson donned his OT uniform and began preparing identity paperwork that would enable his team to ride his stolen German truck to Rouen in the guise of a construction crew.

The plan for PT's six-strong team was to pick up bicycles stashed at the edge of the woods. Even if the Tigers could only move long distances at fifteen kph, they had no time to waste if they were to have a realistic chance of following them on bicycles.

Henderson gave Marc and PT maps, marked with the most likely routes to Normandy and key locations where sabotage might be an option. He then grew irritated as the two squads dragged out their goodbyes.

'Move out,' PT shouted.

'Good luck,' Henderson said, as he quickly shook PT's hand.

Besides PT, Marc, Luc, Edith, Daniel and Michel, more than twenty other Maquis decided to walk to the edge of the woods with them because they had nothing better to do. Henderson worried that this unofficial entourage could attract attention, but he had other things on his mind and knew that nobody would follow them once they'd picked up the bikes.

The tail end of PT's entourage had just vanished between trees when a flash and shockwave burst over the small forest clearing. As Henderson and everyone else hit the deck the sky was lit with bright white light and there was a sound like a thousand twigs snapping.

'Take cover,' Henderson shouted, but nobody heard because the Germans had launched three more artillery shells.

The first attack of the war had involved Hitler's tanks pushing into the forests of Poland. The Germans had quickly learned that sending tanks or artillery into dense woodland was hopeless. But setting shells to explode a few metres above a forest canopy turned trunks and branches into thousands of deadly, high-velocity splinters.

As Henderson looked about, hot wooden spears whizzed in all directions, smashing into the ground, into trees and into flesh. The 108th clearly knew exactly where the Maquis headquarters was, even though Jean had only moved here that morning.

Jean's command tent had been levelled and a man's legs were smashed under a felled trunk less than 3 metres from Henderson's position.

'Team B, move out,' Henderson shouted, as he stood up.

He did a quick three-sixty, seeing every surface covered with charred splinters, from the size of an arm to the size of a pencil stub. Paul's face came out of the dark and Henderson put a reassuring hand on his shoulder.

'You OK?'

'Yeah,' Paul gasped, as he eyed the sky overhead nervously. There was blood spattered on his face, but it was someone else's.

'We stick to our plan,' Henderson ordered. 'Round the others up and lead them out of the woods to my truck.'

'How do we know there isn't a line of tanks between us and the truck?' Paul asked.

'We don't,' Henderson said bluntly. 'But I don't fancy sticking around here much, do you?'

Before Paul could answer, another triple-shell barrage lit the sky. The first blasts had ripped the tops off the trees, enabling this second wave to penetrate deeper and shred more wood. After finding a couple of members of his team and ordering them to move, Henderson ran towards his tent to grab a leather pouch containing his maps.

Jean got in Henderson's face as he reached under the canvas to pick it up.

'*You* brought this upon us,' Jean screamed. 'I hope you feel *bloody* proud.'

Jean was right, but Henderson felt no guilt. Shitty things happened to decent people. Henderson was a military man and you had to accept that fact if you wanted to wage war.

'Take your men deep into the woods and stay put,' Henderson said. 'The 108th is a mechanised battalion. They've got no infantry to chase you into the woods and they can't stick around long enough to starve you out.'

Jean grunted as Henderson slung a backpack and the leather map-satchel over his shoulders. Before Henderson ran, he realised that there were probably decoded notes and plans in his tent, so he rolled a grenade between the tent flaps and shouted, 'Fire in the hole.'

Meantime, Paul had found Joel and Sam and relayed Henderson's order to head for the truck.

As more artillery shells burst over the clearing, Henderson caught the pair up. 'Where are the others?' he demanded.

'Two dead,' Sam shouted. 'No sign of anyone else.'

'Either ignoring orders or they got hit by something,' Henderson said.

Everyone who could had left the clearing. Henderson looked back at the writhing bodies and desperate moans of those who weren't able to. It would take forever to reassemble his team in the dark, and the longer they stuck around the more chance there was that one of them would get speared in the next blast.

'Looks like it's just the four of us then,' he shouted. 'Let's move out.'

CHAPTER FOURTEEN

While Henderson's squad got halved before it even left the forest, PT and the rest of Team A cleared the worst of the blast zone and shed their entourage.

'They'll need help,' Edith pleaded, scrambling over the undergrowth as Daniel looked forlornly back at the screams and smoke rising out of a clearing that was now almost a kilometre behind them.

'Cower in the woods while others do the fighting and you get what you deserve,' Luc said. 'End of story.'

PT and Marc's responses were more tactful, but Henderson had instilled military discipline in his trainees. They were determined to pursue the 108th, not head back into the woods to administer first aid.

Occasional shell blasts continued as Team A neared the point where the woods turned to farmland. Unlike the Morels' large farm, this remote area comprised small peasant farms linked by narrow dirt tracks. Most were farmed by a single family and ringed by hedgerows several metres high.

This warren was one reason why the Maquis found it relatively easy getting in and out of the forest without being seen. PT's team heard German activity a few fields over as they headed towards a barn stashed with bicycles. When they got close they found part of the road churned by metal tracks and a farm gate that had been bulldozed.

PT studied the tracks before whispering, 'They're too narrow for a Tiger. It's some kind of half-track truck, or motorised artillery.'

The shelling had slowed after the initial barrage, so they all jolted when they saw the muzzle of an artillery gun light up a couple of hundred metres away.

'We should go after them,' Edith said, though she was still keen to help the people stuck in the woods. 'Our job is to wipe the 108th out, isn't it?'

PT didn't answer, but stepped cautiously over the twisted iron gate. A couple of disinterested cows looked his way and there were ruts where the tracked vehicle had crossed the field before exiting by demolishing another gate on the far side.

'Christ!' Daniel said, loud enough to make PT turn around to shush him.

But PT was equally shocked when he saw the horrifically smashed body of an old man. It seemed he'd come out to investigate the noise and been run over by the tracked vehicle. The body was a real mess, but the worst part was that the tracks through the mud swerved towards him.

'Looks like he wasn't armed,' Marc said. 'But the driver went straight for him.'

Edith headed towards the little farm cottage. It was unlikely that any Germans would have stuck around, but she unholstered a pistol before moving inside.

It was a typical peasant home, with one internal wall separating the living area from a tiny bedroom. A gas lamp flickered and a small dog hid in the darkest corner. Edith backed out as the artillery piece fired again. She found the rest of her squad moving briskly across the manure-caked pasture.

Luc reached the second smashed gate first and a muzzle flash gave him enough light to see the German set-up at the centre of the next field.

'Wempe hundred-and-five millimetre,' Luc said. 'Motorised artillery gun. It looks like there's a support truck on the road as well.'

PT looked at Marc and Luc, as Edith, Daniel and Michel caught up.

'Is that gun doing all the damage in the woods?' Edith asked.

'Nah,' Marc said. 'There's got to be at least three of them around.'

'I think I heard some smaller, eighty-eight-millimetre ones, as well,' Luc said.

'It won't stop them attacking the woods, but I still think we should act on this,' PT said. 'The truck will make our journey west a lot easier than pushbikes. We're already close and the hedges give good cover if we're careful.'

Marc nodded in agreement. 'If I run around the front of the mobile gun and crack a few Germans with my sniper rifle, they'll think we're coming out of the woods and it'll draw their fire. The rest of you can flank from the sides. Pick off as many men as you can, but you've got to blow the tracks off the Wempe before it can drive away.'

'Makes sense,' Luc said.

PT agreed, though as he was supposed to be running the show he was irritated by Marc calling the shots.

Marc was equipped for a long journey, but the gear would slow him down. After stashing his pack close to the hedge he set off with his sniper rifle, throwing knife, pistol and ammunition belt covered with spare clips and grenades.

Another huge shell got launched towards the woods as Marc skimmed past a hedge. He sighted the Wempe and a German major standing on the roof of the truck, studying the woods through binoculars. After 100 metres, Marc found a decent climbing tree. He stepped up into a large fork that gave him a view over the hedges, then leaned against a branch and sighted the major through his scope.

Marc held his breath and squeezed the trigger. It was too dark to see subtle movements, but the crack of his rifle scattered at least half a dozen Germans as the major himself crashed backwards on to the truck's canvas awning with a bullet through his heart.

As Marc's second shot hit an observer whose head had popped up from the turret of the Wempe, the area lit up with a succession of grenade blasts. Unfortunately, these blasts illuminated Marc's position and he was forced to jump out of the tree as bullets whistled past.

While the German troops regrouped, the driver inside the Wempe threw it into reverse and shot backwards. The Wempe was less than one fifth the weight of a Tiger tank. While the heavily armoured Tiger was built to plough into battle, the Wempe was designed to fire giant 105-mm artillery shells from safer positions behind enemy lines.

But although it was no Tiger, the big mobile gun still made a fearsome target for a group armed only with grenades and plastic explosives.

Whatever criticism people made of Luc, he was no

coward. He shot out of a hedge on a carefully timed run, aiming to get within a couple of metres of the Wempe and toss a grenade under the side flaps to blow off a track.

But the driver's rapid reverse sent the tank straight towards him. Luc slipped as he turned around and tucked his right leg in half a second before the metal tracks would have mashed it.

He ended up between the mobile gun's tracks in pitch darkness, listening to its whirring driveshaft echo through the armoured floor centimetres above his ear. There seemed to be a lot of shooting going on as the tracks on either side of Luc stopped moving.

Fearing that the Wempe might turn and squish him, Luc had no option but to clamber out at the front and jump on to its armoured hull. He was now on the front running board, with the turret being slowly cranked into a firing position. Judging by how low the barrel was being aimed, the crew were hoping to fire through the nearest hedge, at what they assumed was a frontal assault by Maquis coming out of the forest.

Luc's head was less than a metre and a half from the 105-mm gun's huge muzzle and if it went off while he was this close his eardrums would rupture. His palm seared on the hot gun barrel as he kicked against a metal rung to launch himself to the top of the turret.

Since he'd turned and slipped, everything Luc did

had been for self-preservation. Now he finally had a second to think.

He'd dropped his grenade somewhere along the way, but there was another hooked to his belt and the top of the turret was open, with the bloody face of the guy Marc shot staring at him. As a bullet pinged off the armour somewhere behind, Luc ripped a pin out of a grenade and dunked it past the dead man and into the turret.

Someone shot at Luc from close range as he slid off the turret to the side of the tank. Shouts in German came from inside. Luc didn't speak the language but suspected it was something like '*Oh shit, that's a grenade!*'.

A fuel can strapped to the mobile gun's side jammed into his gut. He pushed off, hitting the dirt on his knees as the grenade exploded.

This explosion instantly killed the mobile gun's four surviving crew members. The much larger secondary blast from the shells stored inside probably would have killed Luc too, but for the fact that the turret hatch was open and most of its energy got directed upwards.

Luc found his feet, but was deafened and completely disorientated. He had no idea if he was staggering towards German machine-gun fire and he felt like church bells were going off in his head as someone grabbed him.

'Luc,' Edith said.

At the same moment Marc closed on the scene and shouted something that Luc barely heard.

'That was amazing!'

As Luc looked around, he realised that while he'd taken out the mobile artillery, the combination of Marc's sniper shots and everyone else's grenade blasts had killed most of the Germans or sent them running away.

'Is Luc OK?' PT asked.

'Quite a burn on his hand,' Edith answered. 'I've got some bandage.'

PT nodded. 'The other German positions can't be far off, so we need to move out. I'll drive the truck. Marc, you speak the best German, so you ride with me up front and deal with checkpoints. The rest in the back. Try and get German uniforms. Grab any weapons you find, and we need fuel. *Especially* fuel.'

'What about the bicycles?' Marc asked.

'We'll still stop and pick them up,' PT said. 'Might need them further down the line, but this truck gives us a real chance to stay on the 108th's tail.'

CHAPTER FIFTEEN

Team A had struck gold with the truck. The only damage during the shoot-out was a smashed side window and some bullet holes in the canvas awning. They also found two large cans of diesel, towing ropes and a mechanic's chest filled with tools and spare parts.

Edith, Luc and Michel faced a rough ride on the bare floor in the rear, with a strong oily smell and the bicycles packed around them. Daniel had found a corner and snuggled on a mound of greasy mechanic's overalls, with a padded kneeling-mat under his head. Up front, Marc and PT had dressed themselves in uniform stripped from dead Germans.

At nineteen, PT was older than the 108th's most recent conscripts, while at sixteen Marc looked young, but not so much that he'd raise suspicion.

'Any ideas on what I should say if we're stopped?' Marc asked.

PT shrugged as he drove fast around a tight corner, making spares and tools crash about in the back.

'Our uniforms show we're from the 108th,' PT said, as he accelerated. 'Whenever I've seen big troop movements the vehicles just get waved through checkpoints.'

'True,' Marc agreed. 'I reckon I can handle a checkpoint, but what if someone looks in the back and sees our passengers?'

'Prisoners, or something?' PT suggested.

'Maybe if we tied them up,' Marc said, then he shouted into the back. 'Hey, Luc. Mind if we tie you up?'

Luc's head popped through the canvas flaps separating the cab from the cargo bay. 'I'll put on a mechanic's overall,' Luc said. 'If anyone asks, Daniel, Michel and Edith were arrested for sabotage before we left and have no proper paperwork.'

'That's credible *and* it explains the lack of documents,' Marc said, as he reached into his slightly-oversized German jacket and pulled out several military IDs stripped from the dead Germans. 'See if one of these looks anything like you.'

As Luc took the IDs and disappeared into the back, PT stopped the truck before turning on to a dirt road that Marc knew well.

'Used to walk down here every day, between the orphanage and my school,' Marc said.

PT was more interested in the chunks of bark stripped from trees growing close to the road. 'Gotta be tanks did that,' he said.

'Slow down then,' Marc warned. 'Probably not a good idea to run into them.'

'Tanks aren't subtle,' PT answered. 'We'd hear 'em way before we saw 'em.'

It was a warm night, so the side windows were down and Marc caught a whiff of smoke. He knew that the only thing close by was a row of peasant cottages, with a small farm-supply store at the far end.

PT slowed as they passed a flattened hedge, and while there wasn't much light, they could see several sets of huge Tiger tank tracks veering off-road towards the cottages. A 60-tonne Tiger will demolish any wall it hits, and it seemed that a line of tanks had gouged through three homes, knocking down the front walls and making roofs cave.

As with the old man splattered by the mobile gun, there was no reason for this carnage beyond enhancing the 108th's reputation for meanness. Marc recognised most of the distraught people standing beside wrecked homes and glimpsed two bodies laid out, either dead or close to it.

'Bastards,' Marc said.

The locals near the road didn't recognise Marc. They just saw a German truck and German uniforms. PT accelerated because if his home had been demolished, he reckoned he might just be angry enough to shoot at the next bunch of Germans who drove by.

'There was an old girl who lived in the end house,' Marc said sadly, taking a last glance back as they sped on. 'One time a storm broke on our way home from school. I was about six and it was thick mud, so she took four of us boys in and gave us hot milk. I can remember sitting on her floor, with my hair dripping and mud caked up my legs.'

'Was she still around?'

'Haven't seen her in years,' Marc said. 'I know one of her sons worked for Morel.'

As this memory faded, Marc realised the burning smell hadn't. They'd seen no obvious fire at the cottages and the smoke was starting to cloud PT's view down the road.

'It's the orphanage,' Marc blurted anxiously. 'It's over the next hill.'

As his old orphanage came into view, Marc saw its outline lit by orange flames. The main building where the kids slept seemed OK, but the nuns' accommodation and adjoining chapel were ablaze. PT slowed the truck to a crawl, because tanks had smashed through the orphanage's boundary wall, leaving the road strewn with chunks of rubble big enough to rip a tyre off its rim.

'Let me get out,' Marc said urgently. 'We need to know how many tanks we're chasing, and how long since they left.'

Edith and Luc's heads had popped through the canvas flaps to get a view. The nuns had organised a chain of boys passing buckets and bowls of water from a nearby stream. The fire was out of control, so they were dousing the dry grass between the chapel and the orphanage in the hope that it would stop fire spreading to the orphanage proper.

'Don't hang about,' PT told Marc, as he turned through the orphanage gate. 'Two or three minutes.'

Marc barely listened, and as he jumped out of the cab a bullet whizzed past, forcing him to his knees.

'It's me, Marc Kilgour!' he shouted, as he raised his hands to the unseen gunman. 'Don't shoot!'

The arrival of a German truck had made the nuns send the line of boys scrambling into the surrounding countryside. But a young sister named Mary raced downhill, recognising Marc despite his uniform. Jae's father was close behind, and sober for once.

'What happened?' Marc asked.

'They were short of rations and must have known that we preserve a lot of food for the boys,' the sister explained. 'They arrived twenty-five minutes ago, with six tanks and a line of trucks. They threatened to level the orphanage if we didn't hand over every scrap of food, then they made some of the older boys help load their trucks. When that was done, they forced five boys into a truck. Things turned nasty when we tried grabbing the boys back. They beat up Sister Fidelis and threw grenades into the chapel.'

Marc was sickened. 'How old were the boys they took?'

'Lucien's the youngest, he's twelve but big for his age. The others were thirteen or fourteen.'

'Did the Germans say what they wanted them for?'

This time Farmer Morel answered. 'They didn't say anything. But I've read that this tactic has been used in the east. There's a lot of manual labour in the army: latrines, trenches, graves. And why dig yourself when you can force a civilian?'

'What about Jae?' Marc asked.

'They drove across our land tearing through fencing and hedges,' Morel explained. 'Jae is safe. She and some of the labourers are out now, fixing holes and rounding up loose animals.'

'We have to go, Marc,' PT shouted from the truck. 'Are you staying or going?'

Morel looked at Marc. 'Going where?'

Marc felt loyalty to his old orphanage, but there were plenty of nuns and his specialty wasn't putting out fires or nursing scared kids.

'Give me thirty seconds,' Marc shouted to PT, before turning back to Morel and the sister. 'We're trying to stop the 108th getting to Normandy,' Marc said. 'I can't promise you anything but I'll keep an eye out for your boys. Tell Jae that I'll be back in a few days and that I love her.'

It was a token of how much Farmer Morel had warmed to Marc over the past couple of years that he didn't baulk.

'She already knows,' Morel said. 'You all be careful. I ran over here to investigate the flames, and almost got myself shot. There's a broken-down truck on the road, just shy of my farm gates.'

'German truck?'

Morel nodded. 'Identical to yours.'

Marc reboarded the truck and updated the others, as PT steered a cautious path through the rubble. Then they worked up a plan for their imminent encounter with the broken-down truck.

Morel had been right. It was a canvas-covered Opel truck identical to their own, but he hadn't noticed the small, towed artillery gun attached to the rear.

The road was barely wide enough for two vehicles to pass, so PT steered past slowly with one side clattering branches. He stopped when the trucks' front bumpers were level. A bored-looking soldier sat in the driver's seat, Germanically blond and no more than twenty years old.

'We've got a mechanic in the back,' Marc said, in German. 'You want him to take a look under your hood?'

The young German seemed happy taking it easy at the roadside while his battalion charged towards battle in Normandy.

'We'll be OK,' he said. 'My partner headed off to find water for the radiator.'

'Up to you,' Marc said casually. 'But the locals don't like us. I wouldn't want to be in your seat when the resistance works out that the rest of our battalion has left town.'

Marc's line seemed to tweak the young soldier's sense of self-preservation. 'You could be right,' he said thoughtfully.

'So it's just you?' Marc asked, as Luc vaulted from the back of the truck, wearing a baggy mechanic's overall.

The soldier nodded. 'How come you speak like a frog?'

'French mother,' Marc explained, disappointed that strenuous efforts hadn't disguised his accent.

The only things Luc knew about fixing trucks were a few tips he'd picked up while learning vehicle sabotage during his espionage training. He squeezed between the trucks, carrying a random tool pouch he'd found inside.

The broken-down vehicle's radiator had overheated

and the hood had already been loosened to let out steam. As Luc balanced on the front bumper making thoughtful noises, Edith stepped over the little artillery piece and crept in the back.

Shooting the young German would have been easy, but Marc didn't like the idea of revenge-happy troops finding a blood-spattered truck outside the farm where his girlfriend lived.

Edith crawled over boxes of 37.5-mm artillery shells. When she got behind the German's seat she swung a cosh, cobbled together using a sock filled with metal sockets from the mechanic's chest aboard their truck. It was meant to belt the German in the temple and knock him cold, but he glanced around at the last second and it smacked the bridge of his nose.

Luc had been waiting for Edith's blow and he jumped off the bumper and opened the driver's door. As Edith knocked the soldier out with a second coshing, Luc grabbed his boots and yanked him into the road.

Luc looked happy as he put the unconscious soldier in choke hold and throttled him. As the German breathed his last, Marc hopped around the back and inspected the artillery piece.

'Reckon we could use this?' Marc asked, as he looked across to confirm that their truck had a suitable towing bar.

'Do you know how to use artillery?' Michel asked.

Marc shrugged. 'It's basically a gun with massive bullets. How hard can it be?'

As Luc dragged his kill through the roadside hedge and deep into one of Morel's fields, Marc and Michel unhooked the artillery piece and attached it to their truck, along with several crates of small shells.

Edith searched the truck's cab and found a road map. It had a route marked all the way from Beauvais to Caen in Normandy, passing through Rouen as Henderson had predicted. Edith didn't read German well, so she passed the map to Marc.

'PT,' Marc shouted, as he ran back to the cab. 'This map has got *everything*: routes, alternative routes, diversions, weak bridges.'

PT didn't quite believe it when he saw the map. It was a standard German-language road map that had been carefully adulterated with dozens of hand-stamped symbols, which were explained in a separate key typed on waxy paper.

'They wouldn't give a map this detailed to every driver,' PT said.

Marc thought for a moment before replying. 'I guess they have to give it to some of them. With air attacks and resistance raids, the 108th will move in smallish groups. And there's a big risk of getting separated or lost in the dark.'

By this time, Luc was back from hiding the body,

while Edith and Michel had transferred a can of fuel and anything else worth having from the broken-down truck.

'I say we use this map,' PT said, 'find a weak spot on the 108th's route and sabotage as many tanks as we can.'

Edith looked wary. 'Henderson said—'

PT interrupted. 'Henderson thought we were gonna be riding bicycles, harassing stragglers and broken-down tanks at the rear. But our truck can cruise three times as fast as the tanks and we've got a map that shows us where they're heading.'

'We don't wanna fall too far behind,' Marc said. 'Luc can ride up front for a bit. I've got the best German, so I'll study the map in the back and try to find their weak spot.'

CHAPTER SIXTEEN

Thursday 16 June 1944

A hundred kilometres separated Beauvais from Rouen. It was a seven-hour ride for a Tiger tank that couldn't risk breaking its drive shaft, but even with a couple of diversions to avoid tank columns and Maquis-infested forests, Henderson's OT truck reached Rouen's outskirts in two hours. He'd driven fast and Paul, Joel and Sam were thoroughly shaken in the rear.

Rouen's half-million population was divided by the River Seine. The main German fuel depot was in an industrial area south of the city. Heavy bombing had damaged the only bridge here and nothing heavier than a motorbike was allowed across.

Instead, the 108th's advance party had put up signs with directions into the city and Henderson crossed the

Seine in the heart of Rouen, before taking a tortuous route south through narrow city streets. Each sign was guarded, lest some mischievous resistance member decided to meddle with it.

'What's the plan, boss?' Paul asked, as he stuck his head through the canvas flaps behind Henderson's seat.

Henderson tapped the fuel gauge. 'Running on fumes,' he explained. 'So we'll try and kill two birds with one stone. I'll follow the signs to the depot, get a fresh tank of diesel and a good look around. Hopefully we'll be able to work out a way to come back and do some damage before the Tigers get here.'

The French had built the depot close to the river so that supplies could be brought in by tanker. There were three large cylindrical fuel tanks above ground, but these were neglected and Henderson immediately realised that the Germans kept their precious supplies in newer tanks, dug into the ground and shielded by metre-thick concrete.

As the Allied planes now dominated the skies, it was important that the 108th made as much ground as possible under cover of darkness. While the first Tigers wouldn't arrive for at least five hours, many support vehicles due to reach the depot before sunrise had done so. Henderson found himself in a queue of trucks, Kübelwagens, motorised artillery and half-tracked troop carriers.

While he waited, a team pushed bulky handcarts down the line, passing out bread and sausage, pouring coffee into soldiers' enamel mugs and refilling canteens by dunking them into a barrel. Henderson passed out his canteen, but the man cutting off chunks of sausage baulked when he saw his brown uniform.

'OT?' he said, glancing at his colleague.

The colleague shrugged like he didn't care and Henderson got fed. Henderson would have liked to wear a 108th uniform, but it was too risky because he'd been seen around the bars in Beauvais dressed as OT.

'Anyone want this?' Henderson asked, as he passed the sausage back through the canvas.

Sam was hungry. He split it with his older brother Joel, but gobbed it into his hand when he tasted the mouthful of fat and gristle.

'That's vile!' Sam gasped, as he unscrewed the top of his canteen to rinse his mouth.

'Look on the bright side,' Joel said, as he tried swallowing his piece. 'Eating this muck can't be good for German morale.'

Paul couldn't help smirking as Henderson rolled the truck a couple of places further towards the refuelling pumps. 'Good for *my* morale though. Your faces are a picture.'

But Henderson darkened the mood when he turned

back and spoke through the canvas. 'You boys be ready. I don't like what I'm seeing.'

'Ready for what?' Joel asked.

'Keep weapons and grenades to hand,' Henderson warned. 'If you have to run, go left and try getting between the fuel tanks. They're shielded, but hopefully they still won't want to fire bullets towards their precious fuel.'

There was no way to look out of the canvas awning without being spotted by someone in the truck behind.

'What's the problem?' Paul asked.

'We're up to sixth in the queue,' Henderson said. 'There's three pumps and a private with a clipboard is checking everyone off against a list.'

With fuel in such huge demand it was no surprise that security was high, and ticking off vehicles was a standard procedure used to track progress during the movement of a large battalion. Henderson hoped he could bluff a tank of fuel, but didn't feel optimistic as he rolled up to a slim private.

'Vehicle number,' the private asked.

'OT seven-five-six-two,' Henderson said, figuring there was no point lying because of his uniform and the vehicle ID painted on the door.

'Not the 108th?' the man asked.

'I have to get west,' Henderson said. 'I'm part of a survey team.'

'I don't care if you've got Adolf Hitler in your passenger seat,' the private said. 'Our allocation is short. Every drip is earmarked for the 108th and you're not even supposed to be on the road until the 108th has cleared the area.'

'Is there anywhere I can get fuel in town?' Henderson asked.

The soldier laughed. 'Can't miss it, bright red sign. All the fuel you want, all the food you can eat and all the whores have three tits.'

Henderson smiled at the joke, after which the soldier showed more sympathy.

'There's an OT office in town,' he said. 'Drive back the way you came and get them to write up a fuel requisition slip. But I still can't supply you until the entire 108th has passed through.'

'Blast it,' Henderson said, as he looked at his fuel gauge and guessed that he had 10 kilometres' range if he was gentle on the throttle.

'I'd help if I could,' the private said.

'Rules are rules, I guess,' Henderson said, making like he wasn't too bothered. 'I'll head back towards town.'

The concrete refuelling courtyard was wide enough to turn the truck around in a single arc. The private made an absurd show of self-importance as he gave a *halt* signal for the vehicle behind Henderson's truck, followed by grand sweeping gestures to indicate that

Henderson was about to turn back towards the city.

'Could have been worse,' Henderson told the boys, as he drove slowly past the queue that he'd wasted the last hour in. 'Can't see us damaging those buried fuel tanks with our sticks of plastic, but we could hold things up a good while by destroying the refuelling pumps.'

The road into the fuel depot narrowed as it neared the point where it met the highway. Henderson had to stop to let the men dishing out food and water wheel their carts out of his way. It wasn't much of a hold-up, but before he could set off, a man wearing the heavy silver neck chain of a German military police officer stepped from between two queuing trucks making a *halt* gesture.

'Out of the vehicle,' the man said. 'Present your documentation.'

Henderson thought about hitting the gas and flattening him. But his forged paperwork and spoken German were perfect, so he decided to chance it. As Henderson stepped down into the dark, Paul peeked through a tear in the canvas awning.

'I recall you drinking with some of my officers, in Beauvais,' the policeman said suspiciously, as Henderson noted that he wore the stripes of a Hauptmann, which was equivalent to his own rank of Captain. 'You seemed interested in the men of the 108th, and now I find you here.'

Henderson didn't like where this was going. Regular military policemen spent their time breaking up fights, charging drunks and running down deserters. But this guy was a senior officer who clearly packed a decent brain.

'OT seven-five-six-two,' the policeman said, placing one hand on his holstered pistol as he ran his fingertips across the number stencilled on the truck's door. 'OT one-five-six-*seven* was reported stolen after a Maquis ambush north of Beauvais. A few careful brush strokes would change one to the other, I think.'

The officer was clearly proud of his detective job, but as he was alone he ought to have put his suspect in cuffs before bragging about it.

'Turn and place your hands on the side of the truck,' the policeman said, as he pointed his gun at Henderson's chest. Then the officer turned to a group of troops sitting in one of the trucks waiting to refuel.

'Secure this vehicle immediately,' he ordered. 'Make sure there's nobody hiding in the back.'

The policeman had to take a step back to enable the other troops to see him. Henderson planned to use this half-second to kick him in the groin and try grabbing the pistol, but Sam had snatched up a pistol and crawled into the truck's cab. His bullet flew out of a side window, hitting the policeman in the head.

At the same instant, Paul leaped into the driving

seat, grateful for the fact that the engine was still running. He drove a few metres forward, knocking down the first soldiers reacting to the policeman's final order.

Sam threw open the canvas flap at the back of the truck and yelled at Henderson, 'Get in!'

As Henderson jumped aboard, Paul realised he had a problem. One side of the road was lined with trucks and the way forward was blocked by two serving carts and a giant-wheeled water barrel. There was a chance he could smash them out of the way, but they could easily end up beaching the truck, so he didn't fancy his chances.

'Backing up,' Paul shouted to the others, as he struggled to find reverse gear.

Fortunately it was dark and the soldiers in the surrounding vehicles were half asleep. The truck's transmission whined as Paul reversed 100 metres towards the three fuelling pumps.

'I need grenades,' Henderson shouted, as he scrambled around in the back. 'Where have you hidden them?'

Paul was driving an unfamiliar vehicle backwards in the dark, seeing nothing but black shapes in his side mirrors.

'Can anyone see?' he shouted. 'Where the hell am I going?'

Joel and Sam had grabbed weapons and grenades while Henderson had been at the roadside. Sam decided that anything that took attention away from them was a good thing and lobbed several grenades out of the side window towards queuing trucks.

Henderson looked out the back and yelled at Paul. 'Turn hard right. Everyone brace!'

There were a couple of gloomy electric lights in the refuelling area and Paul saw that he'd backed up to the broad concourse on which Henderson had turned two minutes earlier. He swung the steering wheel, half expecting the truck to roll.

The first grenades went off under the waiting trucks as Paul hit the brake. A bullet smashed the windscreen as he crunched first gear and set off towards the fuelling rigs. He thought about ramming one of them, but his main concern was getting away so he aimed between two trucks in the middle of refuelling.

The gap was barely wide enough. Side mirrors broke off and the canvas awning got ripped. They had enough plastic explosive to blow the refuelling rigs, but there wasn't time to set detonators, so Henderson could only lob out grenades while Joel shot up the refuelling crews with a machine gun.

The fuel depot's exit was up a slight ramp, 50 metres ahead. An arrow pointed left towards a wooded area further south where the 108th would hide its vehicles, waiting for the big tanks to catch up before setting off on the second half of the journey to Normandy at nightfall.

Paul had no idea where a right turn would take him, but he figured it was better to move away from the 108th's freshly-fuelled vehicles than towards them. The road was slightly uphill, passing a boatyard with the River Seine at its far edge.

As Paul accelerated, the steering wheel almost ripped his hand off and he realised he had a front puncture. He veered out of control towards tatty pleasure boats and river barges standing on their keels. A large explosion in the refuelling area coincided with the point where a lot of angry soldiers had their weapons ready and had finally worked out who they were supposed to be shooting at.

'It's dying on me,' Paul shouted, as the engine stalled.

He forgot to apply the handbrake and the truck began a slow roll downhill as he dived for the driver's door. But as Paul grabbed the handle, it felt like a thousand machine-gun bullets simultaneously hit the side of the truck.

The vehicle picked up momentum as Paul scrambled out. Sam kicked him in the face as they hit the road on top of each other. Henderson and Joel had already jumped through the torn canvas. As Joel vaulted a low fence into the boatyard and bullets tore up the road, Henderson helped Paul and Sam to their feet.

'You hurt?' Henderson asked.

Sam and Paul both felt OK as they scrambled away from the rolling truck. They'd all made it into a gloomy channel between two beached coal-barges when a light tank annihilated Henderson's truck with a single shell.

Nobody was injured, but Joel had the only gun and they knew next to nothing about their surroundings.

'Shit, shit, shit!' Henderson gasped. 'It'll be a *bloody* miracle if we make it out of here alive.'

CHAPTER SEVENTEEN

While the fuel depot burned, Daniel and the rest of Team A were 40 kilometres east. Daniel had just reached the top of a large tree, with first light coming over the horizon behind him. He held up Luc's binoculars and saw the murky outline of a 30-metre-long road bridge. There were guards at either end and a tow-truck on standby.

Marc had carefully studied the German road map, looking for vulnerable points: tunnels to block, bridges to blast or steep-sided valleys from which you could stage an ambush. But the land between Beauvais and Rouen was flat and the only bridges crossed tributaries of the Seine narrow enough to be bridged at every hamlet. Blowing one of these up would only divert the tank columns a couple of kilometres to the next bridge.

However, the 60-tonne weight of a Tiger tank did create difficulties for the Germans. Many bridges on the map were marked with a cross, which the key translated as *Bridge uncrossable by tanks*, or a cross with a circle which meant *Light vehicles only*.

After careful study, Marc found several points where blowing a strong bridge would add significant time to the tanks' journey to Rouen. The best of these was just past the intersection of three roads on the edge of a small town named Gournay-en-Bray.

Taking out the bridge here would add sixty to ninety minutes to a tank's journey time. It wasn't much, but Marc hoped it would give extra time for Henderson to set up a sabotage operation in Rouen, and the longer the tanks spent on the road in daylight the greater the chance that they'd be located and destroyed by the RAF's rocket-firing Tempest bombers.

'What's it like?' PT asked, reaching up to grab Daniel as his legs dangled overhead.

The whole of Team A were huddled 200 metres west of the bridge, with their truck hidden between two dilapidated barns.

'There's a few guards on either end, but they're just standing around looking bored,' Daniel told the others. 'The river's less than six metres wide.'

Marc was worried by this. 'Tanks might be able to ford that. Were the embankments steep?'

'Pretty steep,' Daniel said.

PT tutted. 'I don't mind risking my life, but not if we blow the bridge only for the tanks to roll down the embankment and drive across the river bed.'

Marc looked at the sun. 'You're the boss, PT, but you'd better decide soon. It's getting murky and it'll be light by o-five-thirty.'

'Plus the tanks can't be more than an hour away,' Luc noted.

'Maybe we're thinking about this the wrong way,' Edith said. 'If we wait until there's a tank, or better still two tanks crossing, they'll be destroyed. There's also bound to be a hold-up while the rest of the convoy works out another way to cross over to this side.'

'And we've got our little artillery gun,' Luc added. 'Thirty-seven-point-five millimetre shells won't penetrate heavy armour, but if we set up a good firing position we could blow tank tracks to shit, maybe damage the wheels as well.'

'You'd have to be fast,' Edith said.

Luc nodded. 'If it's a surprise I reckon you could get three or four good shots in before a tank fires back and destroys the position.'

PT smiled. 'Now this is starting to sound like a plan. Daniel can sit up in the tree and act as our lookout. He can't shout without alerting the Germans, so Edith waits at the bottom and acts as our messenger. It's gonna take some muscle setting up that artillery piece on the riverbank. I'll handle that with Michel, which leaves Marc and Luc to sneak under the bridge and lay the explosives.'

'Sounds good,' Marc said, as he started walking back to the truck to get their equipment. 'Let's get cracking.'

*

The boatyard was pitch black and its puddled floor a minefield of rotten wood, nails and paint tins. Sam sliced his arm on a piece of rusted metal as he charged blindly between coal-barges with rust holes big enough to fit your head through.

A single German Kübelwagen had gone after them, but the men inside either thought his team had died when the shell blew up the truck, or didn't have the appetite to charge into a boatyard that might be crawling with resistance.

The explosions in the fuel dump had destroyed the refuelling equipment and set men and vehicles on fire. But cut-off valves prevented any kind of blowback into the main tanks.

Sam clutched the gash through his bloody shirt-sleeve as he reached the gently lapping river, joining in a gasping pack with Henderson, Paul and his brother Joel.

'Is it bad?' Joel panted.

'I don't think so,' Sam said, as he undid his cuff button and pulled up the sleeve.

As Joel inspected his brother's bloody-but-not-particularly-large cut, Henderson looked upriver, seeing a bridge silhouetted against first light.

'I've got the name of two places where I can potentially contact the local resistance,' Henderson said. 'Maxine reckons they're a funny lot though.'

'Communist?' Paul asked.

'Mostly,' Henderson said. 'But we've got no equipment and the Germans are gonna be looking for me.'

'You want this?' Joel asked, offering Henderson the machine gun.

Henderson shook his head. 'I've got my silenced pistol. Just try keeping that thing out of sight and don't waste any ammunition.'

As he spoke, Henderson flung his brown OT jacket into the part-flooded hull of a rowing boat. Then he ditched the matching brown tie and pulled his shirt out of his trousers. He could now pass as a Frenchman, provided you didn't look too closely at his German military boots, or ask to see his papers.

'You three have civilian ID,' Henderson said, though this comment made all three boys check their pockets to make sure they hadn't left them aboard the exploded truck. 'Nobody knows what you look like and curfew ends at sunup. So we walk north. After a couple of kilometres—'

Henderson stopped talking because an air-raid siren

had kicked in. Things got a little darker as lights went out across the river.

'Think they're after the same thing as us?' Paul asked, as he eyed the sky warily for Allied planes. 'Did you send a message saying the 108th was on the move?'

Henderson shook his head. 'I would have got Edith to send a radio message if we hadn't been forced out of the woods, but it doesn't matter. I expect London will have had a dozen messages from spies and resistance groups by now, all telling them that the 108th is heading west.'

Joel spoke thoughtfully. 'If you figured out that they'd stop here to refuel, chances are the intelligence analysts in Britain came to the same conclusion. Those planes could be after the fuel depot.'

'Heavy bombers aren't exactly accurate,' Paul said anxiously, as he recalled a mission he'd undertaken the previous summer. 'I'd like at least an extra kilometre between me and that fuel dump before I feel safe.'

'They're probably only a couple of minutes away,' Sam added.

Henderson saw how nervous the three boys looked and spoke firmly. '*Never* burn yourselves out worrying about things that you can't control,' he warned. 'Assuming the siren isn't a false alarm, it'll take German minds off searching for us, and give us an opportunity to move towards town while the streets are quiet.'

'Then what?' Joel asked.

'We take a brisk walk north to the city centre. When we get close I'll split off and try to contact the local resistance. I'll let them know what's going on. Hopefully they'll have men and equipment and we can work out a plan to carry on harassing the 108th. I'll set up a meeting point and if I'm not back within three hours, I want you three to assume the worst and board a train or bus. You all know how to contact the Ghost Circuit when you reach Paris?'

The boys all nodded.

'What about going to Beauvais?' Paul asked.

Henderson shook his head. 'Jean was furious with me and we've no idea what happened to the Maquis after we left. Beauvais is the absolute *last* place any of you should go.'

When Henderson's voice tailed off they could all hear the hum of aircraft engines over the sirens.

'Heavies,' Paul said warily. 'Sounds like a lot of them too.'

As they climbed out of the boatyard and began a brisk walk down behind a row of mooring sheds, an American Mustang spotter plane skimmed overhead at less than 100 metres. Its noise made Rouen's anti-aircraft guns and flak batteries begin blasting chunks of exploding metal into the sunrise.

*

France had long feared invasion by Germany. The ability to blow up bridges quickly in front of an invading army was crucial and a law dating back to the 1870s meant that every bridge in France had to be fitted with a mining pan. This large metal shelf was designed to be loaded with explosives beneath the bridge's weakest point.

Marc and Luc had no problem identifying the pan as they crept down an overgrown embankment next to the riveted iron bridge, with packs full of plastic explosive on their backs. Unfortunately, the sun was determined to keep rising and four German guards were now stationed up on the road, less than 5 metres away.

The Germans were having a conversation about sex, joking about each other's wives and the youngest of the quartet being a virgin. The mix of teasing and laughter was lively enough to mask sounds the boys made below. Luc was stronger than Marc, so he clambered 3 metres up into the bridge's iron framework.

A truck rumbled overhead as Luc found a footing next to the pan, which was crusted in thirty years of rust and bird crap. Marc passed up a large rectangular charge first. This comprised two dozen sticks of dynamite with a wired mining detonator at its core. After this, Marc gave Luc balls of plastic fitted with sympathetic fuses that would be set off by the dynamite blast.

Luc put most of these on the pan, but also reached around and placed a couple on the surrounding beams.

Marc was passing up the final three charges when a bearded guard stepped up to the edge of the bridge and whipped out his penis to urinate.

Marc ducked under the bridge, but Luc couldn't move without making a clanking noise. A slight breeze blew the urine against a beam above Luc's head and sent a fine yellow mist into his face. When he turned away, it drizzled through his hair and down the back of his shirt.

By the time the guard shook off Luc was soaked. As the German headed back, Marc gasped with relief, then reached up to Luc with the last of the explosive. But Luc was so furious that he jumped down.

'That's plenty,' he spat.

While Luc crawled up the embankment in a vile mood, Marc kicked the last balls of explosive under the bridge, then knelt down to complete the final wiring.

As they planned to blow the bridge when a tank – or better still two tanks – rode across, Marc had decided on a wired electric detonator. This gave him precise control over the explosion, but the significant disadvantage of having to hide a trail of electrical wire in the undergrowth as he crawled up the embankment to a safe spot 60 metres away.

Luc sat in tall grass unbuttoning his sodden shirt as Marc arrived. Marc was relieved that they'd completed the riskiest part of their job and couldn't hide how much he'd enjoyed seeing Luc get pissed on. To avoid Luc catching his smirk, Marc looked towards a position further from the bridge to see how PT and Michel were getting on with setting up the little artillery gun.

'If you say one bastard word to anyone about this,' Luc warned, as he wagged his finger ominously.

CHAPTER EIGHTEEN

As Henderson predicted, British intelligence had received dozens of radio messages about the 108th's move west. At the Bletchley Park code-breaking centre in southern England, teams of women transcribed coded Morse signals sent on the battalion's radio frequencies, then fed the results into a mechanical computer that filled a large hall.

Once the 108th's daily code was cracked, thirty-four American Mustang spotter planes were dispatched into the air over France. These lightly-armed aircraft could radio information on German movements to British Tempest fighters armed with tank-busting rockets. Most dramatically of all, a planned raid on German industry was postponed and eighty Flying Fortress bombers were diverted to attack the fuel depot south of Rouen.

As Henderson reached the workers' entrance at the side of the Gare de Rouen train station, the sun was up and a thousand bombs had pounded the city. Most landed to the south, damaging crucial roads, destroying a bridge and hitting vehicles belonging to the 108th. But high-altitude bombing was rarely accurate and there were fires all over the city.

Even with the Nazis' grip on France slipping, resistance groups still needed tight security. Ever since he'd been assigned the task of stopping the 108th, Henderson had known he might end up in Rouen. Maxine's Ghost Circuit had some minor dealings with the Rouen resistance and she'd told him the Gare de Rouen was the best place to contact them.

Security was always tight around stations. With no documents, Henderson kept a hand close to his silenced pistol as he stepped through a grimy hallway and approached a counter where workers logged in and out. Two coal-blackened stokers signed off their shift before Henderson reached the grilled counter and used a pre-arranged phrase.

'I'm here to fix the gas lighting.'

The man raised an eyebrow and said, 'Are you indeed? Take a step to the side and I'll fetch someone.'

Railway workers were a powerful force in the resistance. Their jobs gave them ready opportunities to smuggle men and equipment, network with groups in other areas and sabotage German railway operations.

Several minutes passed before a small man wearing a train-driver's uniform arrived. 'Are you the Englishman?' he asked sniffily. 'Ghost said you might show up when the 108th moved, but I need to see this.'

The train driver tapped his lower teeth, and Henderson obliged by popping out his denture plate.

'My name is Gaspard,' the man said, starting to walk now that he was satisfied he'd met the real Henderson.

They passed through a locker room where men showered off coal dust. Spiral stairs took them up to platform level, before a grander staircase brought Henderson to a cobwebbed café. Its soot-caked windows looked down on steaming trains and passengers queuing to have their documents checked before boarding.

'You must have had a busy night,' Gaspard said, as he pointed Henderson towards the only booth that didn't have chairs standing on the tabletop. Judging by the dust, the café had been closed for at least a year. 'I have some excellent coffee. An order sent to German headquarters in Paris that got misdirected.'

A pair of thuggish-looking young men smiled awkwardly as Henderson joined them at a table. Gaspard served Henderson a splash of coffee in an espresso cup and offered him a pick from a basket of freshly made rolls.

'White flour,' Henderson said, as he broke a still-warm roll apart and enjoyed the smell. 'And real coffee.'

Gaspard was in his forties. His two goons maybe half that age. There was a prickliness about the whole situation and Henderson sensed that the food had been brought out to impress him, rather than as a show of genuine hospitality.

This impression was confirmed when Henderson sipped his coffee. It hadn't been stolen from any German military consignment, it was the same stuff he'd been drinking in the woods for the past three months. It came by parachute courtesy of the United States Air Force, along with peanut butter and beef jerky.

'How may we help you?' Gaspard asked.

'I lost my civilian back-up identity when our truck blew up,' Henderson said, trying to keep the mood light as he raised one leg. 'And less Germanic boots might help.'

'Boots, no problem,' Gaspard said. 'Identity is tricky, but I can easily get you a railway-worker's uniform and put you on a train to Paris. I'm sure the beautiful Maxine will sort you out when you get there.'

Henderson drained his coffee and gave a thin smile as his empty cup clattered the saucer. 'I have a task to perform,' he said. 'The 108th has fifty-four heavy tanks. The Tiger is the one German weapon that Allied armies can't handle in the field.'

One of the younger men snorted, then spoke for the

first time. 'The Soviet Union has been fighting Tigers well enough. Britain and America just need to show some grit.'

'I'm sure that's what underground communist newspapers will have you believe,' Henderson said irritably.

'So communists are liars?' Gaspard spat, as the two younger men bristled.

Henderson realised it had been a poor decision to snipe at Soviet propaganda in front of three communists, but he'd missed a night's sleep and his mind was fuzzy.

'There are thousands of French soldiers in Normandy as well,' he pointed out.

Gaspard leaned forward. 'Look here, Mister *English* Officer,' he said firmly. 'We have our own way of doing things here in Rouen. Your operations could disturb the balance of things.'

'I'd rather wait for the Red Army to liberate France,' one of the younger men added sourly. 'Do you think the Allies will liberate France? It might be liberation for aristocrats and politicians, but what about working men?'

'The Soviet Union *is* one of the Allies,' Henderson said. 'And for someone who despises Americans, you seem very willing to drink their coffee, and make your bread with US Department of Agriculture flour.'

Gaspard looked upset that Henderson had caught his lie, but his tone didn't change.

'What they send has already been stolen from impoverished American workers,' he said.

Communists always pissed Henderson off. He'd visited Soviet ports when working for Royal Navy intelligence before the war. The poverty and brutality of the Soviet system bore no resemblance to the teams of happy workers portrayed in France's underground communist newspapers.

'I'm not asking for men,' Henderson said, deciding on one last try for help. 'I need civilian ID, some ammunition and a small quantity of explosives. Your group has *clearly* received plenty of equipment in US parachute drops.'

One of Gaspard's goons leaned forward and jabbed his pointing finger against Henderson's shirt.

'What will happen to our supplies if this Englishman reports that we didn't cooperate?' the goon asked.

Henderson didn't like where this was going. Communist resistance groups were notoriously ruthless, and now they'd floated the idea that he might stop their supplies, they'd surely conclude that the best option was to kill him.

It was three against one, so Henderson had to make the first move. He sprang from his seat, unholstered his silenced pistol and clinically shot the two young men in the foreheads. It was a calculated risk, because he had no idea where the nearest German station guards were, or if the communists had back-up ready to storm out of an adjoining room.

Gaspard was so shocked that he tilted backwards off his chair and started crawling towards the bar. Henderson swung one of his German boots at Gaspard's stomach and yanked the groaning driver to his feet.

'You're only alive because I need your equipment,' Henderson sneered. 'Where is it stored?'

Gaspard hesitated.

'Mess with me, and I'll make sure your death is slower and nastier than it was for your two friends.'

'I can get what you need,' Gaspard croaked.

CHAPTER NINETEEN

With the sun up, Daniel's big concern was getting spotted in the tree. He'd tucked himself in the thickest leaves close to the trunk and a caterpillar dangled off a branch in front of his face as he pushed Luc's binoculars through rustling leaves.

There was a decent view down two of the roads leading to the bridge, but he was picking up sound from a third route which was shielded by trees. He spoke down to Edith.

'I can't see, but there's a *lot* of dust and exhaust smoke.'

'Shall I go and tell the others?' Edith asked.

As Edith said this, a small command tank bristling with radio aerials passed a gap between trees. It was followed closely by something much bigger.

'Tiger!' Daniel said happily.

'You're sure?'

Daniel nodded. 'Get running!'

As Edith scrambled off to Marc at the detonation point, Daniel watched fourteen vehicles passing the gap, including four Tigers, a gunless command tank and several support trucks. By the time he'd counted this lot and made it back to the ground, Edith had alerted Marc and now ran towards PT and Michel in their hidden artillery position.

Marc smiled uneasily at Luc, who'd stripped off his pissy shirt and sat poised with a sniper rifle. The German convoy was led by a truck, with three men manning a 20-mm anti-aircraft cannon on its open rear platform. This crew was on full alert, and things would be hotter than PT's team had anticipated if the men got a chance to swing around and shoot the rapid-firing cannon along the embankment.

'Deal with them,' Marc told Luc.

Luc understood Marc's logic, but was irritated because he was keen to shoot the guy who'd pissed on him. As Luc crawled forward to a better sniping position, the gun truck and command tank reached the bridge.

After that came two of the much prized Tigers. Marc had seen them hidden in the fields around Morel's farm, but these exhaust-belching slabs of armour were far more impressive in motion. When the first set of tracks reached the bridge, its iron structure creaked. Vibration threw up dust and, to Marc's alarm, sent a couple of the plastic-explosive balls sploshing into the water.

As the first Tiger reached the bridge's midpoint the front tracks of a second began the crossing. Marc touched two bare wires together to complete the explosive circuit. He buried his face as the section of road directly beneath the mining pan exploded upwards. The blast was deafening and its heat turned water beneath the bridge into clouds of steam.

The lead truck and command tank had made it across. Clods of earth pelted the ground as Luc bobbed up and targeted the gun crew. He got two men with two shots, but the third swung the gun in Luc's direction, then ducked behind its armoured flanks and opened fire on Luc's position.

As Luc sprinted desperately for cover, PT pulled a lever that sent an artillery shell across the water towards the rear of the convoy. Edith jumped out of cover at the roadside and rolled a stick of plastic with a pressure-sensitive detonator under the track of the command tank.

Flames blinded Marc, and even 50 metres from the blast the water vapour was painfully hot. As this cleared, he saw that the bridge's metal framework had buckled, directly beneath the mining pan. Most of the guards were on the ground, either dead or writhing in agony with blood pouring from burst eardrums.

The explosion had lifted the rear of the first Tiger tank, but its driver had accelerated and made it across the river. The second tank had smashed into the buckled section of road and now balanced precariously over the water, with its crew clambering out of the turret.

An open-topped German staff car had been running between the second and third Tigers. Its driver had slammed the brakes when he'd heard the blast, but the tank behind took longer to stop. Its front track had rolled up on to the Kübelwagen, flattening the rear end and pulverising the two officers in the back seats.

As Edith's plastic successfully blew the track off the small command tank, Marc and Luc used their sniping skills to hit crew members scrambling out of the Tiger stranded in the middle of the bridge. One of the tank crew reached cover as the bridge started creaking again. A slab of road tilted off into the water, followed by the stranded Tiger.

The huge tank hitting water sent an enormous wave downriver. Meantime, the crew of the Tiger which had made it across swung its turret towards PT and Michel's artillery position.

The pair got 20 metres clear before the 88-mm shell tore up their position, but both lads were still knocked down by the mud and plants thrown up by the blast. PT found himself going head over heels down the embankment, before being engulfed in the wash thrown up when the tank hit the water.

Marc and Luc scrambled away from the bridge. They took out two men escaping from the stricken command tank, then watched aghast as Daniel crept up behind the first Tiger. The gun aimer inside had spotted Michel pulling a muddy and half-drowned PT up the embankment about 100 metres away and was making fine adjustments to his second shot.

As the 88-mm blast rang out, Daniel hopped on the back of the tank. Marc thought the eleven-year-old had gone insane. But it was a hot morning, which meant that the inside of the tank was even hotter, and one of the last things Daniel had noticed before climbing out of the trees was that the lead tank was travelling with its turret flap open.

Marc couldn't bear to watch as Daniel clambered on top of the turret, pulled a pin from a grenade and then kept hold for five seconds so that the crew inside didn't have time to lob it out again.

'Run, you crazy little bastard!' Marc screamed.

Daniel took a dramatic leap off the turret and scrambled to the roadside as the grenade erupted. This blast was muffled, but the secondary explosion when the magazine of 88-mm shells exploded was louder than the plastic and dynamite that took out the bridge.

While Daniel grabbed all the glory, Edith had cut

around the back of the 20-mm gun. The truck's driver had been shot by Luc when he tried to run, but there was still a single German shielded behind the cannon and trying to reload. She took him out with a rifle shot in the back.

As the sounds of battle dwindled to a few panicked Germans shooting at ghosts, PT and Michel scrambled away from the river in dripping clothes.

'Are we in control on this side of the bridge?' PT gasped, as he looked at the three wrecked vehicles.

'Truck, command tank and one Tiger made it across,' Luc reported. 'No signs of life.'

'Nice one,' PT said. 'There's more dust coming up behind the trees. I think there's another column of tanks coming. The good news is, there's no way you'll get anything as wide as a tank, or even a car, across the bridge. But it's not completely broken. They can send men after us, so we need to get back to the truck and ship out.'

The six members of Team A set off at a jog, as smoke from the explosions billowed into the sky at their backs.

'Can't be certain we killed every German that made it across the bridge,' Luc warned. 'One of them might be waiting in the bushes with a surprise.'

They were back at the truck within a minute. PT's 108th uniform was a muddy disaster, so Marc got behind the wheel. As the others packed up all the equipment,

Luc stayed on the road and kept lookout until the last second.

'They just sent a couple of men across,' Luc said, as he hopped into the clattering truck beside Marc. 'But they don't seem in any rush to come and see what's over here.'

As Marc turned on to the road, Luc pointed up at the sky. 'Does that look like a Mustang to you?'

Marc nodded as the American plane made a tight arc around the spirals of smoke. 'I'd bet it's a spotter,' he said. 'It's broad daylight. If they can get the Tempests out here before the 108th doubles back, they'll blow the shit out of them.'

The lightly armed spotter plane had four 7.7-mm machine guns. These would be useless against tanks and there was no hope of taking on a convoy protected by anti-aircraft guns. But as the American pilot radioed a squadron of rocket-firing Tempests 30 kilometres north, he saw a single, canvas-covered German army truck travelling west towards Gournay-en-Bray.

The truck would get away before the Tempests arrived, so the pilot swooped low and decided to hunt it down.

'Marc,' PT screamed, as he looked out the back of the truck at the silver plane coming in low towards them. 'Pull off the road. The bloody Mustang's coming right for us!'

CHAPTER TWENTY

'How far are we walking?' Henderson asked, as he glanced around warily.

Gaspard had led him out of the Gare de Rouen and now they were on a cobbled street. Areas close to stations usually had checkpoints, or at least a German presence, but the local garrison was busy dealing with the aftermath of the bombings and securing the route for the 108th.

'Twenty minutes, maybe.'

Henderson wondered if Gaspard was giving him the run-around, knowing that his resistance colleagues would soon find the two bodies in the station café. But on the other hand, it was natural for a resistance group to keep their supplies somewhere remote.

'If you're messing with me . . .' Henderson said.

Gaspard cracked a sly smile. 'You'll kill me in a

horrible way, blah, blah, blah . . . I've heard your spiel already, Englishman.'

The walk took them out of the city centre, passing main roads closed down for the 108th. They saw no military vehicles, because most had arrived before daylight, while the Tigers and their escort vehicles were unlikely to hit town for another couple of hours.

'We have to cross the river,' Gaspard said.

Three of Rouen's road bridges had been shut off for the 108th. The fourth was a melee of locals, queued back a kilometre with bicycles and handcarts. But trains crossed the river too. A pair of railway policemen nodded reverentially to Gaspard as he led Henderson across the Seine via a metal gangway alongside train tracks.

'It's still not too late,' Gaspard said, as he held a hand over his cap to stop a warm river breeze from blowing it away. 'I'll put you on the next train to Paris. My people wouldn't dare follow you into Ghost's territory, although it would be wise not to return to Rouen after what you've done.'

Henderson laughed. 'But I'd report back to my superiors and tell them to stop supplying your group with equipment. Give me some equipment. With luck I'll get myself killed, and you'll have no more bother.'

Gaspard had lost two men, but still laughed at Henderson's logic. At the end of the bridge the two tracks split, with some heading east to Paris and others hugging the side of the river. An express steamed past as Gaspard clambered over a patch of weeds and kicked away gravel to expose a rectangular metal cover.

He strained as he pulled it up. Henderson thought Gaspard was opening a drain, but a metal ladder led down to a narrow concrete chamber with a puddled floor.

'You first,' Henderson said. Then, as his eyes adjusted to the gloom below ground, 'What is this?'

'There was once an engine shed here,' Gaspard explained. 'There were tracks above and this was an inspection pit.'

Henderson was impressed that Gaspard's resistance circuit had such a perfect hiding place. The floor was damp, so metal racks had been run along each side. The neatly organised contents must have come from several hundred containers, dropped by different Allied nations. There was tinned food and milk from the USA, canned beef from Australia and tins of a revolting concoction that the British called MV, short for 'meat and veg'.

There were boots and winter clothes. The British and Americans were generally reluctant to drop weapons into areas where the resistance had communist sympathies. But there was a good selection of knives and grenades, plastic explosive packs disguised as 'Best French Butter', bundles of detonators, machine guns, rifles and stacked boxes of ammunition. Except for a few spots of rust caused by the damp conditions, every piece was in factory-fresh condition.

'Are you planning to start another war after this one?' Henderson asked, as he ran his hand over a shelf of torches and spare radio valves.

'We've fought too hard to hand France back to capitalists,' Gaspard said. 'I hope it never comes to civil war in France. But if it does, we communists will be prepared.'

'I'd love to take you to the Soviet Union some day,' Henderson sneered.

Gaspard spat on the floor. 'I don't care what you say, English Officer. Take what you like, then I'll escort you back over the bridge. And don't waste your time coming back here. We have many hiding places. I'll make sure there's nothing here, should you return.'

*

The Mustang's wings skimmed treetops as Marc floored the brake pedal and swerved off-road. The plane was doing over 200 kph, so the four machine guns had less than a second on their target. Most bullets just chewed up the road, but there were some horrible noises as ricochets pelted the truck's underside.

A big chunk of tree fell into the road ahead as the plane roared up in a wide loop, preparing for a second attack run. Marc's neck jerked painfully as he rolled the truck through a roadside ditch and banged to a stop against a large oak.

As Marc bailed, the plane was skimming treetops again. This second attack mainly ripped off branches. Luc had jumped out the back of the truck and shot wildly into the air with his pistol.

PT wrenched his firing arm. 'What are you doing, he's on our side!'

'Shoot at me, I'll shoot at you,' Luc roared furiously. 'We're the good guys, Yankee bastard!'

'We're in a German truck, in German uniform.'

As PT and Luc squabbled, Marc chased Edith, Michel and Daniel on a mad scramble through a copse of trees. As the plane arced around they reached a field and dived forward into waist-height barley.

Marc rolled on to his back to see if the plane was coming around for a third run, but it kept on climbing.

'I scared him off!' Luc shouted.

'I doubt he even saw you,' PT said.

They'd only driven a couple of kilometres from the bridge. It was well out of sight, but the Germans must have seen the plane and would probably work out that it was their truck being attacked.

'He's gone,' Marc said, as he sprang up. 'All aboard!'

But while there'd been no dramatic explosions, one of the truck's rear tyres was flat and fuel was draining into the road. PT crawled under the chassis to inspect the gas tank. He hoped he'd be able to stop the leak by plugging a hole, but the fuel dribbled from a long crack.

'We're going nowhere in this,' PT declared. 'I hope the bikes are OK.'

The news was better inside the truck. Edith's backpack had taken two bullets, but the grenades and ammunition inside it were intact. Another shot had splintered the stock of PT's rifle, but everything else, including the bicycles, was OK.

'We won't be mounting any more attacks,' PT said. 'But there's enough stuff to defend ourselves and we'll hide the fuel cans in the field in case we find a use for them. Grab what you can carry. Hopefully we'll pick up a track and we can ride cross-country.'

'I'll rig the truck with a couple of booby traps,' Luc said. 'Should blast a couple of limbs off, with any luck.'

The others didn't share Luc's enthusiasm for blowing off limbs, but booby traps were a common resistance tactic. The rest of the team let Luc do his worst as they unloaded the bikes and sorted out what they could carry on their backs.

*

Henderson would have liked to take the precaution of killing Gaspard, or at least tying him up. But he needed the little train driver's influence to get back across the railway bridge. They parted awkwardly, on open ground next to one of the railway bridge's brick pylons.

Henderson broke into a run, made painful by stiff new boots. His pack was stuffed with explosives, detonators and ammunition, but he still had no civilian ID.

Gaspard hurried back towards the railway guards. Henderson suspected he'd walk the tracks back to the Gare de Rouen. Once there, he'd tell his communist buddies that they'd been ripped off by a British officer, who'd ensure that they never got another equipment drop if he made it out of town alive.

Paul, Joel and Sam were waiting close to Rouen Cathedral. They'd hunted down food, but their stolen ration cards could only buy black bread. After they'd all used a tap over a horse trough to rinse the sweat and grime from their skin, Joel had cut the back out of a spare shirt and used it to bandage the gash on Sam's arm.

They'd arranged to meet Henderson on a set of steps close to the cathedral. Instead of speaking to the boys, Henderson stopped a couple of paces away and spoke while faking a coughing fit.

'See if I'm being followed.'

The boys let Henderson go 20 metres before standing up, then they moved off once he'd turned a corner.

'Something must have gone wrong,' Sam said.

They were all tense, but Paul managed a smirk. 'You think, Sherlock?'

It was around 10 a.m. The streets were quieter than they'd been an hour earlier, but still busy enough to make it hard to see if Henderson was being followed. Joel stayed 10 metres back as Henderson walked briskly, heading away from the cathedral into a maze of back streets. Paul and Sam held back even further, hoping to identify any tail and take him from behind.

There was no tail, but Gaspard's men had phoned around with Henderson's description. As Henderson stepped through a brick archway, two men ran out of an apartment entrance. The older of the pair pulled a gun, but Henderson elbowed him in the face before he could shoot. Joel broke into a sprint, barging the younger man to the ground as Henderson ripped the revolver out of his attacker's hand.

By the time Paul and Sam raced in, both attackers were on the ground. Henderson pulled his silenced pistol and shot the older man in the head. The second, much younger man gasped with terror as Henderson rammed the gun in his face.

'On your feet,' Henderson ordered. 'Walk with us.'

It had all happened so fast that they only got a decent look at the young attacker as Henderson began marching him off. The lad wore a white shirt, navy railway worker's trousers and looked no older than fifteen.

'You live near here?' Henderson asked.

The lad nodded.

'Who do you live with?'

'Two sisters, my mother. Plus my aunt's family.'

'That's no good,' Henderson grunted. 'You know anyone near here who lives alone? A friend, an elderly person?'

The kid stuttered. 'I . . .'

Henderson punched the kid's kidney so hard that he sobbed with pain.

'We need a spot to hide for a few hours,' Henderson explained menacingly. 'Pick a good place, because you're gonna hide there with us. If anyone finds us, the first thing I'll do is shoot you in the head. Clear?'

The kid nodded. He paused to snivel, but spoke rapidly when Henderson threatened another punch. 'There's a house down the road. The woman hid two Jewish kids there until the Milice took them all away.'

'Nobody else has moved in?'

'It just happened, like ten days ago.'

'How long to walk?'

It was only a couple of minutes. The small detached house still had a big Milice boot-print on the front door. The lock was busted and people had stripped the place, ripping out wood for cooking fires and mindlessly smashing what the Milice hadn't bothered to steal.

'Joel, Sam,' Henderson said, boots crunching broken glass as he threw the trembling railway worker to the floor. 'Check out every room, then I need your eyes front and back until we're sure nobody saw us come in.'

'So what happened?' Paul asked, as Sam thumped up the stairs.

'Well, I won't be exchanging Christmas cards with the local communists,' Henderson explained. 'So far I've killed three of them, held their leader hostage and ripped off their armoury. Hopefully they'll stop searching if we hole up here for a few hours.'

'Wouldn't we be better off trying to get out of town?' Paul asked.

Henderson shook his head. 'The communists are based at the railway station and I've got no civilian ID to board a train. Major roads in and out of town are for Germans only until the 108th blows through, and in case you've forgotten, we're still supposed to be stopping the 108th.'

'So what's our plan?'

'Haven't got one, yet,' Henderson said. 'But our snivelling friend down there on the floor is about to start telling us everything he knows about Rouen and his resistance friends.'

CHAPTER TWENTY-ONE

Team A was shaken and tired as they carried their bikes through fields of barley, being careful not to leave obvious tracks behind them. Half a kilometre from the truck, Luc stripped his mechanic's overall, while PT and Marc switched 108th uniforms for civilian gear.

'We've got two days of rations,' PT said. 'We blew almost all of our explosives back at the bridge. So, I say we ride a few kilometres to put space between ourselves and the Germans, then find a decent place to hide. Hopefully we can grab some sleep and move on once the rest of the 108th has passed through.'

Marc nodded in agreement. 'Paris is about ninety kilometres. We can stick to small roads and tracks and ride through the night. Even if we don't push hard, we should make Paris by late tomorrow morning.'

They were about to resume walking when a swarm of Tempests dropped out of the clouds. It was unlikely the rocket-firing fighter planes would come after a group dressed like regular teenagers, but it seemed best not to take chances with 500-kph rocket-firing planes so they took cover at the edge of a field and watched the action through branches.

The German anti-aircraft gun protecting the second tank convoy started the battle, but a single British pilot swooped in on a curving course and used two of his eight rockets to destroy the gun. Once this cannon was out of action the Germans' only defence was to drive under trees, or abandon their vehicles. Over the following three minutes the Tempests took turns, making sweeping runs and firing rockets.

Team A had no view of the bridge, but they could see the planes dive and hear the distinct whoosh of rockets firing. Based on the explosions they heard, most of the first dozen rockets hit something, but the pickings got slimmer on their second and third attack runs.

'I counted eleven big explosions,' PT said, as the RAF's finest shrank into summer haze.

'They'll want an accurate report when we get to Paris,' Marc said. 'If we head for higher ground, we can send Daniel up a tree.'

They headed north-east across gently sloping fields

and eventually found a footpath they could ride bikes on. It was tough to ride fast because the day was getting warm, and even though they were a couple of kilometres from the bridge there was a smell of burnt fuel that made it hard to breathe.

Daniel was always eager to prove his worth, so he was disappointed when a vista opened up, showing the bridge and its surroundings without any need for his climbing skills. The bridge itself had now completely given way. The scene on the near side was more or less how they'd left it, with one Tiger, the truck and the command tank out of action.

The Tempests had done all their work across the water. By the time the aerial attack started, the Germans had planned their diversion and turned their vehicles around. What remained of the first group and the whole of the second had been caught on open road that offered little cover.

Much of the view was obscured by smoke, but Luc raised his binoculars and reported what he saw between gusts of smoke.

'They've lined about ten dead up by the road,' Luc said. 'There's at least two dozen in the field getting medical treatment.'

'What about vehicles?' PT asked.

'Looks like the planes hit four Tigers, two motorised artillery and wrecked at least ten trucks or cars. There might be another Tiger. It looks like a busted track sticking out of a ditch.'

PT took the binoculars to confirm Luc's estimates.

'So four or five Tigers,' PT said happily, 'added to the one on our side and the one that tipped over when we blew the bridge. If they started with fifty-four, they're now down to forty-seven or forty-eight.'

'Almost fifteen per cent of the 108th's heavy tanks,' Marc noted. 'And Henderson's team might do more damage in Rouen.'

'Not bad for a few kids setting off on bikes with no plan and a couple of bags of explosive,' Michel said proudly.

But the mood was less triumphant once they'd all looked through the binoculars. Edith passed them on after the briefest glance and retched on an empty stomach.

'What's the matter?' Marc asked.

Edith smudged a tear. 'There's a guy down there with half his face hanging off,' she said. 'He's no older than PT.'

'Screw him,' Luc said forcefully. 'I hope he's in as much pain as my brother was when the Nazis killed him. If I thought I could pull it off, I'd sneak down there and lob a couple of grenades at the wounded.'

Edith sobbed as Marc spoke furiously. 'Luc, for once in your life can't you shut up? We've *all* lost people we love. Your brother isn't an excuse for you to act like an arsehole.'

Marc and Luc had a long history of kicking off, so PT forced himself between them. Before he could say anything, a boom echoed from the direction they'd just walked.

'Bet that's our truck,' Daniel said. 'Someone found Luc's booby trap.'

PT looked alarmed. 'That means the 108th sent men after us before the Tempests blew the bridge, or the local garrison has been called out from Gournay-en-Bray. Whichever it is, I want as much distance between us and them as possible. So let's stop the bickering and start pedalling.'

*

The fifteen-year-old railway worker was called Xavier. He was no hard-core communist, just a kid who wanted to fight with his local resistance group. He looked desperate as Henderson grabbed him by the throat and thrust him backwards into a chair.

'We're gonna be here for at least a couple of hours,' Henderson said. 'If you answer my questions like a good boy it might not be so bad. If you mess me around it'll get painful, and you'll still answer my questions in the end.'

To make his point, Henderson ripped a jagged-toothed hunting knife from a sheath clipped to his belt.

'I don't like all this,' Xavier blurted, as his hands trembled. 'Why do resisters fight each other, instead of the Germans?'

'Good question,' Henderson said, giving a smile. 'You hungry? I've got some chocolate.'

Xavier shuddered at the thought. 'I'm more likely to puke right now.'

'Forgive me if I lack sympathy,' Henderson said. 'But you and your pal tried to shoot my brains out. So what do you work at on the railway?'

'Station porter,' Xavier said.

'You must see a lot of comings and goings, with Gaspard and his friends?'

'A bit,' Xavier agreed. 'But they're careful. I'm only ever told what I *need* to know, and usually that's not much.'

'Seen a lot of action?'

'Not a lot. It's all woodland south and west of the city,' Xavier explained. 'I've been out there helping when Americans parachute equipment.'

'Gaspard organises the drops?'

Xavier nodded. 'He has a radio operator who gets instructions. Gaspard splits what we get with Maquis who live in the forest.'

'And what does he use it for?'

'A lot of the others come up with schemes,' Xavier said. 'But Gaspard never wants to do much.'

'The Ghost Circuit notified Gaspard that the 108th was coming. Did they make *any* plans to slow them down?'

Xavier shook his head. 'They say it's not necessary. They say it's not about *if* the Allies win the war, but *when.*'

'Who's *they*?' Henderson asked.

'Gaspard and his cronies. They have an unofficial arrangement with the German command. The Germans turn a blind eye to the parachute drops. In return, Gaspard keeps the Maquis out of Rouen and nobody shoots at the Nazis.'

'So does the resistance do anything?'

'The railways are our turf,' Xavier explained. 'We sabotage trains and steal cargo, but targets in town are off-limits.'

'So Gaspard's positioning himself for a big communist uprising?'

'He wants to be Mayor of Rouen, as soon as the Germans are gone.'

Henderson laughed. 'Gotta love politicians! Soldiers fight and die less than a hundred kilometres west, and that communist prick's only worried about winning an election when it's all over.'

Paul came into the little kitchen as Henderson spoke. 'Are you hearing this?'

'Most of it,' Paul said. 'I checked with Sam and Joel.

There's no sign that anyone saw us come in here. I reckon we're OK.'

'Good,' Henderson said, then he pointed at the backpack filled with explosives. 'Any bright ideas on how to sabotage the 108th with that lot?'

'You might destroy one or two tanks,' Paul said, as he peered down into the bag. 'But security will be on red alert after our grenade attack on the fuel depot. We got lucky last night, but we can't rely on air raids enabling our getaway a second time.'

'I'm no fan of suicide missions either,' Henderson said thoughtfully. 'But from what young Xavier tells me, the resistance in this town has got way too chummy with the Germans. So while the Nazis concentrate on protecting the 108th, I reckon we should try making life a bit less cosy for Gaspard.'

CHAPTER TWENTY-TWO

Team B had slept a few hours in shifts and eaten out of tins, and it was getting dark as Henderson, Joel, Sam and Paul got ready to leave the house.

'You've been a massive help,' Henderson told Xavier, as he tied the fifteen-year-old to a dining chair. 'I wouldn't want you to rot in here. I've written a note to go through the door of that butcher's shop up the street. I'll put it through the letterbox and they'll untie you in the morning.'

Xavier nodded as Henderson prepared a gag, made from one of Xavier's socks with a ball of candlewax stuffed inside it.

'Joel did wash it out,' Henderson said. 'You're a decent kid and I wish we'd met under better circumstances. You've got a few bruises coming out. Tell everyone that I tortured you for the information and you should be OK.'

Xavier made a muffled groan as Henderson forced the gag in and secured it with a leather dog collar they'd found in a kitchen cupboard.

Then, to Xavier's surprise, Henderson grabbed his knife and slit the base of his earlobe. As Xavier moaned in pain, Henderson tipped the chair on to its side, making it look like Xavier had been kicked into the dirt and broken glass on the floor.

'That's for your own good,' Henderson said. 'I didn't tell you because there's no advantage having time to think about it. The cut will bleed across your face for ten or fifteen minutes and you'll look a proper sight when they find you in the morning.'

As a final thought, Henderson grabbed two ten-franc notes from his trouser pocket and tucked them into Xavier's trousers.

'Who's ready?' Henderson asked, as he grabbed his backpack.

Paul, Joel and Sam were all dressed for a warm evening.

'I've got no ID, so you three need to walk ahead and warn me of any checkpoints,' Henderson said. 'Are you all clear on your roles?'

The boys nodded, then said awkward goodbyes to Xavier before heading out into darkness. The first part of their journey was a six-minute stroll to a laundry. Henderson banged angrily on a grille and spoke with a German accent.

'You have my uniform?'

Clothes were in short supply, so even bags of dirty laundry had to be guarded. A fat old Frenchman puffed a cigarette as he waddled to the door.

'We're closed,' the guard said, pointing to a sign as he shone a torch in Henderson's face. 'We open at five tomorrow morning.'

Henderson used information Xavier had given him. 'You live at twenty-one Rue Beaumont, don't you?' Henderson asked.

'And if I do?' the guard asked.

'I've heard rumours that your daughter passes communist newspapers,' Henderson said. 'Perhaps I could arrest her. Put her in a cell for a night of interrogation.'

To seem extra sinister, Henderson made a gesture like he was cupping a pair of breasts. This threat made the guard stiffen up like he'd had iced water tipped down his back.

'If you give me your ticket I'll fetch it for you. But your uniform might be wet. There's nothing I can do about that.'

Henderson didn't have a laundry ticket, but he made like he had one in his wallet. As the guard reached through the grille to take it, Henderson grabbed the man's shirt and slammed him against the inside of the grille as Joel pointed a silenced pistol at his head.

'Let us in or I'll blow your head off,' Joel hissed.

The guard bent awkwardly, undoing a bolt with his free hand before turning a latch. Henderson barged in, knocking the guard backwards.

'Two German uniforms,' Henderson told the guard, as he pointed at Joel. 'An officer's uniform for me. Enlisted man for him.'

'Who are you?' the guard asked, as he backed up down a short hallway. 'We don't do things like this in this town. If the Nazis don't catch you, the resistance will.'

'I'll bear that in mind,' Henderson said. 'Now where can we get uniforms?'

They'd entered at the back, so they had to cross through an area full of wooden washtubs, mangles and steam irons. The floors were puddled and there were mounds of smelly washing ready for the next day's work. They reached a collection area where suits and uniforms hung from rails behind a counter, while unironed laundry was stacked up in numbered cotton sacks.

'Tie him up,' Henderson ordered.

As Paul and Sam made the guard lie on the floor and trussed him up, Henderson and Joel picked uniforms that fitted. Joel found a cloth soldier's cap, but the laundry didn't deal with the stiff braided caps worn by army officers and there were no belts or boots.

Fortunately Henderson's plan relied on getting close to the Germans, not on passing a detailed inspection. They left in a hurry through the laundry's front door. The 11 p.m. curfew was getting close and people were hurrying home. Streets that had been closed for the 108th to pass through had been reopened and unlike earlier there was a large security checkpoint in operation on a road leading to the station.

The quartet avoided this route. Instead they turned on to a side street which was lined with parked cars – a highly unusual sight during a fuel shortage. One was an impressively long Mercedes staff car, but the rest were shabby French vehicles that had been seized from civilians for use by officers in the local army garrison. Some even had large metal containers on the roof, indicating that they'd been converted to run on coal gas.

Henderson looked at Joel and spoke quietly. 'Steal something that looks like it'll shift and check there's at least a quarter tank of petrol before you start the ignition.'

'Will do,' Joel said.

Beyond the parked cars lay a small, pedestrianised square, set up exactly how Xavier had described it. There were no signs banning Frenchmen, but there were three cafés and a restaurant around the square and their street terraces were dominated by men in German uniform enjoying a warm summer's evening.

Xavier hadn't been able to name the restaurant where the most senior Germans drank and dined, but the expensive look and the stripes and pips on customers' uniforms made identifying it easy. There were even several black-uniformed SS officers drinking at an outside table.

As Joel prepared to break into a car, Sam came to a halt by the giant Mercedes, Paul walked to the square's entrance and Henderson strode on towards the restaurant with the senior officers sitting outside.

A bell jangled over the doorway as Henderson entered a muggy restaurant. The hot weather meant that the tables outside were much busier, and none of the diners inside paid any attention to Henderson's slightly out-of-kilter uniform as a waitress approached.

'Is it too late to dine?' Henderson asked.

'I'm very sorry,' the waitress said. 'Our chef has to get home before the curfew.'

'Ahh,' Henderson said. 'Then is there at least time for some drinks with my friends?'

The waitress turned back to look at a smartly dressed Frenchman behind the bar, who nodded.

'Any table you wish,' the woman said.

Henderson took the large pack off his back and

selected a table at the front, close to the tables outside.

'This pack is heavy,' Henderson said. 'I'll stick it here while I run out to tell my friends that I've found a table.'

'No problem,' the waitress said.

As Henderson set the backpack down, he sneaked a hand under a flap and snapped a glass time-pencil detonator. This detonator was rated for one minute, but they weren't the most accurate devices so he actually had somewhere between thirty seconds and two minutes to get away.

Running across the square might alert the waitress, so Henderson could only go at a brisk walk, making signals like he was beckoning his imaginary friends towards him. When Paul saw Henderson exit without his pack, he reached up as though he was stretching into a yawn.

Joel had already shorted out the car's ignition to start the engine and he pulled out on Paul's signal. Sam glanced around furtively before unfurling a bed sheet on which was scrawled a message:

THE REAL ROUEN RESISTANCE
ACCEPTS NO COMPROMISE WITH NAZIS

Below the message, Paul had carefully drawn out the resistance's Cross of Lorraine emblem.

Sam quickly draped the bed sheet between the Mercedes' silver-star hood ornament and the driver's side door-mirror. Joel stopped the car just past the square's entrance. Paul hopped in the back, followed closely by Sam.

As Henderson scrambled into the front passenger seat, his backpack exploded in the restaurant 100 metres away. The entire glass and wood façade got blown out, instantly killing everyone inside and spitting a powerful fireball.

As a dozen of Rouen's most senior German officers got incinerated, shards of hot glass and debris flew across the square, causing serious injuries and leaving almost nobody sitting around the small square without burns or cuts.

The quickest way out of town and the most direct route to Paris would involve crossing the Seine, but the bridges would all have a German checkpoint, so they headed south. Cars were a rare sight, so the plan was to drive 4 kilometres and abandon the car when they reached the Dominaile Forest.

They passed the heavily-guarded gates of the fuel depot they'd sabotaged the night before with no problem, but as the terrain turned rural and the first trees scrolled past the side windows a truck roared out of a side turning and T-boned them.

Joel fought the steering wheel, but the truck was

much heavier and their little car tilted on to its side. Injuries might have been far worse had the sideways skid not been absorbed by a huge hedge. The car had no seatbelts and Henderson found himself lying on top of Joel with a smell of fuel and the sound of free-spinning wheels.

When he looked in the back, Sam was clambering out, but Paul appeared to be unconscious. The car windows had been open. Paul's shirt was in shreds and his shoulder bled profusely where it had been dragged along tarmac.

Henderson realised he had a slight concussion himself, because it seemed like one second he was looking at Paul, then his memory blanked and Sam had him halfway out of the car.

The truck was 30 metres away, stationary. The way it had come out of nowhere had to be deliberate and there appeared to be a group of scruffy young men peering cautiously around it.

'Let's move,' Henderson said, as he flopped to the ground and found his feet.

There were dense trees on both sides of the road. Henderson grabbed Sam's arm, but he was trying to climb back into the car.

'My brother's still in there,' Sam protested.

The young men were still cautiously moving around the truck and it was now clear that they were local

Maquis, not Germans. Finally, the bravest of the young men shouted, 'Surrender.'

Henderson gave Sam a tug and the teenager found branches scraping his face as Henderson dragged him into the woods.

*

Team A's mood relaxed after a few hours' sleep in a barn. An accidental encounter with a lonely old farmer earned PT, Edith, Marc, Luc, Daniel and Michel a generous cooked dinner of eggs and wild mushrooms, served with local wine.

The farmer told them about a downed British airman he'd helped two years earlier and as he regularly foraged for mushrooms, he gave excellent information on the best paths for riding bikes and likely places for German checkpoints.

They left the farm at sunset and the Germans were now spread so thin that the convoy of bikes went 20 kilometres before seeing any sign of the enemy.

It was an abandoned Tiger tank. At first they thought it had been shot by an Allied plane or blown up by local resistance, but the outside was in good shape and when Luc climbed cautiously on to the turret he caught a strong whiff of burnt rubber and saw dials and controls melted from some kind of electrical fire.

'Shorted out in the heat, I guess,' Luc said.

The Germans were sure to be back. Even if the tank

couldn't be repaired, undamaged parts could be used for spares, so PT reached inside and dropped their last ball of plastic and a thirty-minute timed fuse down by the gunner's position. Hopefully the small explosion would ignite all the ammunition and blow the tank apart when it went off.

Their next encounter with the 108th came an hour later and *had* been caused by Allied bombing. Two Opel trucks had been hit by rockets. One must have been full of ammunition crates because its blackened chassis had burned so hot that it had melted to the surface of the road. The second truck had a burned-out cab and they'd already rolled past when Edith looked back and saw something like a face.

'Wait,' she gasped.

It was a short night so PT looked frustrated as he turned back. Edith had spotted three boys laid out on the roadside. The only obvious damage was blood congealed in their ears, which meant that delicate blood vessels inside their skulls had been ruptured by the shockwave from a large explosion. Most likely when the truck full of ammunition blew up.

The boy in the middle didn't seem to be bloody and Edith reached forward to see if there was a weak pulse. As she was about to lift his arm, Luc grabbed her slim waist and yanked her backwards.

'Don't touch me,' Edith shouted furiously, as Luc

threw her down in the dirt. 'Why'd you do that?'

Instead of answering, Luc shone a small torch between two of the bodies. When Edith stood, she saw the torch beam illuminating a grenade nestled in the middle boy's armpit. The pin was pulled, and had almost certainly been wound down to a one- or two-second delay.

'You just saved my life,' Edith gasped, and she was so relieved that she kissed Luc's cheek.

'Would have got me as well,' Luc said coldly. 'The 108th are bad-asses. There's always gonna be a trap if they lay bodies out like that.'

PT and Marc were the last to double back. 'Are they from your orphanage?' Daniel asked.

Marc choked back tears as he looked into young dead faces and nodded. 'I grew up with those three.'

Marc, Edith and Daniel all started crying and for once Luc kept his mouth shut.

'We can't leave 'em like that,' PT said. 'It's disrespectful, but the poor bastard who turns up next might get their arms blown off.'

They all got back on their bikes and rode about 100 metres. Marc was the best shot, but he was in a state, so Luc knelt on one knee and aimed Marc's sniper rifle at the body in the middle. The bullet jerked the body and the exploding grenade made a gory mess across the road.

Marc was sobbing. 'I wonder what's happened to the other two?' he said.

PT put an arm around his back. 'Don't let it get to you. The Allies are landing more equipment every day. They're gonna break out of Normandy and push every Nazi out of this country.'

'Hope you're right.' Marc sniffed. 'Because I don't think I can take much more of this shit.'

Part Three

August 15th–August 24th 1944

Resistance and Maquis activity meant that the 108th Heavy Tank Battalion arrived at the front lines in Normandy three days late, critically short of fuel, spares and ammunition, and with a quarter of its Tiger tanks destroyed or out of action.

It took two months of brutal fighting for the Allied armies to break out of Normandy. But once they'd smashed through German lines they began a rapid advance, sweeping west to Lorient and Nantes and south to the River Loire.

In mid-August, Operation Dragoon saw 95,000 Americans landing in southern France. They advanced further in one week than the Normandy invasion managed in its first two months. In the north, a vast Allied army now charged west towards the River Seine and the cities of Rouen and Paris which lay on its banks.

An increasingly desperate Hitler made arrangements to

send heavy artillery and huge quantities of explosives to the French capital. Many people believed that Paris was the most beautiful city in the world, but if Hitler got his way, scorched-earth tactics would see it razed to the ground.

CHAPTER TWENTY-THREE

Tuesday 15 August 1944

Marc stood peeing. The little window in front of him was open and he stared over rooftops at the hilly and affluent suburb of Saint Cloud, 9 kilometres west of central Paris. The sun was bright and already hot enough to make his brow bead with sweat.

He washed his hands, but kept them wet. Marc's bedroom was tiny. All the covers were on the floor and Jae was sprawled on his bed, face down and naked. Marc held his fingertips above her shoulder blades and let the cold water drip.

Jae's slim body shuddered as drops hit her skin and she moaned as she rolled on to her back.

'Hey you,' she said, smiling.

The bed was a single and Marc shivered as he laid on

sheets cold with sweat. The air felt thick and there was a smell of stale breath and armpits that would have been gross coming from anyone but a girl he was madly in love with.

As Marc snuggled up, Jae threw a surprise by swinging a leg across his midriff and sitting astride his chest.

'You're putting on weight,' Marc gasped. 'Get off.'

'Make me,' Jae teased.

Marc raised his right leg and effortlessly knocked her off. As Jae slid off the bed on to the floorboards, Marc snatched her ankle. Jae went into a spasm as he tickled the sole of her foot.

'No!' Jae shrieked.

'Ticklish there, aren't you?' Marc said.

Jae squirmed and giggled helplessly as Marc let go of her foot and started tickling her under the arms. Drool spilled out the corner of Jae's mouth as Marc moved in for a kiss.

'Aye-aye, what's going on here then?' PT said.

Marc sprang up as Jae dived under tangled bedclothes.

'Haven't you heard of knocking?' Marc asked, half smiling, half angry.

'Where's the fun in that?' PT replied, as he rattled a single-sheet newspaper. 'I need a quick word.'

Marc tutted. 'It *better* be important.'

The two lads ended up in the kitchen. The five-bedroom apartment was on the third floor and the living-room's giant bay window gave a sweeping view downhill, across the Seine towards central Paris. On a good day you could see the Eiffel Tower, but right now the heat made it too hazy.

Jae was visiting from Beauvais, but Marc, Luc, Sam, PT, Edith and Henderson had been living here for eight weeks. They'd done a few little delivery jobs for Maxine's Ghost Circuit, but they'd mostly been twiddling thumbs and slowly turning the apartment into a tip.

'I know Henderson's gone to Rouen,' Marc said. 'But where's everyone else?'

'Sam and Edith are out looking for food. I haven't seen Luc this morning, but I expect he's two floors down, with that married mother of two.'

Marc laughed. 'Must be tough not having a girlfriend when even a scumbag like Luc is getting some action.'

'I certainly need something to relieve the tedium,' PT said, as he pulled a chunk of hard black bread from a loaf and tucked it in his cheek to soften. 'Remember our old friend, Milice Commander Robert?'

'He killed Rosie,' Marc said. 'I'm not likely to forget, am I?'

'Read this,' PT said, as he handed over the underground newspaper.

The two-day-old paper was tissue thin. Some sections were smudged where several people had already read it.

'This is a communist paper,' Marc sneered, then more

angrily as he saw the depleted loaf on the kitchen dresser, 'How much bread have you scoffed? That's all we've got between seven and who knows when we'll find more?'

'Second article,' PT said, as he struggled to chew. 'The Nazis would still be winning the war if they built their bunkers out of this bread.'

Marc took the sheet. With paper and ink in short supply, the headlines in underground newspapers were only a few millimetres high. Stories stayed short and usually stirred propaganda into the news.

DON'T LET THE MILICE GET AWAY!

As the Allies advance towards an inevitable battle in Paris, France's vilest traitors are abandoning their Milice uniforms and going into hiding.

These sub-humans use stolen identity papers and take new names so that they can avoid retribution by the communist brotherhood.

Comrades are urged to root out this cancer! Destroy the Milice! Act before they vanish!

THEY SHALL HAVE NO PART IN THE NEW COMMUNIST FRANCE.

'I don't know about you, but I don't much like the idea of Rosie's killer vanishing on us,' PT said. 'I found a map of Paris. The address Paul found for Robert's café is only four stops from here on the Métro.'

'And when did you last see the Métro open?' Marc asked. 'We haven't had electricity at all for the last three days.'

'An hour's walk, then,' PT said. 'What else are we gonna do all day?'

'Henderson ordered us to stay here,' Marc said.

PT laughed. 'Since when did his orders bother you?'

'Look,' Marc said, as he glanced back over his shoulder to make sure that his girlfriend was still out of earshot in the bedroom. 'It's not that I don't care about Rosie, but Jae's only here for one day. She'll get in a right mood if I say I'm leaving.'

PT understood where Marc was coming from, but still felt a bit irritated. 'All right then,' he sighed. 'You stay here working up a sweat with your little farm girl. I'll track him down on my own.'

*

Paul shuffled back nervously when he heard boots clank on the wooden hatch in the ceiling.

'Joel,' he whispered, reaching across the tiny black space and tapping his fellow prisoner's foot.

When the hatch opened a shaft of light made both lads shield their eyes. For the first three weeks they'd been hauled out of the basement every few days for a nurse's visit. But that stopped once their cuts from the car accident healed. Now, their guard just threw down scraps of food and hauled up their slop bucket on a rope.

'How's the weather down there?' the doughy guard asked, finding his own joke hilarious.

Paul and Joel couldn't hold their eyes open in the dazzling light, but the sound of a revolver being cocked made them try. Getting shot would be unfortunate, but Paul reckoned he might choose a bullet over another eight weeks holed up in darkness.

'I hear you can be tricky,' the guard warned. 'So I want you to climb out one at a time. Real slow.'

Paul was nearest the ladder. He knew the layout of the little cellar well enough to find anything with his eyes shut, but when he tried climbing his brain went into meltdown, as if his muscles had forgotten how to do stuff.

'Ain't got all day,' the guard barked. 'Move out!'

'I can't see,' Paul shouted back, panicked by his state of mind. 'My eyes need to adjust.'

'What are you bringing us out for?' Joel asked.

'It'll be for an arse whooping if you don't hurry up.'

Paul eventually got it together. Hands on the side of the ladder, one clumsy step at a time. It was getting so that his eyes would stay open for a couple of seconds at a time when he got to the top. He breathed clean air and felt sun-warmed tiles on the soles of his feet.

'Through there,' the guard said, as he shoved Paul towards an open door.

The place sparked vague memories of the night they'd arrived. It was a boarded-up ticket office but the trains that regularly shook their cell never stopped at the platform outside.

Two thuggish railway workers leaned against the far wall and there was a bucket and some clean rags on a table. Paul and Joel were both ordered to strip and wash, which wasn't easy because the water was cold and there was no soap.

Paul didn't shave yet, but Joel was handed a cut-throat razor and gave himself a couple of nicks as he sheared off 3 centimetres of ragged beard. Paul could almost tolerate the light by the time he got told to put on some army boots and a tattered railway worker's uniform.

He still needed to think about every routine movement and he was fascinated by scabs and lumps that he'd only been able to feel in the darkness. His torn shoulder muscle had healed, but he had scars where he'd scraped across tarmac through the car's open window.

'What's happening?' Joel asked, as he buttoned his shirt.

'It's on a need-to-know basis,' one of the railway workers said.

'And the likes of us don't need to know,' the other added, as he smiled at his colleague.

Paul felt cautiously optimistic as he was led out of the

ticket office and on to a deserted platform. The nightmare had always been that the Nazis would get them, but Rouen's communist resistance wouldn't bother getting them washed and dressed up for that.

CHAPTER TWENTY-FOUR

The Nazis banned civilians from driving in Paris soon after the invasion. The occupied city had always been quiet, but now it was eerily so. The Germans kept their own journeys to a minimum, saving fuel for battle or a retreat. The Métro opened for one hour in the morning and one in the evening, but only if the electricity was on. Mainline trains couldn't go south or west because the Allied advance had cut the lines off.

PT got lucky and found a horse-drawn taxi-cart for a sunny half-hour ride to an industrial district on the other side of the Seine. There weren't even food queues now. The Germans wanted to discourage any kind of public assembly and all official rations had been reserved for the army.

Parisians ate what they grew, paid extortionate prices

on the black market, or trekked into the countryside to forage or steal. Cats had vanished and pigeons landing in the wrong spot were liable to end up in a cooking pot.

The address Paul had found on Commander Robert's water bill was a small café-bar with a single apartment above. A sign in the window said *Closed Due to Shortages*, so PT walked down an alleyway at the side. A ground-floor window was open because of the heat, and since nobody was around he leaned against the wall behind the rubbish bins and listened to sounds coming from inside.

There were two, perhaps three, little kids running around and a baby screaming. A woman occasionally told one of them off, but if there was a man inside he was either asleep or ignoring the brats. After peeking in to make sure the downstairs room was empty, PT opened the window wide and pulled his shoulders in to get through.

He was in a narrow space that was a kitchen for both the home upstairs and the café out front. He was surprised to see plenty of food: a full sack of potatoes, a big box of carrots with their tops on, a hanging sausage and a basket filled with German-labelled food tins.

After breakfasting on stale black bread, PT couldn't resist picking up a carrot and taking a bite before heading up the stairs.

A little set of eyes peeked out on to the top landing.

'Mummy, there's a man,' he yelled.

The eyes belonged to a boy aged about four, who bolted back into the upstairs front room and dived behind a couch. PT put a hand on his hunting knife as he raced up the stairs.

He found the woman of the house in a back room. PT had guessed she was the mother of all the brats, but she was too old. She looked at least sixty, sitting on a sofa with the baby alongside and her swollen ankles on a table top.

'How dare you!' the woman shouted, pulling her feet down and reaching for a set of knitting needles as PT closed in.

'I didn't mean to startle you,' PT said, before taking another bite out of his carrot. 'I'm looking for Pierre Robert. When did you last see him?'

'What's it to you?' the woman asked back, as she screwed up her face and made a pathetic stabbing gesture with one of the knitting needles.

The little boy and two slightly older girls peered nervously through the doorway as PT swiped the knitting needles from the elderly woman's grasp.

'I'm a nice guy,' PT said. 'I don't *want* to make trouble, but Pierre owes money to some friends of mine. They're not the kind of people you want to get on the wrong side of. People get hurt, cafés get burned to the ground. You understand?'

The woman's lips went very thin before she spoke reluctantly. 'He's my son-in-law.'

'Are these his kids?'

'The two girls are. The others are their cousins. I look after the kids while their mothers work in a factory.'

'So where's Pierre?'

'I never see him,' the woman said.

PT took a step closer and tried to look menacing. 'If you never see him, why did we find his name on a utility bill for this café? And who supplies all these nice black-market carrots?'

The woman stayed silent, so PT leaned forward and grabbed the baby off the sofa. She tried to stop him as the baby started bawling.

'You're a cute one,' PT said, as he stepped backwards, rocking the baby in his arms. 'How old is he?'

The elderly woman now sounded short of breath. 'Ten months,' she said nervously. 'What did that poor, helpless baby ever do to you?'

'Nobody will get hurt,' PT told the baby in a sing-song voice. 'Because Grandma's going to tell me *all* about Uncle Pierre.'

'Pierre Robert doesn't live here,' she blurted. 'He went off with another woman, but he's good to the kids. Dropping by with food and stuff.'

'Where can I find him?' PT asked, as he stepped back towards the sofa.

'I don't know where he lives. But if he's in town, he'll roll up at Bistro le Baron sooner or later. It's two streets over and he hangs out there with a bunch of gangsters.'

'Has he quit the Milice?'

The baby settled down as the woman gently stroked his head. 'I already told you. I have nothing to do with the man.'

'I'll see if he turns up at Bistro le Baron then,' PT said. 'Thank you.'

'Kiss my arse,' the woman said, as PT headed for the stairs.

*

Paul felt light-headed as he moved along a set of curving train tracks. Joel and one thug walked in front, and the other one walked behind. Every now and then Paul got told to pick up the pace. But when the goon finally lost his temper and gave Paul a shove, he sprawled out helplessly in the trackside gravel and stumbled up with his railway uniform covered in dust.

'I can't help it,' Paul said, as he scowled angrily at his tormentor. 'I've not moved out of that cellar in weeks and you've been feeding us scraps.'

The guard reluctantly let Paul drape an arm over his back before setting off again.

Their destination was a set of overgrown railway sidings, close to the river. Paul and Joel were told to sit inside a dilapidated goods shed. Its wooden cladding was badly holed, so they had no trouble watching the scene that developed outside.

More railway workers arrived, followed by at least a dozen Maquis. The heat made Paul thirsty as they all milled about for more than an hour. Snippets of conversation told him that they were waiting for a train to arrive, but it was late because the tracks had been bombed and it had been diverted along a much longer route.

The sun was high when a train finally reversed into the deserted sidings. The small steam engine was pulling three goods wagons and surprised everyone by stopping 50 metres short. Three men jumped out of an open cargo door. They held machine guns, which set off a panic among the waiting Maquis and railway workers. Some went for weapons, but most ran for cover between the goods sheds.

Paul was pleased to hear Henderson's voice. 'I need to see my boys,' he shouted.

'I need to see our goods,' the most senior railway worker shouted back.

A guard made Paul and Joel stand by the shed's doorway and wait for a signal.

'Bring the boys out,' Henderson said. 'You can send two unarmed men across to check the wagons.'

As two Maquis men walked towards the train, Paul and Joel got led out on to the tracks.

'I'm told you're in good health,' Henderson said.

'Not too bad,' Joel shouted back.

The two Maquis climbed in the wagons and came out a minute later, making thumbs-up signs. As a railway worker began decoupling two of the three cargo trucks, Paul and Joel were told to begin a slow walk towards Henderson.

Joel smiled and Paul had a tear running down his face, but Henderson's voice remained tense.

'Get in the front truck, fast as you can manage.'

As Paul and Joel climbed aboard, Henderson signalled the train driver. The engine was already starting to move as Henderson and his two machine-gun-toting accomplices stepped into the cargo wagon.

The interior had straw-filled pillows strewn across the floor. As Henderson slid the wagon's wooden door shut, he looked back at the Maquis and the railway workers, frantically unloading the two wagons they'd left behind.

Joel and Paul took turns gulping tepid water as the train accelerated. A man also handed across a basket filled with apples, chocolate and bread.

'We're still in the Rouen resistance's territory,' Henderson warned. 'So let's all keep our guard up.'

Paul smiled. 'So how much are we worth? What was in the two wagons?'

'Food and fuel, mostly,' Henderson said. 'They were desperate.'

'What happened after the café bombing?' Joel asked.

'Things got hairy,' Henderson said. 'The bombings did exactly what we'd hoped. Half the senior Gestapo were killed in the blast and Rouen's military commander was sacked. The regional governor staged a crackdown. Gaspard and at least twenty of his cronies were arrested, tortured and hanged on a specially built gallows outside the main station.'

'It's a miracle the communists didn't shoot us,' Paul said.

'Fortunately for you two, there wasn't much love lost between Gaspard's communists and the Maquis who captured you. Maxine used her contacts to find out that you were both alive and sent envoys to Rouen to negotiate your release.'

'But it was all railway workers who guarded us,' Paul said.

Henderson nodded, as Joel hungrily licked the foil from a bar of melted chocolate. 'I sent a message to Boo on campus. The Rouen communists still had a radio operator in contact with Britain. We made it clear to their new leadership that they'd never get another parachute drop if you two were harmed.'

'Still took eight weeks,' Paul moaned.

Henderson explained. 'The Maquis made ransom demands that were impossible to meet. They wanted heavy weapons that no resistance group has and vast quantities of food and fuel. I had to give some ground in the end, because I didn't like the idea of you two being locked up if the Allies swept into town.'

Paul gasped. 'So our guys finally broke out of Normandy?'

'And a lot more,' Henderson said. 'We're having difficulty getting regular radio broadcasts in Paris because there's rarely any electricity to charge the batteries. But the Allied armies seem to be on track to reach the River Seine before the end of this month.'

CHAPTER TWENTY-FIVE

PT had no idea how fast news would spread about his encounter with Pierre Robert's mother-in-law, so he had a quick sniff around Bistro le Baron and its neighbourhood before taking refuge in another café opposite. The only dish on the menu was vegetable soup. It cost what three courses in a fancy restaurant would have done a couple of months earlier, but the place was heaving and the waitress laughed when PT offered a ration ticket.

'Just your money,' she said.

PT found a stool with a view out on to the street and kept an eye on Bistro le Baron. Men in porter's overalls came and went and it looked like shady business was happening in the rooms above the bar.

Most of the visitors were going back and forth between the bistro and a storage depot 100 metres up the road.

It had high wooden fences topped with barbed wire, and all PT could see beyond them were the pitched roofs of warehouses stretching back more than 50 metres.

Carts came and went. People knocked on a wooden gate in the fence. Their baskets went in empty and came out full. The contents were always covered, but the odd protruding celery stick or a glimpse of an aluminium can gave the game away. This was clearly a major black-market operation. And as it had taken PT ten minutes to work out what was going on, there was no way it could operate without the local Germans taking a cut.

'Do you want another bowl?' the waitress asked.

PT patted his stomach and turned on the charm. 'I can't – unless you're offering credit.'

The girl smiled back, but spoke firmly. 'We have a queue. I must ask you to leave.'

PT wanted to watch some more. 'I'll get a coffee,' he said.

'No. I'm sorry, sir,' the waitress said. 'It's lunchtime and we're busy.'

PT pointed his thumb back at some men near the counter. 'They've not taken a bite since I got here.'

'They're friends of the owner.'

Rather than argue further, the waitress made a hand signal to the men at the counter and backed away. A mountainous man who couldn't have looked more villainous if he'd tried moved up to PT's stool and cracked his knuckles.

'Is there some difficulty with the house rules?' he said, in a voice that sounded like it was coming through organ pipes.

PT didn't hang around to be asked a second time. He thought about heading off, but as he stepped off the kerb a bicycle squealed to a halt and a tall man stepped off a bike. He wore a linen suit rather than a navy Milice uniform, but it was clearly Pierre Robert.

Gangsters obviously ran things around here, so it wasn't the kind of place where you could stand around gawping. Excited by the sighting of Robert, PT decided to take a risk. He strolled purposefully across the street and approached the entrance of Bistro le Baron a few paces behind his target.

The place could seat a hundred, but the only customers sat at two distant tables. Robert leaned his bike against a wall near the door and joined a group of eight men at the room's biggest table. PT found a table by the window. It was close enough to overhear most of what Robert's group said, without making it seem obvious that he was listening.

PT ordered coffee. It was no surprise when a couple of senior German officers emerged from upstairs with sacks over their shoulders. One even had a large box of Swiss chocolates tucked under his arm.

'What brings you here?' the waitress asked, as she put down a cup of coffee that smelled like the real stuff.

PT wondered if the waitress was bored, or under orders to be nosy. 'Came out for a walk and ended up here,' he said, before blowing on his hot coffee.

'I always wonder if it really makes a difference,' the waitress said.

PT looked confused. 'What makes a difference?'

'Blowing,' the girl said. 'Does it cool your coffee down?'

PT laughed. The girl was attractive and seemed to like him, but he felt conned when she crossed to the big group sitting with Robert and used the same banter on them.

He spent fifteen minutes sipping a coffee and pretending that he wasn't listening to the conversation between Robert and his friends. They spoke about the war and the Germans looking jumpy. A few comments suggested that most of them had put on Milice uniform at some stage, but mostly they discussed the Allied advance.

'New rulers, same tricks,' Robert said. 'I don't care if communists, Yanks or Free French take over from the Nazis. There's not a regime in history that hasn't been open to a black market, bent politicians and swindles.'

This line raised a big laugh.

PT was getting frustrated. He had a hunting knife

and a small .22 pistol under his shirt, but it would be suicidal to attack Robert while he was sitting on home turf with eight friends.

His bladder got the better of him halfway through a second coffee. The waitress pointed him to a toilet up a narrow staircase and he followed his nose to a foul-smelling urinal. As PT came out, a bulky man with a ginger beard blocked his way down. He was one of the guys who'd been drinking with Robert.

'Have you been earwigging us?' he asked.

PT smirked, like the idea was mad. 'Not many places sell real coffee,' he said. 'It was a nice cup, so I had another and took my time over both.'

'Expensive though,' the man said, as he ran beefy fingers through his beard. 'And I saw you have lunch across the street. Did someone pay you to nose around?'

A door clicked at the top of the stairs and a stocky, well-spoken man came out.

'Who's this?' he asked.

'Young man drinking coffee, boss. Two coffees. Been sitting on his lonesome for over half an hour.'

'Is that right?' the boss asked.

PT looked over his shoulder at the boss. Even German officers had got shabby because of all the shortages, but this guy looked like the war never happened. He wore immaculate black leather shoes, a silk shirt with the sleeves rolled up and the eccentric touch of a gold watch on each wrist.

'I'll leave if you want me to,' PT said, raising his hands. 'If you don't want people coming in you should put up a sign.'

'You're telling me how to run my business now?' the boss said irritably.

'There's nothing going on,' PT said.

'Do I look that green?' the boss asked.

'What's in your bag?' the ginger fellow added.

'Not much of anything,' PT said.

The boss tapped the sheathed knife bulging under PT's shirt. '*That* looks like something,' he said. 'I think we need a proper chat in my office.'

PT wondered how to get out of this as he reluctantly followed the boss upstairs. He hadn't been patted down properly, so he still had the gun holstered under his shirt and there was no sign that anyone had heard what had happened to Robert's family above the café.

The office was a proper villain's lair, with thick red rugs and an ornate desk. PT's eyes fixed on an alcove off to one side where an elderly man sat counting money and writing the amounts into a ledger.

'Open your bag,' the boss said.

PT put his backpack on the rug and undid two buckles. As the boss peered inside, PT reached across the desktop and grabbed a chunky marble desk lighter.

He lashed out, smacking the boss in the eye socket. As he crumpled, PT slugged the ginger guy in the guts and reached for his gun as he backed out of the office.

PT took the stairs in three rapid leaps. The men sitting with Robert had stood up to see what was going on and PT shot one of them in the chest before they got a chance to see the gun. PT looked for his target as he moved into the restaurant, but Robert had stayed back at the table and PT couldn't get a clear shot.

The waitress hurdled the bar gymnastically as PT grabbed Robert's bike. The glass in the door shuddered as PT booted it open. After a running start, he swung his leg over the saddle and started pumping the pedals.

CHAPTER TWENTY-SIX

'Good to have you back!' Marc said, eyes tearing over as he wrapped Paul in a tight hug.

As Paul got hugged by Edith, PT, Jae and a decidedly less enthusiastic Luc, Joel enjoyed a blurry-eyed reunion with younger brother Sam across the apartment's living-room.

'Thought I might never see you again,' Sam said.

Joel laughed. 'You think I'd get myself killed and leave you to fend for yourself?'

Henderson came out of the kitchen holding two magnums of champagne. 'Picked these up a couple of weeks back,' he said. 'There's no ice, so I hope you can stand it warm.'

'I'll stand for anything that has alcohol in,' Joel said cheerfully.

The first cork sailed across the high-ceilinged room and Henderson drank from the foaming bottle before handing it across. Joel took three foamy gulps, then passed the bottle on to Paul as Henderson began untwisting the wire clamp that held the cork in the other magnum.

'I've really come to admire and respect you boys,' Henderson said, as he gave a nod to Edith. 'And the odd girl, of course.'

Henderson paused, making a rare display of emotion as everyone looked his way.

'Marc, you've been with me from the start,' Henderson said. 'You're the one that taught me what young people are capable of doing. Paul, you probably have the biggest brain in this room. You're not the strongest, but I'll always respect how hard you had to push yourself to get through training. Joel and Sam, you have guts and integrity and I know you'll go a long way together when this war is over. Edith, you've never trained on campus, but over the last eight months you've become one of us where it matters: in the field. PT, you've swindled and conned your way into my heart!'

Everyone went stiff as Henderson turned towards Luc, apart from Jae, who was passing out a mixture of unmatched glassware and enamel mugs so that they didn't have to keep slugging champagne out of bottles.

'I'm not going to pretend that I like you,' Henderson told Luc, to a couple of uneasy laughs. 'I *wish* I could dig into your soul and rip out whatever makes it so dark. But I can honestly say that with my back to the wall in a scrap, there's nobody on earth I'd rather have on my side. So for one night, let's forget about the war and welcome back our friends. I raise my glass – well, my tin mug – to all of you, and a toast to the future.'

Everyone moved towards the middle of the room and chinked glasses, mugs and bottles together.

'The future!'

PT raised a second toast. 'Henderson's boys!' he shouted.

Things got noisy as they went for a second toast. Then they all settled around the room, breaking into separate conversations as they drank the champagne. Henderson liked a drink and even in these hard times he'd amassed a cache of four magnums, a bottle of whisky and some revolting red wine which they left until everything else had run out.

Booze, mixed with evening heat and a sparse diet, meant they were all soon drunk. Luc had invited his girlfriend Laure up from her apartment two floors down. She was a dark-haired woman of twenty-two, and while she canoodled with Luc, her five- and six-year-old sons rampaged through the apartment.

Marc, Paul and Sam acted like drunk kids, chasing

the little lads around, having mock fights and swinging them by their ankles. It was a taste of childhoods that had ended too soon.

Maxine knocked on the door at nine. She carried cold beer and a bag filled with butter, paté, tomatoes and fresh white baguettes. Paul ate greedily, but the rich food lying on top of champagne made him queasy. He curled up on Marc's bed, feeling a mattress under his body for the first time in almost two months.

Henderson rarely smoked, but once they'd eaten Maxine's food, he shared a cigarette with her on the balcony. Eyebrows were raised as the pair discreetly moved into Henderson's bedroom.

'How's your wife, Captain Henderson?' Luc shouted.

'How's your girlfriend's husband?' Henderson shot back.

Laure looked annoyed, but Sam and Marc broke into fits of drunken laughter.

As the sun set, Luc helped Laure carry her dozing boys downstairs and by the time he came back up, everyone was either asleep or getting ready for bed.

The electricity had been off all night, so Luc helped Edith collect plates and glasses before joining her at the sink.

'You wash, I'll dry,' Luc said cheerfully.

Luc usually dismissed domestic chores as women's work and Edith's jaw almost hit the floor.

'If this is what having a girlfriend does for you, I'm all for it,' she said.

'Laure's *so* nice,' Luc said. 'I know she's older and she's got a husband in Germany, but I really like her.'

There was no soap or detergent, so Edith only had tepid water and a square of old cloth to get things clean.

'You seem to get on with her boys as well,' Edith said admiringly.

Luc walked to the dresser with a stack of dry plates. 'Did you enjoy tonight?'

Edith nodded. 'How often can we forget about everything and have a laugh?'

Once the plates were dry, Luc put out the last gas lamp and stepped into the bedroom he shared with PT. The room had two single beds, but was barely wide enough to walk between them. PT had fallen asleep drunk, with his shirt unbuttoned, one leg hanging off the side of the bed and his hairy balls catching a breeze through the window.

PT's trailing foot touched the floor. It would have been easy to step over but Luc couldn't resist stepping on his toes.

'Jesus,' PT gasped, as he sat up and clutched his foot.

'Sorry,' Luc said, smirking in the dark. 'Hope it didn't hurt.'

'Thought you'd be downstairs, with Laure,' PT said,

as he inspected his big toe. 'Was Mr Penis out of order after all that champagne you drank?'

'Laure doesn't like me staying overnight, in case the boys blurt something to her mother-in-law,' Luc explained.

'You wanna make some cash?' PT asked, as Luc dropped his trousers.

'How?' Luc asked.

'You and me don't have much in common,' PT began, 'but money – or rather the lack of it – is one of them. Paul's inherited from his folks. Edith was left property by Madame Mercier; Marc's got a rich girlfriend. But the war will end sooner or later, and you and me'll have no money and no family.'

Luc looked intrigued. 'Keep talking.'

'I tracked down Pierre Robert today,' PT explained. 'I think he's reverted to being a full-time gangster, no Milice uniform.'

'Milice don't work where they live,' Luc pointed out. 'The resistance would crucify them.'

'Robert's associates run a black-market food racket. Food goes out of a little depot, money winds up across the road to a place called Bistro le Baron. I got up in the boss's office today and there's a guy with a ledger. He sits there counting piles of money, all day long.'

'Definitely interested,' Luc said. 'Is it just about the dollars, or is killing Commander Robert still part of the plan?'

'I loved Rosie and watched her die,' PT said. 'I've worked out a plan that should enable us to do both.'

'Why pick me?' Luc asked.

'Exactly like Henderson said earlier: if it comes to a scrap, there's nobody I'd rather have on my side.'

'Just the two of us?' Luc asked.

'Three would be better. I'll ask Marc in the morning. So are you in or not?'

Luc nodded slowly. 'I'll look at your plan when I'm not boozed up. If it's any good I'm in for sure.'

CHAPTER TWENTY-SEVEN

Wednesday 16 August 1944

Paul slept solidly and woke feeling rested, with morning sun warming his bare midriff. He found Marc, PT and Luc sitting on the living-room floor, around a low coffee table.

'Morning,' Paul said, before looking at Marc. 'Sorry about your bed.'

Marc waved a hand dismissively. 'Couldn't make you sleep on the floor after all you've been through. You really knocked that champagne back. How's your head?'

Paul smirked. 'Not great, but it was a good night. So what are you guys plotting?'

PT explained about finding Pierre Robert and that they'd worked up a plan to take him out and rob the gangsters' cash.

'You can come if you want,' PT added.

But Paul didn't seem enthused. 'Killing Robert won't bring my sister back,' he said dourly, as he settled on a couch. 'You guys do what you have to, but I'm not interested.'

Marc nodded sympathetically. 'You're better off resting, after all you've been through.'

'Henderson's still holed up in his room with Maxine,' PT explained. 'It's a bit early, but we want to sneak out of here before he starts asking what we're up to.'

'I'll try and cover for you,' Paul said. 'Where's everyone else?'

'Joel and Sam are still sleeping off the booze,' Marc said. 'Edith's chasing a rumour that there's gonna be some bread on sale in the market and Jae's riding her bike back to Beauvais.'

PT, Luc and Marc made final preparations as Paul went to the kitchen. He took the last of the hard black bread and smeared it in the synthetic gloop that the German food scientists tried to pass off as jam.

Although the Nazis were increasingly focused on the Allied advance, there were still Gestapo teams out hunting the resistance. Henderson made sure there were enough guns and ammo stashed to put up a fight if the front door got kicked in, but their supplies of automatic weapons, grenades, ammunition and explosives were stored under a drain cover in the building's basement.

The cache wasn't huge, and the boys had to travel light because there was a chance they'd be stopped at a checkpoint. Large bags were the most frequently searched, so Luc carried a large suitcase filled with clothes. The idea was that he'd join any checkpoint queues first. Hopefully, Marc and PT would get waved through while the Germans searched his bag.

The road they lived on ran 100 metres down a steep hill, before reaching the banks of the Seine less than 50 metres from a road bridge. There were often a couple of taxi-carts standing around here, but the boys were out of luck.

'Always the way when you've got stuff to carry,' PT moaned.

'You said Robert didn't get to Bistro le Baron until lunchtime yesterday,' Luc said. 'If he's a creature of habit, we've got bags of time.'

The checkpoint on the bridge was unmanned. Once they reached the Seine's east bank, Luc walked ahead and Marc dropped back. The Germans were less likely to stop one young man than a group of three, and if one of them got hassled by a patrol there was a chance that the other two could rescue him.

They kept to back streets as much as possible. There was more traffic noise than usual, but they were almost halfway to Bistro le Baron before they had to cross a major road.

Luc stopped at the kerb as three Kübelwagens sped past. This was notable, because German vehicles usually travelled alone and took unpredictable routes to avoid resistance attacks. All three cars were so heavily laden that their rear bumpers almost scraped the road. One had suitcases lashed together and poking out of an open trunk. Another had crates of wine and a large, landscape painting on the back seat.

The streets had been quiet for so long that Luc felt strange having to look both ways for traffic. He crossed behind a truck crammed with OT officers and their luggage. As he reached the opposite kerb a convoy of two dozen German vehicles, ranging from motorbikes to trucks, rumbled into the street.

PT and Marc wouldn't be able to cross until this line of vehicles passed through, so Luc turned into a side street and waited by a beautifully-kept flower garden in front of a community meeting hall.

A frail voice surprised him. 'Why dig up my flowers?' the man said, as if he was asking himself. 'If I plant vegetables, they'll get stolen.'

Luc turned and studied an old man, holding a rake and chuckling. He wore glasses with one lens cracked and had his shirt done up in the wrong button holes.

'How long have they been driving past like this?' Luc asked.

'Oh!' the old man said dramatically. 'I've seen

hundreds. All packed up to leave town. I'm told there's been trouble.'

'How do you mean?'

'Smashing windows, stealing things they want to take back to Germany.'

'Good riddance,' Luc said firmly. 'Though you can bet it's administrators and bureaucrats clearing out, not soldiers.'

The old man gave a wry smile. 'They're getting out before the city turns into hell,' he said.

The convoy had now passed and Luc looked behind and saw Marc and PT. The pair dashed across the road, almost in step but acting like they didn't know each other.

Ten minutes further on, a police checkpoint asked all three for their papers, but didn't search any bags and the three boys reached their destination at noon. After the previous day's chase, PT couldn't show his face anywhere near Bistro le Baron. He found a hiding spot amidst the rubble of a bomb-damaged building, while Luc headed towards the place where PT ate soup the day before.

There was a thirty-strong queue waiting for the café to open. Luc joined the end and kept a discreet eye on Bistro le Baron. Robert's mother-in-law had told PT that he'd always turn up at the Baron if you waited long enough, but that was no guarantee. Did he come every day? Was it always at the same time? Robert might already be upstairs out of sight, away on Milice business or even have gone into hiding after PT threatened his family.

Luc took time over his soup and watched comings and goings, exactly as PT had done the day before. He left when the waitress was about to make him and as Luc walked back to the bomb site, Marc joined the queue outside the café and took over the surveillance.

Marc maxed out his stay with a second bowl of soup. After leaving the café he crossed the street and looked in at four men at a table inside Bistro le Baron, including a man with a ginger beard who fitted PT's description of the person who'd stopped him coming down the stairs.

'Nice soup; no Robert,' Marc reported, when he met up with Luc and PT on the bomb site a few minutes' walk away.

Luc looked at his watch. 'I'll give it half an hour, take a stroll past and see if there's any sign. Then I can stroll back in the other direction half an hour later. If Robert's still not turned up, Marc can do the same thing.'

'I'm worried that the depot might soon close for the day,' PT said. 'I bet they don't leave all that money in the bistro overnight.'

'Why don't we go in now, grab the cash as planned and come back for Robert later?' Luc asked.

Marc shook his head. 'If we rob the money, the place

is gonna be swarming with gangsters and Germans. It'll be too hot to come back for Robert.'

Luc looked frustrated. 'Well, there *must* be some other way to find him. His wife worked in a factory. If we could get hold of her . . .'

'*If* we knew what factory she worked in,' Marc said.

'We know Robert visits his kids,' PT said. 'The mother-in-law told me he brings food for the kids.'

'But how often?' Marc asked. 'Every day? Every third day? Once in a blue moon?'

PT spoke firmly. 'We're not running off on tangents. I made a plan and we're sticking to it. If we spot Robert we follow the plan. If he doesn't show, we can try again tomorrow, or work out some alternative.'

Luc scoffed. 'Henderson will be pissed off that we disappeared today. There's no way he'll let us disappear a second day.'

'How would he stop us?' Marc asked.

PT laughed. 'Our beloved captain may have gone all misty-eyed on us last night, but he's *still* Henderson. If the only way he could stop one of us from disobeying a direct order was to shoot us, I reckon he'd do it.'

Luc smiled at PT. 'Henderson *loves* Marc, but he'd shoot you or me without batting an eye.'

When the time came, Luc walked past Bistro le Baron in both directions and drew another blank.

But when Marc made his first pass just after 3 p.m. there was a group playing dominoes at a table by the bar and Pierre Robert was among them.

'Got him,' Marc said when he got back to the bomb site. 'And when I walked past there were still porters going in and out of the depot.'

Luc, Marc and PT exchanged wary smiles as they squatted behind a blast-damaged wall, sorting out their kit. Marc assembled his sniper rifle and handed it to PT, while Luc went down his bag and pulled out a lump of plastic explosive the size of a ping-pong ball.

'All set?' Marc asked.

Luc nodded as PT took the safety off on Marc's rifle.

'Let's do this shit!' Luc roared.

Marc walked the long way around, passing the depot as he headed towards Bistro le Baron from the top of the street. A girl in a servant's uniform came out of the depot's front entrance with a basket of vegetables straining on each arm. Marc didn't like the idea of hurting her, so he slowed his pace and glanced at a handcart being loaded with sacks of potatoes down a side alley.

The girl was 20 metres clear when Marc neared the depot's high fence and dropped down on one knee. He tied his shoelace, but as he stood he cracked a glass time pencil, pushed it into the ball of explosive and squished it against the wooden fence. Plastic explosive was naturally a sandy beige colour, but he'd pre-rolled it in dirt so that it blended in perfectly.

The time pencil was designed for one minute. As Marc gave an *All good* signal by scratching his scalp, PT hid in a side street with the sniper rifle poised and Luc strode into Bistro le Baron. The men playing dominoes eyed him suspiciously as he approached the bar.

'Two coffees,' Luc said.

The waitress looked curious. 'Two?'

Luc nodded as he peeled out a ten-franc note. 'My friend will be here any second.'

Marc stepped in as the waitress turned to face the coffee machine. He'd only got two paces when the explosion went off. Nobody was within a metre, so the small charge just blew a hole in the fence. As Bistro le Baron's windows rattled and people in the street took cover, Pierre Robert and his fellow domino players charged towards the exit to see what had happened.

There was broken glass in the street as PT raised the sniper rifle and took preliminary aim at head height, just past the Baron's exit. Keeping one eye shut and holding his breath, PT watched different heads in his telescopic sight.

Robert glanced around as PT pulled the trigger, almost as if he'd spotted the muzzle poking around the wall across the road. PT hadn't done sniper training like

Marc and Luc, but he was still a decent shot and the range was less than 50 metres.

The bullet split Robert's head like a boot stomping a ripe pumpkin. Bullet fragments punched through the bistro's window as PT took his second shot. Everyone was diving for cover, so PT lowered his aim and shot the guy with the ginger beard.

At such close range, any half-decent marksman could take PT out with a pistol, so he slung the rifle over his shoulder and began a sprint.

Inside the bistro, Marc and Luc dived as glass flew and pieces of the bullet that killed Robert shattered glassware behind the bar. Marc led a fast crawl towards the stairs and they charged up while the gangsters huddled on the floor near the entrance. Luc had a crowbar hooked on his belt in case the boss's office was locked, but the door was half open.

There was no sign of the boss, but the elderly accountant sat in his alcove with his ledger and his stacks of money. As Marc stood on the landing, covering the stairs with his pistol, Luc opened his suitcase and ditched the bundle of tatty clothes inside.

'Fill the case,' Luc ordered the old guy.

Downstairs, a couple of the gangsters had worked out what was going on. But it was a straight staircase, so Marc could easily take out anyone who tried coming up. There was more money than would fit in the case, but they couldn't take more than a case full without seriously impeding their getaway.

'I'm ready,' Luc shouted.

As Luc opened a window behind the desk, the boss came out of the toilet, with his braces dangling and tailored trousers held up with one hand.

'Can't I take a shit in peace?' he yelled as he stepped on to the landing. 'What's all this bloody noise?'

His expression turned to shock when he saw Marc right in front of him.

Startled, Marc took a low shot, hitting the boss in the thigh. As the boss collapsed, Marc sent him tumbling downstairs with a knee in the back.

'I'm done,' Luc shouted. 'Let's move out.'

Marc backed into the office and kicked the door shut. The accountant had his hands in the air and Luc had one leg on the window ledge, ready to jump down into an alley behind the building. He made the 3-metre leap, then Marc passed the suitcase down before jumping himself.

The pair belted down an alleyway that emerged much closer to the depot than they would have liked. PT had made a long sprint and covered the pair with the sniper rifle as they turned left into a sloping street. Once the trio met up, they turned right and sprinted between rows of tiny houses built for factory workers.

The boys ran half a kilometre together, with no sign

of a chase. When they reached a turning into a large road, PT stopped and did a quick disassembly job on the sniper rifle. Luc took a right and strained from the weight of money as he strode towards three waiting taxi-carts.

Marc whispered, 'See you back home,' to PT before crossing the street and walking briskly down the first turning.

CHAPTER TWENTY-EIGHT

PT walked the opposite way to Luc and had less luck finding a taxi-cart, but he was astonished by an open Métro station. People were so used to it being closed that he rode four stops in a near-empty carriage, while the trains going back towards the city were crammed with German infantrymen carrying their full kit.

Marc was the only one who made the journey back to Saint Cloud on foot. The roads were still full of Germans heading out of town and he had to make a long diversion because they'd closed the bridge nearest home for a movement of military vehicles.

Marc expected a bollocking as he stood inside the apartment's front door, gently sliding boots off his blistered feet.

'Living-room,' Henderson said brusquely.

Maxine rarely stayed in one place for long, so Marc was surprised to see her in the middle of a sofa. PT and Luc sat on another sofa facing towards her and the money-filled suitcase rested on the coffee table between them.

'Sit,' Maxine snapped, sounding like she was ordering a dog.

Paul and Edith hovered in the doorway as Marc squeezed on to the sofa between Luc and PT. He'd been on his feet all day and would have loved a glass of water and a cool flannel.

'I'm told Pierre Robert and another man are dead,' Maxine said. 'Plus one critically injured.'

'How do you know that?' Marc asked.

'Telephone,' Maxine said. 'The network is as useful to us as it is to the Germans, so we've done nothing to damage it.'

The boys knew this, but gave respectful nods like they were learning something.

'The Ghost Circuit has put significant efforts into tracking down Milice,' Maxine said. 'If you'd had the common sense to ask, I could have easily found out where Pierre Robert sleeps at night. And if I'd known you planned to kill him, I'd have ordered you to wait. Robert's girlfriend is a member of a resistance group. She was using him to gather intelligence on Milice members.'

The three boys all gawped.

'We had no idea,' Marc said weakly.

'How *can* you know if you don't ask?' Maxine said irritably. 'Fortunately, Commander Robert's involvement with the Milice had almost come to an end and the overall Milice threat is a fraction of what it was. They've been deserting in droves now they've worked out that they've sold their souls to the losing team.

'But that doesn't excuse your cavalier behaviour. Paris belongs to the Ghost Circuit. No resistance operation goes down without me, or one of my senior commanders, approving it. Even the communists wouldn't commit murder and robbery without letting me know first and my circuit has only lasted this long because we have strict rules and severe punishments for those who break them.'

The boys looked anxious as Maxine let the threat sink in.

'Just this once I'll turn a blind eye,' she said finally. 'Especially as you're making such a generous contribution to resistance funds.'

Maxine stood up and pulled the suitcase of stolen money off the table.

'Paul, come here,' Maxine said.

Paul approached warily, though he was only guilty of lying to Henderson about Marc, Luc and PT's whereabouts. Maxine opened the suitcase and pulled out a 3-centimetre stack of twenty-franc notes.

'Rosie was a hero of the resistance,' Maxine said. 'When things calm down, you can use that money to give her a proper funeral, and buy her a headstone.'

Paul had learned to cope with Rosie being dead, but he wasn't over it and his eyes glazed as he took the money.

'Now I have other matters to attend to,' Maxine said, as she stood up and strained under the weight of the suitcase.

She stopped to kiss Henderson's cheek on her way to the door. 'See you at the cinema later, Charles.'

Marc looked back at Henderson once Maxine had left. 'You'll have a hard job finding a cinema that's open.'

'An even harder time getting one where the power stays on for the whole film,' PT added.

Henderson grunted. 'If there's one lesson you boys should have learned today, it's that Maxine is a lady who gets what she wants. And thank you *so* much. I trusted you lot and you've repaid me by making it seem like I can't even control my own people.'

'We didn't mean to cause trouble,' PT said. 'But I'm not gonna apologise for going after a Milice scumbag who killed Rosie.'

For a moment Henderson looked as if he was about to blow up, but his voice was calm when he spoke.

'You've been through a lot, but you're still young,' Henderson said. 'I was doing espionage work while you lot were in nappies. I know you think you know it all, but you don't.'

*

Two hours later, Henderson led a 9-kilometre bike ride from the eastern suburb of Saint Cloud to l'Odéon in central Paris. He was trailed by Marc, Luc, Paul and PT.

The district was known for restaurants, bars and especially cinemas. Managers had kept Parisian cinemas open through all the shortages and power cuts by switching to candles or gas lanterns, and converting projectors to run off car batteries. But as the Allies closed on Paris, city administrators became concerned that any public gathering might turn into an anti-German demonstration and had ordered all screens to close.

Despite shuttered cinemas and extortionate prices in the few cafés and bars that had something to sell, there were hundreds of people out for an evening stroll as Henderson and the four teenagers padlocked their bikes to railings around the Métro station.

They passed the major cinemas on Rue de l'Odéon and cut into a back street. Their destination was a basement news theatre. These places were much smaller than main cinemas and typically showed short programmes of news and documentaries, for customers who dropped by during lunch breaks, or after work.

The cinema lobby was padlocked, so they went down

a staircase that stank of drains and entered through an emergency exit that brought them in right beside the screen. Fifty rows of seats stretched down a narrow space, lit only by paraffin lanterns hanging on a side wall.

Henderson nodded to Maxine, who sat in the front row next to the American liaison officer, Colonel Hawk. There were a few other people scattered in the front three rows. The ones Henderson recognised were either Maxine's most trusted lieutenants, or influential members of other resistance groups.

PT, Marc, Luc and Paul went to grab seats, but Henderson smiled and shook his head. 'Maxine has a special job for you four. Go right up the back, and knock on the projection booth door.'

'Why?' Marc asked.

'Just do what you're bloody told for once,' Henderson snapped.

The rear of the cinema was pitch black. PT led the way, brushing a hand along the wall to guide himself. A pretty teenaged projectionist led them up to the projection booth. It was cramped, but there was a small skylight and a wall had been crudely knocked down so that the space continued into what had once been the cinema manager's office.

The four boys were nearly flattened by a stench of BO. There was an array of car batteries wired up along the office floor and two standing bicycles. These had their back wheels off the ground and rigged up to drive large dynamos.

'You need to get a move on,' the projectionist said. 'The American said that his film lasts thirteen minutes. Pedalling both bikes for three minutes makes enough charge to run the projector for one minute.'

The boys looked appalled, not so much by the prospect of forced exercise but by the smell of those who'd gone before them.

'I've already walked twenty kilometres today,' Luc moaned.

Paul shrugged. 'Look on the bright side – Maxine didn't have you shot.'

The projectionist picked a voltage meter off the floor. 'Don't make this needle go into the red,' she explained. 'If you generate too much current you'll fuse the charging circuit.'

PT and Marc put their legs over the stationary bikes and both almost shot head first over the handlebars when they gave their first push on the pedals.

The projectionist smirked. 'It is heavier turning the dynamo than riding a bike.'

'*Now* you tell me,' Marc said, before shaking his head and giving the pedal a slower but more powerful push.

As PT and Marc began making their contribution to the room's aroma, Paul looked out of a small opening and watched more resistance leaders arriving. An argument broke out as one man turned up with a retinue of bodyguards and hangers-on. Maxine furiously ordered them to the back of the auditorium, hemmed in by members of her own security team.

By the time Maxine was satisfied that everyone had arrived, PT and Marc were stepping off the bikes.

Marc pulled a wringing-wet shirt over his head before giving Paul a slap on the back. 'Your turn, old pal.'

Paul was weedy and, with a hangover and weakened from eight weeks in a cellar, he could barely get the pedals turning.

Luc showed his typical lack of sympathy. 'If I have to do all the work I'm gonna beat the shit out of you.'

The projectionist saw Paul's struggle and took pity on him. 'I can take over from you,' she said.

PT was the oldest and couldn't stand by while a girl did the work, so he quickly drank some water and stepped back to the bike. Paul felt humiliated as he got relieved.

'I don't know what Henderson was thinking after what you've been through,' PT told Paul. 'Get out of here, go watch the show.'

As Paul stepped down from the projection booth and took a seat in the back row, Colonel Hawk was finishing a brief introduction.

'. . . My role is to ensure that Allied command and

the resistance in the Paris area are all working to the same end. The military values all the work the resistance has done, but you must now work with us if we are to avoid unnecessary loss of life.

'Over the past few days, groups inside the police, the railways and communist resistance groups have increasingly called for a general uprising among the people of Paris. Today's mass evacuation of German administrative staff and non-essential personnel is sure to ramp these feelings up further.

'As I'm sure none of you need reminding, at the start of this month a similar resistance uprising took place as Soviet troops neared the Polish capital. But the Warsaw resistance acted too hastily. The Soviets didn't advance into the city and the Nazis staged a merciless crackdown. Entire streets were dynamited and thousands of civilians rounded up and slaughtered. The resistance was forced down into the sewers and incinerated with flamethrowers. Those captured alive were hanged, or strapped to German vehicles and used as human shields.

'As soon as the projector batteries are charged, I'll be showing you some remarkable film footage smuggled out of Warsaw by a Swiss journalist. This footage is extremely graphic. Once you've seen it, I hope that you'll drop any thoughts of a premature uprising.'

A communist leader in the audience shot to her feet. 'The Germans have massive reinforcements heading to Paris from Germany. If we give them time, they'll wire our city with explosives and we'll be left fighting over rubble.'

'The Warsaw resistance was weak,' a voice out of the dark added.

There were several murmurs of agreement before another leader shouted, 'Colonel Hawk, is it true that the Americans plan to bypass Paris, leaving us to our fate while your tanks ride on towards Germany?'

'I don't know the intimate details of the American battle plan,' Hawk replied.

'Then what's the point you being here?' someone shouted.

'It would be *ludicrous* for me to be dispatched behind enemy lines if I had detailed knowledge of the Allied battle plan,' Hawk explained.

Henderson got to his feet and spoke in Hawk's defence. 'The prime goal of the Allied armies is to reach Berlin and end the war in the shortest possible time. The idea of bypassing Paris and leaving its population in a siege situation with desperate German forces is not a pleasant one. But the Allies can't afford to get bogged down in a street-by-street battle through a city of five million people.'

'Is that the official British position?' someone shouted.

Henderson sounded irritated. 'Of course it isn't. I'm just stating the obvious fact that there's no tactical reason for the Allies to spend weeks fighting through the streets of Paris.'

'And the Parisians are left to starve and be slaughtered?' someone shouted.

Henderson and Hawk both sensed that they were losing the argument as applause broke out.

'I for one will not stand by while Paris burns,' a beefy communist woman shouted.

Hawk sensed the room turning against him and tripped on his words. 'I . . . You must, er, watch the film. I *beg* you to watch the footage from Warsaw. If you rise up too soon, thousands will die unnecessarily.'

'No, no, no!' the beefy woman shouted, stamping dramatically with each word. 'I have no wish to sit through your American propaganda film. The Allies are within twenty-five kilometres of Paris. If they don't have the guts to take our city, we'll take it for ourselves.'

Cheers and clapping erupted as the woman set off for the exit. Paul was surprised to see that even a couple of Maxine's Ghost Circuit deputies were applauding the communist.

'I'm leaving,' the communist woman shouted. 'I say we strike, we bomb, we harass. Better to die fighting, than die of starvation after a siege like Stalingrad.'

Maxine stood up and blocked the woman's exit. 'No,' Maxine said. 'Please listen. There should be no resistance uprising until the Allies give us a signal. We have no heavy weapons. If we start fighting the Germans will rip us apart.'

The beefy woman was a good ten years younger than Maxine and looked genuinely sad as she faced her off.

'Maxine, you've been a great leader for Paris,' the communist said. 'But you are wrong about this. It's time to stand up and fight. You've become so addicted to British and American assistance that you have become their pawn.'

Maxine looked devastated as the woman left the meeting, followed by a dozen other communist leaders, plus representatives of resistance groups within the railways and public utilities such as electricity and water.

When the walkout ended, a representative of the police officers' union stepped up to Henderson and Maxine.

'I'm inclined to agree with your position on this,' he began. 'But things are moving beyond our control. The city's civilian administrators have been sent home and replaced by a fanatical Nazi general named Von Choltitz. One of his first orders was to disarm all French police officers, because they can no longer be trusted. There's a meeting later tonight, but our men aren't going to hand over their guns. The police will be going on strike. The railway workers have promised to do the same and I expect other groups to follow.'

Maxine looked shocked. 'With a general strike and

no police on the streets, the communists will start an uprising for sure.'

Colonel Hawk had overheard and hurried over to them, sounding desperate. 'Is there nothing you can do?'

'There's going to be a vote,' the policeman said. 'But the mood is militant. I'd be astonished if it wasn't overwhelmingly in favour of a strike.'

Maxine, Henderson and Hawk gathered into a huddle as the police representative left. Apart from the projectionist and the boys up the back, the only people left in the cinema were five deputy leaders of the Ghost Circuit – and Maxine had seen at least two of them clapping the walkout.

Maxine smudged out a tear and addressed them. 'If I give orders now, will you follow them?'

To Maxine's surprise the five leaders all nodded.

'There wouldn't be real resistance in Paris if you hadn't nurtured and protected it,' one of the men said.

'That's appreciated,' Maxine said, before pausing to think. 'I don't want an uprising. But it seems there's going to be one and I give you free rein to support it in any way you wish.'

Hawk sounded shocked. 'Maxine,' he blurted. 'You can't support—'

Maxine turned to the colonel. 'Get a message to Allied command. Tell them what's about to happen and *beg* them not to bypass Paris.'

At the other end of the cinema, Paul stepped back into the projection booth. He had to shout over the whirring dynamos.

'Good news, bad news,' he yelled. 'The good news is, you can stop pedalling. I don't think they'll be showing the film.'

'Are you bloody kidding?' PT said, gasping for air as he stopped his bike.

'And the bad news?' Marc asked.

Paul took a deep breath. 'It looks like the resistance is about to start a war with the Germans.'

CHAPTER TWENTY-NINE

Thursday 17 August–Saturday 19 August 1944

Thursday was a day for rumours. Henderson ordered his team to stay out of the city centre, so the boys climbed up on the apartment block's roof with binoculars to try and see if there was anything exciting going on. Heat made the city shimmer, but they could only speculate on the pillars of smoke and the odd bang in the distance.

Had the uprising kicked off, or were the Germans setting things on fire as they continued their evacuation?

A neighbour who'd phoned a friend in the city told Henderson that the police had taken control of the central prefecture; railwaymen hadn't reported for work and resistance groups had begun shooting at German patrols.

At the bottom of the hill by the bridge, Edith got hold

of an underground news sheet. It backed up the information from their downstairs neighbour, but led on a cry for the whole of Paris to rise up and start killing Germans.

At 7 p.m., BBC Radio France confirmed widespread strikes and a minor uprising in central Paris. It also reported that Allied troops were less than 15 kilometres from the city's western suburbs.

As night fell there were gunshots and German convoys rumbling across the bridge near the bottom of their street. Reassuringly, there were no signs of large-scale fighting, or heavy artillery. Nobody in the apartment could sleep because of the heat and tension, so they sat up through the early hours playing low-stakes poker and talking about what they all planned to do when the war ended.

Friday morning brought even hotter weather and more gunfire. Luc asked if he could take a sniper rifle into town and kill some Germans. Henderson said he wouldn't stop him, but not to bother coming back if he did. Luc stayed, because for all his tough-guy act, Henderson and his team were the closest thing he had to a family.

'So we spend another day sunbathing while it all happens without us?' Luc asked sourly.

Luc was always the boldest in confronting Henderson, but Marc, Sam and Joel didn't like being cooped up in the apartment either, and shared most of his feelings.

'You can train an infantryman in four weeks,' Henderson said. 'I've been training you lot for four years. I'd rather wait until we can do something that makes a real difference, than to risk your lives taking a few pot-shots at a German patrol.'

Everyone understood Henderson's logic, but that didn't make sitting around while momentous things happened a few kilometres away any less frustrating.

Paul tried to kill off Friday afternoon by sketching the city from the roof, while PT sunbathed next to him. Luc went downstairs to Laure's place, Edith read a novel and Joel, Sam and Marc headed out on to the street for a kick-about.

You had to go downhill to the riverbank to find ground flat enough for football. Kids were all on summer holidays, so they joined a game with a group of youths ranging from twelve up to about sixteen.

Heat and hunger meant long sprints and hard tackles were off the cards and players dropped out and joined teen girls sitting on the kerbs when they got knackered. Little kids played skipping, chasing and fighting games on steeper ground at the base of the hill, while grandmothers on apartment balconies kept an eye out for grazed elbows and tantrums.

Sam had the ball 10 metres from goal when the lad marking him caught his heel on an uneven cobble and hit the deck. Sam neatly rolled the ball back from the kid's outstretched legs and flicked it across to a shirtless thirteen-year-old making a run on goal.

The kid brought the ball down nicely, but scuffed his shot and kicked it limply at the keeper. Since they were playing on cobbles, the goalie punted the ball with an outstretched foot rather than diving to scoop it up.

Marc saw the ball coming and flung his leg out, more in hope than expectation. The resulting volley arced through the air, glanced off the keeper's shoulder and passed between goalposts marked by rusty buckets.

'Genius!' Marc roared, as cheers broke out among his teammates.

A couple of younger lads slapped Marc on the back, while a kid on the other team moaned that Marc shouldn't be playing because he was too old.

'Aww, go cry to your mummy,' Marc said. 'You've got two players bigger than me.'

'They went home!'

'And how's that my fault?' Marc said, backing off as he realised that he was acting more like he was ten than sixteen.

Kick-off got delayed because the keeper Marc volleyed was getting abuse from his teammates and didn't want to stay in goal. When nobody volunteered to replace him the keeper headed home in a strop.

The game was about to resume with Joel in goal, when everyone got distracted by a tiny, ruby-red Peugeot coming down the hill with its horn blasting. The engine was misfiring and judging by the thick plume of exhaust it was running on black-market petrol of less-than-premium quality.

At the bottom of the hill the car turned so sharply that it almost rolled before stopping on the edge of the football pitch by the main doors of Saint Cloud's municipal building. By some extraordinary act of contortion, six young men emerged from the tiny two-doored car. Two carried aged revolvers, while the other four were armed with fire axes and garden tools. All wore white armbands with the handwritten initials FFI, which stood for Forces of the French Interior.

Judging by their youth and unkempt hair the men were Maquis. Three were local enough to get recognised and kissed by some of the girls, while one found two younger brothers and had a tearful reunion.

It was a jubilant scene, but Joel, Marc and Sam all worried that things could turn nasty if the Germans turned up and tried to arrest the young draft dodgers.

A crowd of thirty kids and youths watched as the leading Maquis tried getting into the government offices. He'd expected to find the door open and looked disappointed as he read the opening times and discovered that it closed at 1.30 p.m. on a Friday.

He rattled the door, then made a fairly feeble shoulder charge.

'Shoot the lock,' one of the watching kids suggested.

One of the Maquis seemed to consider this, until his mate reminded him that they only had fourteen bullets. Eventually, one of the Maquis lads forced a small window and lifted an eleven-year-old boy through the opening. The boy opened the door from the inside, and bowed theatrically as the crowd gave him a cheer.

Five Maquis charged in, while a sixth rushed back to the car to grab a flag. Within a minute they were all up at a second-floor window. There were more cheers as one lad unfurled a grubby-looking French tricolour with FFI painted across it. There was no flagpole, so he tied it to the balcony and shouted.

'Long live France, long live the resistance!'

Exuberant youngsters cheered and clapped. Some had begun a charge into the building and tore Hitler's picture off the wall and took turns stomping on it.

Marc looked nervously across the river, then at Sam and Joel. 'One shot from a tank on the opposite embankment would kill the lot of 'em.'

As Sam nodded, an elderly lady stood below the hanging flag and started yelling. 'Yves Raimond, stop being an idiot and take that flag down.'

Yves identified himself with a wave from the balcony.

'Hello, madame. Do you still teach at the primary school?'

The teacher wagged her finger angrily. 'Yves, this is not a game! All of you kids get out of there before the Germans see what you've done.'

'I'll fight the Germans!' Yves shouted, managing to sound brave and pathetic at the same time.

Marc shook his head and spoke to Sam. 'They're sure to hold 'em off with fourteen bullets and two old revolvers.'

Joel had just spotted Laure's two boys jumping around in the crowd. 'Go home, right now,' he ordered.

The older lad shook his head. 'Mummy said I can stay out until she calls me,' he said firmly. 'Unless the Germans come.'

Joel pointed at the French flag. 'If the Germans see that, they'll come all right. Now run straight home before I boot the pair of you up the arse.'

A few adults had come down the hill to see what was going on and the little Peugeot's horn blasted as kids jumped about on the driver's seat.

'Bloody idiots!' a man in a vest was shouting. 'This is a peaceful neighbourhood. Why invite trouble?'

'Take that flag down!' the elderly teacher repeated.

'We'll fight and die for Paris!' one of the Maquis shouted. 'We're not scared.'

Marc looked at Sam and Joel. 'I don't know about

you but I'm getting out of here.'

Joel spotted Laure's boys hiding in a doorway. 'What did I just tell you?' he shouted, as he grabbed both boys by their wrists and started marching them uphill.

'If this is the standard of the resistance fighters, we're *really* in the shit,' Sam said.

*

By Saturday morning the outbreaks of gunfire had spread from central Paris to the suburbs. From apartment roofs you could see French tricolour flags and bursts of gunfire erupt every ten or fifteen minutes. Henderson and Edith walked downhill to see what was going on and found the six lightly-armed Maquis had been bolstered by several Maquis colleagues and a couple of elderly locals.

As a military man, Henderson saw little point in setting yourself up to be shot inside a building that was of little strategic value. But there was a festive atmosphere amongst the Maquis and the young people hanging around in front of the municipal building. For all their foolishness, Henderson couldn't help but feel roused by the young Frenchmen, standing under their own flag with the confidence to shoot at Germans.

Henderson was halfway back up the hill towards the apartment when he heard vehicles crossing the bridge. After four years of not being allowed to drive, it was remarkable how many resistance fighters had taken cars out of mothballs and found a few litres of illicit petrol to get them running.

The two cars speeding across the bridge had FFI painted on the doors and the lead driver blasted his horn when he saw the French flag draped off the building. The atmosphere changed a minute later when a medium-sized Panzer tank started rattling across the bridge.

Girls and younger boys poured out on to the cobbles and started running home. Henderson took cover in a doorway 50 metres up the hill, with Edith gripping his arm nervously.

'I doubt he'll shoot,' Henderson said, as they were joined in their hiding spot by a pair of teenaged sisters.

'Why?' Edith asked.

'No need to get this close,' he explained. 'Tanks can strike accurately from half a kilometre.'

But as the tank neared the end of the bridge it slowed down and swung its turret towards the municipal building. One of the Maquis hurled a rock off the building's roof. He missed by several metres, but a few more got thrown and at least one plinked harmlessly off the side of the tank before it moved off without firing.

Henderson smiled at Edith as the tank rumbled away. 'Told you,' he said.

Edith laughed. 'Your brow's awfully sweaty for someone so confident.'

'It's a warm day,' Henderson said, smiling as he stood up to start walking again.

Edith spoke more seriously as they neared the apartment. 'If the Germans attack, are we really going to sit in our apartment and let them kill everyone?'

Henderson avoided a direct answer. 'Let's hope it doesn't come to that, eh?'

*

The BBC's 7 p.m. bulletin announced that Allied troops were now within 12 kilometres of Paris. It also warned that large-scale German reinforcements were on their way, and that heavy fighting could be expected either in or around Paris in the coming days.

The Germans deliberately switched all electricity off during the BBC's evening broadcasts, but it came back on at ten to eight, so that people with mains-only radios could listen to the news on German-controlled Radio France.

The pro-Nazi broadcast began with a bombastic report, explaining how trainloads of soldiers, tanks and artillery had already begun pouring into Paris to defend the city. This propaganda lacked credibility because everyone knew that the railway workers were on strike and that the lines between Germany and France had been repeatedly cut by the resistance and blasted by Allied bombs.

The second report was more intriguing. Radio France

had never previously mentioned the three-day-old resistance uprising, but it now announced that the administrators of Paris had '... *generously offered a midnight ceasefire with troublemakers within the capital.*' It then went on to say that leaders of the troublemakers had agreed to stop all anti-German activity. In return, the Germans agreed that there would be no reprisals.

Henderson and his team were all gathered around the radio as the broadcast ended and the apartments' electricity supply flickered and died.

'Why a truce?' Edith asked.

Marc looked at Henderson as he struck a match for paraffin light. 'Why would either side agree to a ceasefire?'

'Have you spoken to Maxine about this?' PT added.

'I haven't heard from Maxine since she left the news theatre on Wednesday night,' Henderson said. 'I'm sure she'll be busy and she's probably not keen to use us for anything after your little freelance operation to kill Commander Robert.'

Paul spoke thoughtfully. 'Remember how Maxine said that neither the resistance nor the Germans went after the telephone network, because they both found it useful? I guess this is similar. Both the Germans and the resistance need a truce at the moment – all the resistance groups are scared of German reprisals with heavy weapons.'

Marc nodded. 'And if the Allies are only a few

kilometres from the city, the Germans want to focus their attention on fighting them, not getting bogged down with pockets of resistance.'

'I doubt the ceasefire will hold for long,' Henderson said. 'But our food situation is getting critical and this could be our chance to resupply. Marc, have you got the energy for a ride out to Beauvais tomorrow?'

A loud artillery boom sounded from the Allied lines to the west.

'Doesn't sound any closer than it did last night,' Marc said.

Henderson nodded. 'Supply lines will be holding the Allies back, as much as anything. They've got plenty of men and machines, but the food and the fuel has to make a long voyage across the Channel to Normandy and then trek halfway across France to the front lines.'

'Tanks drink a lot of fuel,' Paul agreed.

Marc returned to Henderson's question about making a food run to Beauvais. 'We'll know the ceasefire's working if the gunfire stops at midnight. If it does, three of us can ride out to Morel's farm. We'll put baskets on the bikes and we've got that little tow cart.'

CHAPTER THIRTY

Monday 21 August 1944

Marc opened one eye. The sun was up and he could hear bodies moving around the apartment, but his legs were stiff from the previous day's seven-hour bike ride and an all-too-brief reunion with Jae. He'd have liked to go back to sleep, but he was stuck to the sheets and it was way too hot.

Marc was careful not to wake Paul as he stepped over his mattress. Deep thuds rumbled out from central Paris as he entered the kitchen.

'Morning,' Marc said. 'That sounds ominous.'

Edith had boiled some of the eggs they'd picked up from Morel's farm the day before. Marc joined Luc and Henderson at the dining table and began peeling a speckled eggshell.

'The ceasefire gave both sides a breather,' Henderson said. 'But judging by the noise, the Germans have taken their big toys out of storage.'

'Any word from Maxine?' Marc asked.

'Nothing,' Henderson said. 'I expect she's busy.'

'I think she's forgotten all about us,' Edith said. 'Either that or she's been arrested.'

'Speculation's pointless,' Henderson said, his voice dismissive but his face unable to hide deeper concern.

Shouting erupted in the street as Marc bit the top off his egg. Edith dashed out of the kitchen and crossed to the living-room to see what was going on. The room shuddered as she peered downhill.

'They're getting shot at down by the river,' Edith reported.

By the time Marc, Luc and Henderson reached the window a cloud of white dust was billowing up the street. There was also some kind of megaphone announcement being made. It was too distant to catch every word, but the gist was that the Germans had fired warning shots and given the Maquis inside the municipal building one minute to surrender.

Edith looked round at Henderson. 'Well?'

Henderson took a pensive step back from the window. 'Maxine clearly doesn't need us,' he said finally. 'Go fetch the weapons, but we'll need a clearer idea of what's going on before wading in.'

As PT, Henderson, Edith, Sam and Joel charged down to the basement, Marc hurriedly pulled on his boots. Luc had been two floors down with Laure, and had already gone out on to the street to see what was happening.

'I grabbed some woman running up the hill,' Luc told everyone as they joined him outside. 'She reckoned there's a German truck. Eight to ten troops hiding on the bridge, and a tank further back.'

'Damn,' Henderson said. 'Did she say what kind of tank?'

Luc shook his head.

'OK. Marc, Luc—'

Henderson got interrupted by a second tank blast. They were too far up the hill to have a view of the bridge or the municipal building, but there was the sound of masonry shattering and a new dust cloud gave an opportunity to move without being seen.

'Marc, Luc – find sniper positions and see what you can pick off,' Henderson said, as they all scrambled into the lobby of an apartment building. 'The rest of us can keep moving downhill, but stay out of sight.'

A German speaker announcement wafted through the dust. 'Surrender immediately or we shall storm the building.'

Still in his pyjama bottoms, Marc took a sniper rifle and a bag of ammunition clips off Joel.

'I'm going for the balconies where the old grannies sit watching the kids,' Luc said.

Marc thought Luc's idea was smart, but didn't tell him so. He had to squint as he charged after Luc into the white dust cloud. As they sprinted 60 metres, a couple of feeble revolver shots rang out from inside the municipal building. The pair went through the rear entrance of the last apartment block in their street. They charged up to the second floor and pounded on an apartment door.

It got answered by one of the elderly women who usually sat out watching the little kids play.

'We need your balcony,' Luc said brusquely.

The woman didn't look keen, so Luc forced the door and bundled her out of the way. She made a kind of cackling sound as she fell backwards and slid down the wall.

'Sorry,' Marc said as he stepped over her legs and followed Luc.

Dust blew into a sunny living-room as Luc opened the balcony doors. The old woman had found her feet and started shouting about it being her private home and them having no right to charge in.

'Shut up or I'll punch you out,' Luc said, getting his usual kick out of being nasty.

Marc gave the old girl a guilty smile. 'Just go into the back room. Close the door and try to stay calm.'

The balcony gave a superb view of the municipal building, the riverbank and the bridge. For all his threats, the German commander hadn't given the order to storm the building because it would involve an open approach across the broad cobbled area that local boys used as a football pitch.

Marc and Luc crept on to the balcony as the tank launched another shell at the building. A couple of 88-mm shells from a heavy tank like a Tiger would have flattened the building. But this was an outdated Panzer, equipped with a much less powerful 20-mm cannon.

The situation looked like a classic stand-off. The Germans had jumped out of their truck and crouched securely behind the low wall running the length of the bridge. The Maquis were all holed up inside the municipal building and if they had any sense they'd have moved to rooms at the rear so they wouldn't get hit by the tank blasts.

Marc looked at Luc. 'Any bright ideas?'

'The Germans might advance using the tank as cover,' Luc said. 'Charging in with the truck could be risky, but if they came in at speed they'd only be exposed for a few seconds. Or, they could wait for a heavier tank to arrive and pound the whole place to rubble.'

'Have they got heavy tanks in the city?' Marc asked as Luc peered through the scope on his sniper rifle. 'I've never seen one if they have.'

'Aye, aye!' Luc said excitedly.

'What?' Marc asked.

'From this height we can get a clear shot through the floor of the truck.'

Marc looked confused and Luc tutted impatiently.

'What's below the floor of a truck, just behind the cab?' Luc asked.

'Oh,' Marc said, feeling dumb as he worked it out. 'We could shoot through the floor and hit the fuel tank.'

Luc nodded. 'With any luck the Germans will panic when the truck goes bang and we can pick a few off as they scramble away.'

'Henderson and the others should be in position by now,' Marc said. 'You wanna take the shot?'

'You're Mr Bull's-eye,' Luc said.

It was awkward firing between iron railings from the balcony floor, but standing and taking a shot from the top of the railing would make it too easy for the Germans to spot their position and shoot back. Luc glanced inside to make sure that the elderly woman wasn't up to anything, as Marc spread out on his belly and took aim.

'Range three hundred and twenty metres,' Marc told himself quietly, taking deep breaths to calm his thumping heart. 'Strong breeze coming off the river from my right.'

The fuel tank was a large target. On a good day Marc could hit a walnut from this range. But the shot was complicated by having to estimate the position of the unseen fuel tank, and there was no way to predict the bullet's trajectory after it punched through the truck's canvas awning before hitting the floor.

'Here's goes nothing,' Marc said, as Luc took a slightly higher firing position, ready to blow off any German heads that bobbed up during an explosion.

Marc was about to shoot when he was startled by the tank firing another shell towards the municipal building. The two previous shells had flown high with the aim of punching holes in masonry and frightening the men inside. This one went in a much lower arc, turning the building's double front doors to splinters, smashing up the staircase inside and creating a shockwave that blew a dozen windows.

'Looks like they're preparing to attack,' Luc said.

'Shall I shoot now, or wait until they move?'

Luc was about to say *wait* when Marc saw something bob up above the line of the bridge's side wall. The soldier responsible was trying to keep his head down, as a colleague strapped on a large backpack that comprised two metal cylinders and a long hose.

'Flamethrower,' Marc said.

He made a tiny adjustment to his aim and pulled the trigger as the cylinders started going out of view.

The bullet caught the top of a cylinder, knocking its wearer backwards. Nothing happened for a second, but as Marc zeroed back in on the truck's fuel tank there was a flash of blue flame. The man in the backpack was rolling around on fire and as men ran in to save him, Luc took aim at their chests.

Marc re-aimed his original shot, going for the truck's fuel tank. A spark ignited the fuel and the canvas awning, forcing more Germans to break cover as they scrambled back down the bridge. The German commander was shouting orders for his men to back off, while simultaneously ordering the tank to come forward and give them cover.

The men crouching on the bridge hadn't seen where Marc and Luc's shots came from, but the tank crew had a clear view. They swung their cannon towards the balcony as the tank advanced across the bridge.

'Time to leave!' Marc yelled, as he scrambled inside with Luc pushing against his back.

They dived for cover as the 20-mm cannon began pounding the balcony. Wood and glass flew across the old woman's living-room as rounds tore holes through thin plaster walls and opened a view into the neighbouring apartment.

'Little bastards!' the old woman screamed, waving a fist as she leaned out of her bedroom door. 'I've lived here in peace for thirty years.'

As Marc and Luc charged out of the apartment and raced upstairs to find a different balcony to shoot from, Henderson's ground-level team made the most of the chaos they'd created.

The tank was now moving too fast to continue shooting at the balcony. There was a crash of glass and metal as it smashed the burning truck out of the way. When it broke on to the open cobbles, the tank slowed to a brisk walking pace, with half a dozen soldiers hiding behind its flank. The gunner zeroed in on the municipal building and began firing shells at the French flag.

The Germans assumed they were fighting inexperienced Maquis and perhaps a few locals who'd taken a lucky shot from the balcony. But Henderson had anticipated the possibility of the tank being used as a shield. He'd sent Sam and Joel on a flanking manoeuvre, jumping walls and crossing flat roofs to emerge on the opposite side of the tank.

The brothers waited until the Germans were within 10 metres, then jumped up behind a wall and opened fire with STEN machine guns. These weren't accurate weapons, but from this range they didn't need to be.

As the tank's entourage got ripped apart, 20-mm shells continued pounding the municipal building and a section of its façade turned into a waterfall of rubble.

Back in the apartment building, Marc and Luc reached the fourth floor, where a woman with a baby welcomed them into her apartment.

'I watched what you just did,' she told them admiringly,

as she grabbed her baby and ran towards a neighbour's apartment across the hallway. 'The Germans killed the father of my child and my landlord's a shit, so let them have it.'

But by the time Marc and Luc reached the young woman's balcony there was little to do but spectate. Sam and Joel had advanced and taken out a couple of Germans who'd stayed on the bridge. The only surviving German infantryman was retreating to the other side of the river as the tank juddered up the municipal building's steps and smashed into the front entrance.

Ironically, it was masonry weakened by the tank's own shells that thundered down and beached it. The tank's commander threw the tracks into reverse, but the stairs had left the Panzer at an awkward angle and the tracks couldn't get any purchase.

With no Germans in shooting range, PT sprinted towards the tank and squished a hunk of plastic explosive with a thirty-second detonator on the underside of the running board above the tracks.

Inside, the tank commander rocked the tank backwards and forwards, as Henderson and several others shouted at the Maquis, telling them to jump out of the municipal building's back windows before the charge went off.

Several Maquis were trapped on the second floor and threw themselves from windows into a big tree at the building's rear. Seconds before the plastic exploded, the tank commander finally found some grip. As he reversed across the cobbles towards the bridge, another huge section of the municipal building's façade collapsed, throwing up choking white dust.

It was tough to breathe and impossible to keep eyes open. Nobody on the ground saw the explosion at the rear of the tank, but four floors up Marc and Luc got a grandstand view. The orange blast lifted the Panzer's rear off the ground and shattered its right track. The armour hadn't been penetrated, but the shockwave from the blast killed the tank's engine and mangled the exhaust system.

The three-man crew was deafened and found their cramped quarters filling rapidly with exhaust fumes. There were two clanks as one desperate German opened the turret flap and another released an emergency escape hatch in the floor.

'Please!' the German shouted as he stood up, making a surrender gesture.

Luc caught the German's bald sweaty head in his scope and took him out with a headshot.

'He was surrendering,' Marc blurted.

Luc gave an evil laugh. 'We can barely feed ourselves, and in case you didn't get the memo: the resistance ain't got any prisons.'

Down at ground level the two Germans who'd crawled

out through the escape hatch had even less luck as newly confident Maquis closed in and dished out merciless beatings. It wasn't clear if the Germans were dead or just unconscious as the jeering lads dragged them up to the riverbank and flopped their bodies over a wall into the Seine.

As the dust continued to swirl, nervous locals came down from their hilly streets to inspect the tank and the remains of the municipal building. Henderson, Joel, Sam, PT and Edith tried making a discreet exit, but their actions hadn't gone unnoticed and their weapons made them obvious.

'Hey,' one of the Maquis lads shouted. 'Who are you?'

Henderson carried on walking, but several Maquis kept up the chase and he eventually stopped and turned to face five scruffy lads.

'Name's Charles.'

'You have excellent weapons, Charles,' one of the awestruck young men noted. 'Your team saved our lives *and* destroyed a tank!'

'Was anybody hurt?' Henderson asked.

'A man named Dominic. He was afraid to jump and got buried in the collapse.'

As the Maquis spoke, Marc and Luc came out of the apartment block with their sniper rifles. They found themselves with their own crowd of admiring teenage girls. Marc was too in love with Jae to care, but Luc was awkward around girls and enjoyed being the centre of attention.

As Henderson turned to walk away, the young Maquis pulled off his FFI armband and thrust it at Henderson.

'We need a leader to fight the Germans.'

'What's your name?' Henderson asked.

'Jean-Claude,' the young man answered.

Henderson smiled wryly. 'Jean-Claude, you need to go home to your family. Have a shave and a bath. Try and find a decent meal and pray that the Allies get here before the German reinforcements.'

Jean-Claude looked crushed. 'We want to make a difference.'

For all their naivety, Henderson couldn't help admiring the balls of young men who wanted to take on the German army with rusty revolvers and a few rounds of ammunition.

'Well,' Henderson said, after a second's thought, 'I'm not doing anything else, so I might as well do what I can to stop you boys getting yourselves killed.'

CHAPTER THIRTY-ONE

'You're all dusty,' Paul said, as PT led the gang back into the apartment. 'What's going on?'

Marc cracked up laughing and shook his head as he put the sniper rifle down on the couch and moved into the kitchen to wash his face. 'You *seriously* slept through all that?'

'I was knackered after riding to Beauvais and back,' Paul said defensively, as more dusty bodies came into the apartment. They included Jean-Claude and a couple more scruffy Maquis lads. 'Mind you, I *was* dreaming that I was in the middle of an air raid.'

'We didn't miss you,' Luc said. 'You're shit at everything anyway.'

As Paul jogged back to his room to put trousers on, Henderson stood at the centre of the living-room and looked at Jean-Claude.

'So, what's your objective?'

'To defend our neighbourhood,' he said proudly.

Henderson shook his head. 'Defend it from what?' he asked. 'The only reason this neighbourhood got attacked was that you put a dirty great French flag on the front of a building that could be seen from the other side of the river. You might as well have stood in the street with a target around your neck saying *Please shoot me.*'

Jean-Claude looked a little upset. 'So what *do* we do?'

'Think like a bullfighter,' Henderson said. 'Your opponent has speed and muscle, so you have to tease and dodge. What's your fighting strength?'

'There are ten of us now Dominic is gone,' Jean-Claude said. 'Plus the older men who joined us from the neighbourhood.'

'Weapons?'

'Four pistols and two rifles. But ammunition is critical.'

'Food?' Henderson asked.

'Virtually nothing,' Jean-Claude admitted. 'But we still have the Peugeot.'

'Explosives or grenades?'

Jean-Claude shook his head.

'Hardly brilliant,' Henderson said. 'But the tank didn't blow up and hopefully there's still fuel in there. We need to siphon it off, then gather up as many empty bottles as we can and use them to make petrol bombs. If there's a pharmacy nearby, there are chemicals we can add to give them a real kick.'

Marc had stepped out of the kitchen. 'You want me to show them how to make them?'

Henderson nodded. 'Get the fuel out of the Panzer first. German forces are at full stretch, but there's still a chance they'll come after someone who blew up a tank. Station lookouts on the bridge and if there's any sign of trouble, don't stay around and fight. That last little skirmish used up nearly half of our ammunition and I don't see where more will come from in the short term.'

'What do we do once we have petrol bombs?' Jean-Claude asked.

'If you want to fight the Germans, it's better to pick off soft targets than try to hold territory,' Henderson explained. 'There's been regular German traffic going over the bridge. We need to find some good ambush points. Snipers can take out drivers of cars. If anyone can get hold of some piano wire we can string it across roads to decapitate motorcyclists. Petrol bombs are most effective against canvas-sided trucks. If we ambush the right vehicles, we might even get lucky and nab some additional supplies.'

For the next hour the neighbourhood hummed with jubilation and fear. Marc found the tank's armoured refuelling cap and the dipstick indicated 125 litres in the tank. They had no tubing to syphon it off, so Marc clambered into the tank's cramped engine compartment and disconnected a fuel line.

While local kids scoured apartments and houses for empty bottles, Marc drained diesel into saucepans and lowered them out through the floor hatch. Two mates aged eleven took turns crawling under the tank to grab them, before walking to a production line set up in front of a house near the bottom of the hill.

Here, Sam and Joel supervised a team pouring the fuel into bottles. A retired pharmacist had been located, along with small supplies of sugar and sulphuric acid that would turn the diesel from a flammable liquid into a sticky explosive. Lastly, a pair of young women cut and rolled pieces of rag, which were pushed into the bottles to serve as wicks.

If the Maquis' arrival had made much of the neighbourhood nervous, the battle and ambush planning brought out a powerful sense of community. As Henderson scoured the streets around the bridge looking for good ambush spots he was greeted warmly and offered food. He also picked up an entourage of teenagers and old men volunteering to fight.

There was no sign of a German counterattack, and no traffic either. As there were several other bridges in the area, it seemed probable that the Germans had switched to using other routes when they saw the stranded tank and burned-out truck.

By noon 190 petrol bombs had been made. Henderson had identified four key spots on the approach roads leading to the bridge and placed teams of six at each one. The teams comprised a mixture of local men, Maquis and boys in their early teens. If anything happened, Henderson's own team would take sniper positions and act as back-up.

The ambush points were supposed to be concealed, but the heady atmosphere meant that women kept bringing out trays of drinks and kids loitered nearby, tasting the excitement.

As the afternoon wore on, people began cycling across the bridge to inspect the stricken tank. Several posed for photographs and someone arrived with a pot of white paint and daubed FFI on its side in large letters.

Henderson was uncomfortable with this. These 'tourists' would attract attention and the riverfront location would always be vulnerable to shells aimed from defensive positions across the water.

Beside cameras and curiosity, some visitors brought the latest underground news sheets. These sheets usually ran different stories reflecting the politics of their editors, but there had been some kind of coordination and Henderson saw three sheets, all with near-identical lead stories below generous headlines.

MAKE BARRICADES!

The uprising has begun. German patrols, once proud, now scuttle through Paris like rats, taking shots from all directions!

Now we must take Paris back. Free your own neighbourhood by building barricades to keep out Nazi scum.

Take up the cobbles and paving. Sacrifice your furniture and tear up railings.

Once you have built your barricade, stand bravely behind it to defend your city and your nation.

This is the order of the FFI and the duty of EVERYONE!

'Where did this *FFI* suddenly come from?' Marc asked, as he showed Henderson and Edith yet another version of the barricades story. 'Who are its leaders?'

Henderson smiled. 'I reckon the FFI is anyone who puts on the armband. If there's any leadership I've neither met them, nor heard of them. But it does no harm if it gives the people a sense of unity and sends the Germans after an imaginary organisation.'

'So are *we* making barricades?' Edith asked.

Henderson shrugged. 'I don't see much tactical value in them. Loose stones and railings won't stop anything heavier than a truck. On the other hand, they'll do no harm as long as they don't stop the Germans getting to our ambush points.'

'If we had them in the right places they might help filter cars and trucks *towards* our ambush points,' Marc reasoned.

News sheets got passed around, while people in upper-floor apartments could see barricades being erected across the river. As the neighbourhood's unofficial leader, Henderson found himself besieged by people who wanted to make barricades.

Partly, it was residual enthusiasm from the battle and the bomb making, but people also worried that they'd be a soft target for the Germans if they had no barricades when other neighbourhoods did.

Despite his doubts about their effectiveness, Henderson suggested that a 15-metre barricade be constructed across the cobbled street between the wrecked municipal building and the riverbank. This would provide a good shooting point from which to ambush enemy vehicles crossing the bridge.

Henderson also gave the go-ahead for a smaller barricade at the top of the road they'd been living in, and several other residential streets radiating up from the river. This would force any German traffic to either demolish a barrier or run the gauntlet of their ambush points.

Within twenty minutes there were three dozen adults

and close to a hundred kids at work. It was decided that the stricken tank would form the barricade's centrepiece and they built out from either side of it.

People brought out barrows, pickaxes and shovels. Broken cobbles were taken up, then kids worked with hammers and crowbars to loosen more. Elderly men worked in teams, plundering the rubble in front of the wrecked municipal building and dragging the biggest sections into place with ropes.

It was hot work and the mix of unstable mounds of stone and kids running around led to crushed fingers and other minor injuries. Paul was no fan of manual labour, but he rounded up six metal fire-ash cans and some paint. He put bright yellow stripes on the cans and found two pieces of board, on which he painted black skull icons and *Danger Mines!* in both French and German.

By the time Paul's artwork was dry, the chest-high barricade had a few people finishing off the section closest to the river, while everyone else had moved uphill to start building the smaller barriers. After stripping several lengths of electrical cable out of the municipal building, Paul arranged his brightly-painted ash cans and warning notices in front of the barricade and ran pieces of wire between them so that it all looked like some fiendish explosive trap.

CHAPTER THIRTY-TWO

The tide of goodwill that took Henderson's suburban neighbourhood through morning and afternoon gave way to anxiety as the sun faded. Barricades or not, you could still hear Germans attacking resistance strongholds throughout the city. There had been no sign of army vehicles in Saint Cloud, but their return was surely only a matter of time.

Henderson's apartment had become a kind of neighbourhood headquarters. The sofas had been pushed back against the living-room walls and the kitchen table put in the middle of the room with a local map spread over it.

At 7 p.m. Henderson, his team, plus several Maquis and locals gathered around the radio for BBC France's daily news broadcast. They all hoped for triumphant news, but the announcer calmly stated that American and French forces had now reached the Seine at Fontainebleau, while resistance fighters faced increasingly heavy German retaliation in central Paris.

'Fontainebleau is south-east of here,' Luc's girlfriend Laure said sourly. 'The Allies are going *around* Paris.'

People nodded solemnly in agreement.

'If they get across the Seine they can quickly cut off German supply lines to Paris,' Jean-Claude added.

'They said nothing about the German reinforcements,' Luc said, as he slid an arm around Laure's back.

'If the reinforcements arrive and the city gets cut off, there could be a siege,' Jean-Claude said.

Henderson shook his head. 'Paris is huge. There could be pockets of German resistance, but it would take hundreds of thousands of soldiers to secure the whole city.'

'And we're almost ten kilometres from the centre,' Marc added.

The mood was dark as people filtered out of the apartment. Henderson sent Marc and Sam out to check on one of the ambush points. Three of the six men had gone home as the initial eagerness of the volunteers gave way to anxiety and hunger.

The other ambush points were similarly depleted, so Henderson reduced their number from four to two, and sent some men home to rest with orders to return in the morning. He also added two of his own people to each team.

It was 2.30 a.m. and Marc was keeping lookout on a flat roof when he heard a truck coming downhill towards the bridge.

'Showtime,' Marc shouted, giving PT a nudge. 'Everyone wake up.'

There were five men on the team, plus Marc and PT. The most alert was a local lad of about fifteen who whipped a lighter from his pocket and grabbed a petrol bomb. Marc went for his sniper rifle, while PT and a couple of the other men grabbed bombs.

When the truck drew close they lit the wicks on their bombs, but the driver surprised them by slowing down.

Marc looked at PT. 'He can't have seen us, can he?'

The truck stopped 15 metres from the point bombs would have been dropped on to his canvas awning. Three men managed to pull the burning wicks out of their bombs, but the fifteen-year-old lost his nerve and lobbed his into the road in front of the truck.

Apparently lost, the truck's driver was reaching for a map in the door pocket. But he threw the gearstick into reverse the instant he saw the explosion. The flames enabled Marc to see the driver and his trigger finger was faster than the driver's foot engaging the clutch.

Marc shot the German through the chest and as his body sprawled sideways the truck began rolling downhill.

'Don't burn it,' PT shouted. 'There might be food, or ammo.'

As the truck accelerated, Marc took a second shot and blew out a front tyre. This made the vehicle lurch sideways. It scraped noisily along a garden wall and stopped just shy of the dying petrol bomb.

While Marc shot, PT had clambered over a sloping roof and now lowered himself on to cobbles directly behind the truck. He pulled out a pistol as he opened the truck's canvas rear flaps and shone a small torch inside.

He briefly glimpsed racks of blue-green cylinders, before getting distracted by a skinny figure cowering at the back.

'High explosive,' the man said, in strangely-accented French. 'Shoot and you kill us both.'

'Come out slowly,' PT ordered. 'Hands where I can see them.'

Marc had jumped off the roof and approached the front of the truck. He was surprised to see that the dead driver wore the insignia of a senior SS officer. Marc opened the passenger side door and grabbed a blazer resting on the seat. The ID inside confirmed the officer's rank and listed him as part of a *Special Demolition Team*.

'Don't kill your pal back there,' Marc shouted to PT. 'I don't know what we've got here, but it might be important.'

PT allowed the skinny man to crawl out of the truck and stand up.

'Not German, Polish!' he said pleadingly. 'Polish. Osttruppen!'

The guy was so underweight that you could see every bone in his face.

'You said high explosive,' PT said. 'What are those cylinders?'

'From torpedoes,' the man explained.

Marc turned to the fifteen-year-old and told him to run and fetch Henderson from the apartment.

'I know what a torpedo looks like,' PT said disbelievingly.

The Pole shook his head. 'They make torpedoes at Saint Cloud, but the Germans have no more submarines.'

'What do you mean they make torpedoes in Saint Cloud? We're in Saint Cloud now.'

One of the locals answered this question. 'The Germans did make torpedoes in a factory near here, but all the workers got laid off months ago. A friend who worked there said the factory was full of torpedoes, but that there were no U-boats left to use them.'

The Pole didn't speak good French but nodded eagerly at the old man's story. 'They take torpedoes apart. Then they remove explosive, for demolition of the city.'

PT peeked back inside the truck and realised that he

was looking at the explosives from more than thirty disassembled torpedoes. His jaw dropped as he looked at Marc.

'If we'd dropped petrol bombs on this lot we'd have killed ourselves and blown up half the neighbourhood.'

But Marc still didn't completely buy the Pole's story. 'So the Germans sent out all this explosive with just one guy and an Osttruppen?'

The Pole shook his head. 'We had a puncture. The other trucks wanted to reach the city centre before dark, but we stayed behind and I guess my driver got lost.'

'So how many trucks were in the convoy?' Marc asked.

The Pole shrugged. 'Fifteen. Perhaps twenty.'

Marc did a calculation in his head. Twenty trucks with thirty large warheads inside made 600 bombs. That amount of explosive dropped from aeroplanes would be nasty, but the destruction would be hundreds of times more effective if the bombs were expertly positioned rather than lobbed out of aeroplanes.

Henderson came running towards the scene with unlaced boots and his shirt buttons undone. Before the war he'd run the Royal Navy's Espionage Research Unit, which specialised in spying on rival navies' technology.

'Two-hundred-kilo torpedo charges,' Henderson said. 'The design's been refined since I last saw one, but they'll still blow a nice hole in whatever you want them to.'

Henderson then shocked the skinny prisoner by switching to fluent Polish. 'How long since the other trucks left the torpedo factory?'

The man's face lit up. 'Are you Polish?'

'Good with languages and accents,' Henderson said. 'Now answer my bloody question.'

'We took almost an hour finding a spare tyre after the other trucks left.'

Henderson nodded, then spoke to Marc in French. 'Use the telephone in the apartment below ours. Contact the Ghost Circuit on five-four-nine-three. It's probably too late, but someone may be able to identify the trucks with the other bombs in. And they can get word out, asking all resistance groups to keep an eye out for demolition teams using blue cylinders.'

As Marc ran up the hill, Henderson looked at the skinny Pole and pointed inside the truck.

'I don't understand what that thing does,' he said.

'What thing?' the Pole asked.

As the Pole turned, Henderson slipped an arm around his neck and started choking him.

PT looked shocked. 'He told us everything we asked.'

'Don't care,' Henderson said, once he'd dropped the dead Pole between his unlaced boots. 'Osttruppen betrayed their own country. They swore an oath to

Hitler to save their own skins. I might have done the same thing under desperate circumstances. But once someone's crossed that line, how can you ever trust them?'

PT looked furious. 'The guy was half starved. He was no threat to anyone.'

'Don't you *dare* question my decisions in front of strangers,' Henderson spat. Then he paused, before reverting to a more normal tone. 'We need to stop worrying about one dead Polish traitor and start thinking about the best way to kill Germans with all the explosives that just landed in our laps.'

CHAPTER THIRTY-THREE

Tuesday 22 August 1944–Wednesday 23 August 1944
'Take cover,' Sam yelled, equipment clattering as he ran frantically uphill, tailed by half a dozen armed men and a bunch of kids.

It was Tuesday, almost noon, and three medium Panzer tanks had rolled on to the far end of the bridge. As the lead tank came off, it slowed to a crawl and turned its turret towards the long barricade less than 15 metres away.

A few seconds felt like hours as the two tanks behind slowed up.

'Panzer mark four,' a girl crouched in a doorway beside Sam said.

He was no tank expert, but you didn't need to be one to appreciate the difference in destructive power between the broken 20-mm cannon of the tank that formed the centre of their barricade and the huge muzzles on these beasts, designed to pump out 75-mm shells.

Then, with a rumble of its engine and a blast of sooty exhaust, the lead tank accelerated aggressively across the riverfront. It tore bricks out of a low wall as it pulled on to the street where the truck had been captured the night before.

The second and third tanks did the same and people began returning to the barricade as their noise faded.

'Those guns were huge!' a worried-looking boy who'd been on the barricade with his grandfather said. 'Do you think the German reinforcements have arrived?'

The grandfather had no way of knowing and shrugged.

People looked to Sam, expecting some pearl of wisdom because he was part of Henderson's team, but he could only copy the shrug.

'Whatever you do, don't try and fight 'em,' Sam said.

'There's less noise from the city centre now,' the doom-faced boy said. 'Maybe they've swept up the resistance there, and now they're moving out here to the suburbs.'

'Or it may be a good sign,' a woman added. 'If the Germans are sending tanks out of the city centre, it could mean that the Allies are closing in.'

'The Allies have already gone around Paris,' another

man insisted. 'So don't go holding your breath on that theory, flower petal.'

The woman took the insult personally. 'I am not your *petal*, old man. And watch your mouth, or I'll knock you out.'

The woman looked tough, but Sam didn't get a chance to see the argument pan out because Paul was yelling at him.

'Henderson wants us indoors for a meeting.'

It took a couple of minutes to walk to the apartment building and up to the third floor. Henderson's whole team was present and the Maquis and other hangers-on had been conspicuously locked out.

'Did you see the guns on those three Panzers?' Sam asked. 'I damn nigh shat myself when the lead tank turned his turret!'

Joel spoke next. 'If we'd placed some of that torpedo explosive on the bridge, we could have blown them into the water—'

Henderson interrupted noisily. 'I need *everyone's* attention. I've had a bit of a run-around, but in the early hours of this morning I re-established telephone contact with one section of the Ghost Circuit. I'm told that the situation in the city centre is tense, but that resistance groups still control large areas and important buildings, despite the increased German pressure.'

'What about the German reinforcements?' Paul asked.

'The resistance has seen no sign of German reinforcements arriving by road, and railways coming from the east are now bombed and sabotaged out of action. I'm also told that several vehicles in the convoy of torpedo explosives were attacked and destroyed. The rest of the convoy is being hunted and I understand that the Germans are now finding it difficult to move any non-armoured vehicles through Paris without incurring constant sniper attacks.'

'That almost sounds like we're winning,' Sam said cautiously.

'Things could certainly be worse,' Henderson said. 'But when the Germans surround buildings with tanks, the resistance is helpless and there have been significant casualties. Putting two and two together, it's not difficult to conclude that we should be using the torpedo explosives we seized last night to target tanks.'

'I said we should blow up the bridge—' Sam blurted.

Henderson cut him off. 'Blowing up bridges suits retreating armies far more than advancing armies. And the more bridges that get destroyed, the more likely it is that Paris will get drawn into a siege.

'Most of the Paris Garrison's tanks are being kept in city parks. I've been told that one of the largest tank facilities is just across the river, in Bois de Boulogne. German vehicles are distributed throughout the park, and camouflaged to avoid attacks from the air. The

Germans have no reliable way of bringing more fuel or spares into the city so we'll be targeting a refuelling and maintenance depot.'

'Who's we?' Edith asked.

'It's a simple blast and run operation,' Henderson said. 'So it'll be me, and I'll take Marc because he speaks the best German. We'll only need about half of the explosives, so we'll leave the rest behind for a rainy day.

'While I'm gone, I want PT to take overall charge. Luc and Joel can run the ambush points. Sam, Paul and Edith concentrate on the barricades. Questions?'

'What if you get blown up?' Luc asked sarcastically.

Henderson looked irritated. 'You're all trained. You know how to contact the Ghost Circuit if needs be.'

*

The truck's windscreen had been shattered by Marc's bullets, but not so badly that Henderson couldn't see where he was driving. He wore the dead SS officer's uniform. Marc sat next to him, dressed in a beige mechanic's overall. He'd tried putting on the dead Pole's jacket, but it was absurdly small.

'Like old times,' Marc said, as they set off.

Marc was thinking back to the weeks after the Nazi invasion when he'd first met Henderson in Paris. They'd depended on each other and Henderson felt like the father-figure Marc, as a twelve-year-old orphan, had always craved. But nostalgia could only take Marc so far.

He was now old enough to see Henderson's flaws, and his heart belonged to Jae.

Paris wasn't much like old times either. They got over the bridge with no bother, but after that every street was dead. They imagined resistance snipers looking at their German truck from rooftops and balconies. There were fewer barricades than they'd expected and many of the ones they did see were unmanned and looked like a good stiff breeze would flatten them.

Henderson drove flat out, but the truck still caught a couple of bullets as it pulled on to a large crossroads. A German motorbike messenger had crashed some hours earlier, possibly after being shot at. The bloody rider lay unattended at the kerb, covered with flies as documents from his attaché case caught the wind.

The journey was less than 3 kilometres and, given their explosive cargo, Henderson was relieved to reach parkland where there was far less chance of getting shot at.

The tank park was blocked off with coils of barbed wire. The wooden security booth was burned out and a sturdier entry gate had been built further back, using sandbags and ribbed steel plates which were usually laid flat to help vehicle convoys cross boggy ground.

'Special destruction unit,' Henderson told a guard, as he flashed the dead SS officer's military ID papers, on to which he'd skilfully grafted his own photograph.

The guard looked baffled.

'I'm carrying demolition explosives,' Henderson explained. 'I can't get into the city centre, so I have orders to transfer my cargo to an armoured vehicle.'

The elderly German guard walked cautiously around the vehicle and peered in the back.

'Strange explosives,' he said.

Henderson spoke in his most irritable, pompous German, as two small Panzers drove out of the compound in the opposite lane. 'This has all been cleared in advance. I was told a vehicle was being prepared for me in the refuelling area.'

The guard shrugged. 'Nobody tells me anything, sir. You need to drive six hundred metres. Branch left when you see a turnoff to your right, after the two felled trees. You'll see the maintenance and refuelling sheds right in front of you.'

Henderson and Marc exchanged relieved smiles as they set off through the gate. Most of the park was woodland, but there were also areas of grass. These were beyond the shooting range of any resistance sniper and they drove past German soldiers sunbathing or playing football.

As Henderson drove slowly, Marc stepped into the truck's rear compartment. He grabbed a bunch of pre-wired detonators and began pushing them into the sockets on twelve drums of torpedo explosive.

There was no additional security around the maintenance and refuelling compound and nobody paid attention as Henderson parked up in front of a 50-metre-long canopy. The corrugated metal roof was covered in camouflage netting and teams worked in the shade beneath, performing routine maintenance on a selection of aged Panzer tanks.

'I count sixteen tanks in blast range,' Henderson said, as Marc passed him a pair of trigger wires.

'All connected up,' Marc said.

Henderson plugged the wires into a simple clockwork timer. 'I reckon eight minutes.'

Marc looked surprised. 'It's quite a walk, and then we've got to find a way through the perimeter.'

'Change of plan,' Henderson said. 'I fancy a quick tan and a chance to see how it goes off.'

As Marc jumped out and walked to the back, he jammed his hunting knife in one of the rear tyres, in case someone tried to move the truck. Henderson moved quickly, but not so fast that anyone would pay attention.

Henderson walked past the fallen trees and started unbuttoning his shirt as he crossed the road and headed towards shouts coming from a football game.

'Reckon this is far enough?' Marc asked.

'Plenty,' Henderson said, as he glanced at his watch. 'Just open your mouth in four minutes and fifty seconds, so that your eardrums don't pop.'

They found a spot in the shade. Marc peeled his overall down, exposing a well-muscled chest, while Henderson rolled up his blazer and tucked it under his head.

'When the bomb goes—'

Henderson paused as a tatty football rolled their way. Marc kicked it back at a lanky German who gave him a *thank-you* wave.

'Everyone will duck,' Henderson said. 'Then they'll move towards the explosion to see what's happening. While everyone's distracted we'll back into the trees and cut our way through the wire.'

'Makes sense,' Marc said. Then after a pause, 'How many people do you reckon will die?'

'If we put those tanks out of action, we'll save more than we kill,' Henderson said.

'You know, I've lost count of the number of people I've killed,' Marc said solemnly. 'When did we get so cold-blooded?'

'War's shit,' Henderson said, as the sun broke between clouds and made him squint. 'People do what they have to.'

'I just hope it ends soon,' Marc said.

'It will,' Henderson said firmly. 'And you've got your whole future. Don't waste it torturing yourself over the past.'

CHAPTER THIRTY-FOUR

Wednesday 23 August 1944–Thursday 24 August 1944
Marc didn't sleep that night. He thought about the truck exploding. Men not much older than himself grabbed their shirts off the grass and ran towards other men not much older than himself who'd just been killed or had bits of their bodies blown off.

Part of what troubled Marc was how easy it had all been. Finding the explosives was a stroke of luck. There'd been no problem getting into the compound. The escape was uneventful and once they'd switched to civilian clothes, the walk back to Saint Cloud was no bother either.

Marc thought about Jae and got scared. What if she was caught up in a battle near the farm? What if he got trapped inside Paris, or died somehow before he ever saw her again? Most of his stuff was already packed in a bag on the bedroom floor. There were bikes downstairs and if he rode off now he'd be with Jae by sunrise. And if anything went wrong, they'd at least die in the same place . . .

Paul spoke softly from his mattress down on the floor. 'Are you OK, mate?'

'Fine.'

'I can hear you sniffling. What's the matter?'

'I'm just sick of everything,' Marc said. 'The sniper scope, plastic explosive, grenades, petrol bombs, trucks, dead bodies. And Henderson.'

Paul was surprised. 'You've always been his favourite.'

Marc felt guilty as Paul sat on the corner of his bed and put a hand on his shoulder.

'Look at me crying,' Marc said. 'You're the one who lost everyone. Your mum, your dad . . . Rosie.'

'You never had family in the first place,' Paul said, feeling tears well up. 'I'm not sure if that's better or worse. I keep remembering one time. Me and Rosie were really little. Playing in the bath, and my mum sitting in a chair laughing at us. The memory hurts, but at least I lived it.'

'I wanna make new memories with Jae,' Marc said, choking back a sob. 'The only ones in my head are shit.'

*

Marc was still depressed when he wandered down to the

barricades on Thursday morning. His mood wasn't helped by sickening tension in a community that didn't know which to fear more: sudden death, or slow starvation.

Not long after sunrise there was a series of blasts across the river. A woman who usually walked over the bridge with communist news sheets came today in tears with a party of refugees.

Eighty Germans had been killed in the blast at the tank park. As day broke, tanks had poured on to the streets across the river, seeking revenge. Tanks smashed through homes, apartment blocks were set ablaze with flamethrowers and anyone who tried escaping the burning buildings had been shot at or beaten up.

Thick black smoke billowed across the river. Plenty of people around the neighbourhood knew that the explosives had been ambushed nearby and that Henderson was responsible for the attack on the tank park.

Besides grieving for people across the river, there was a terrible fear that the Germans would come here seeking revenge if they found out the truth. Henderson's status as neighbourhood leader evaporated just as rapidly as it had taken hold a few days earlier. Nobody bothered manning the barricades or ambush points and Henderson found people looking away, or taking cover indoors when he approached.

He called a meeting of his own people in the

apartment and gave a blunt assessment. 'I have no vehicles apart from bikes. Guns and ammunition are critically short. Worst of all, half the neighbourhood knows I'm here and that I'm behind the blast at the tank park. The Germans are weak, but there's still a chance they could send in a snatch squad to arrest us.'

'That's if the locals don't shoot us first,' Luc added.

Henderson continued. 'Our only realistic option is to leave the area and head towards Beauvais. We'll get food there and we left a significant amount of equipment with the Maquis in the woods. Assuming that our set is intact, we'll also be able to re-establish direct radio contact with campus.'

'Err, pardon me,' Joel said. 'But didn't we leave Beauvais when the Maquis were under heavy shelling? Jean and his men aren't *exactly* going to welcome us back with open arms.'

'It could be delicate,' Henderson admitted. 'But there's a lot of room in the woods and it'll certainly be a lot less precarious than it is here.'

Edith looked at Marc. 'You've been back to Beauvais – what do you reckon?'

'The Milice are still in the woods. Jean's only interest is in keeping the boys alive and I've not heard of any trouble.'

Luc felt miserable because the move would take him away from Laure, but he tried to hide his emotions. 'When are we leaving?' he asked.

'It's less conspicuous if we travel in two or three groups,' Henderson said.

Marc nodded. 'Everyone knows us here and things could turn nasty if they see us making a run for it.'

'We'll wait until darkness,' Henderson agreed.

'What about the curfew?' Paul asked.

'What curfew?' Marc said. 'Germans are way too scared to stand out in the open at checkpoints now. If anything we're more likely to get stopped and harassed in daylight.'

Henderson spent a few seconds thinking. 'Don't tell anyone we're leaving. We'll keep showing our faces around the neighbourhood and act like we're trying to get people back behind the barricades.'

Marc was longing to get back to Jae and cheered up knowing they'd soon be close. Henderson sent Luc and Edith down to the barricades, but everyone was indoors and even the Maquis had vanished.

Not long after 2 p.m., a German convoy crossed the bridge from the city. Twenty tanks thundered west towards the front lines, followed by half-tracks, motorised artillery and two dozen open-sided trucks crammed with soldiers.

Jean-Claude knocked on the apartment door just

before 7 p.m. When he stepped inside, it was clear that Henderson's team was preparing to leave.

'I wanted to listen to the BBC,' he said.

Everyone gathered around the radio, apart from Luc, who was downstairs enjoying a final chance to spend time with Laure. The broadcast mentioned that British troops had reached Rouen, while the Americans were across the Seine at Fontainebleau. Paris didn't get a mention.

'I'm sorry you're leaving,' Jean-Claude said. 'At least you have the balls to fight.'

'You'll have to stay here now you've seen us packing,' Henderson said, as he reached for a key off the table and held it up. 'But it's a decent apartment – you might as well make use of it once we've gone.'

'Your radio?' Jean-Claude asked.

'It came with the apartment,' Henderson said. 'It's staying here.'

As Henderson passed the apartment key to Jean-Claude, an American spotter plane skimmed noisily overhead.

'Jesus,' Paul gasped. 'That practically stripped tiles off the roof.'

Marc and Edith watched out of the window as the aircraft turned, using moonlight reflecting off the Seine to navigate towards the city centre.

'Bye-bye, Paris,' Edith said gently. 'I just hope the

Germans don't blow you up before I get to come back and see you properly.'

*

It was a quarter past one on Thursday morning as Marc's bike led Edith's and Joel's away from the apartment. He had a pistol and knife on his belt and a few pieces of clothing in his backpack, along with his disassembled sniper rifle.

Marc led the group because he knew the route to Beauvais better than anyone. The plan was for Paul to follow twenty minutes later with Sam, then Henderson, Luc and PT would leave half an hour after that.

Marc was keen to get back to Jae, but he always got a tiny bit sad when he left somewhere. The hot weather had finally started to break. The cobbles were slippery under his slim tyres and there was a gentle drizzle in the air as he pumped his legs up the steep hill.

He had to dismount and lift the bike over the unmanned barricade at the top. After checking behind to make sure Edith and Joel were keeping up, he rolled left and started down a gentle slope.

The cobbles made things rough, but there was childish pleasure to be had from the shuddering handlebars and the drizzle felt refreshing after so many hot days.

Marc picked up more speed than he should have and the brakes squealed as he neared the bottom of the hill. The narrow road turned in a gentle arc, but he was shocked by a vehicle shooting out of a side-turning less than 20 metres ahead. Its headlamps were on full beam, which broke every German regulation, and the compact, open-topped vehicle was something he'd seen before but didn't instantly identify.

Marc's first instinct was fear but, as he braked hard, aiming to turn around and make a fast getaway, he worked out that it was a Jeep like the ones American aircrews used on the roads near CHERUB campus.

But what was a Jeep doing here?

As the bike stopped, Marc raised a hand to shield his eyes from the beam of light. A tall man stood up on the passenger side, looking downhill through binoculars. Edith had joined the dots much faster and rolled right into the light.

'Are you Americans?' she squealed, grinning helplessly. 'Tom and Jerry? Mickey Mouse? Bugs Bunny?'

While Edith was reduced to spluttering the names of cartoon characters, Marc trembled and spoke half-reasonable English.

'Do you need any help, sir?'

The tall man lowered his binoculars and was clearly surprised to hear English. 'How's the bridge down the hill?'

'Intact,' Marc said. Since it was dark and the headlight beams were blinding him, the scene felt a lot like a dream. 'You've got a clear run down the bridge from here.'

'What about Krauts?'

'Not in this neighbourhood,' Marc said. 'It's all residential. Turn left on to the bridge and it's pretty much a straight ride to the city centre from there.'

The American gave Marc a little salute. 'You might want to step off your bikes. This road's about to get busy.'

As the tall American sat down, his driver spoke into a radio microphone. 'Pathfinder six reporting. Bridge fifty-four is clear to go. Repeat, fifty-four clear to go. Over and out.'

Marc, Edith and Joel exchanged wary smiles as they stood astride their bikes.

'Do we keep riding, or what?' Joel asked.

'In pitch dark, with a convoy on the way?' Marc said. 'We need to go back and warn the others.'

They'd been pacing themselves for a four-hour ride to Beauvais, but Joel had no need to hold back as he led the return, pedalling as fast as he could and almost losing it on the damp cobbles. When they got to the apartment, they bolted up to the third floor and encountered Paul and Sam coming downstairs with their luggage.

'Nobody's riding anywhere tonight,' Joel said.

Edith charged up to the third floor and burst into the

apartment. 'Americans!' she shouted jubilantly. 'They're at the top of the hill.'

Henderson shot up off the couch, but when he spoke he sounded suspicious. 'What do you mean? Tell me *exactly* what you saw.'

'Americans!' Edith shouted, as she jumped in the air and clapped.

Marc arrived last and began a more detailed explanation. As he spoke, he became aware of a rattling sound. It was clearly tank tracks, but they moved faster than the German tanks they'd grown used to and their petrol engines purred, in contrast to the slow chug of German diesel.

'*Now* I believe you,' Paul said, as he opened the front window to get a proper look.

Several other locals had thrown their windows open and shouts came from all directions.

'They're coming,' Paul screamed. 'We're gonna be all right!'

Luc burst in with Laure as the lead tanks started to cross the bridge. As Edith joined Paul at the window a squadron of British escort fighters swooped overhead, but apparently found nothing worth shooting at.

A nervous silence broke out as the American pathfinders made a dash for the city centre, but as clocks neared 02:30, the sound of Jeeps, tanks and trucks again filled the street. This time people shouting thanks to the

Americans out of their windows found indignant shouts coming back in French.

'We're no bloody Yanks. We're French!'

Even in daylight it would have been an easy mistake. The Free French Army wore rebadged American uniforms and rode in American-made vehicles. They poured down towards the bridge in such numbers that they were forced to knock down barricades and use other routes.

A church bell clanged as everyone headed downstairs. Luc caught up with Laure on the way down and raised one of her lads to his shoulders. As people poured out of their doorways, the street backed up with tanks and trucks painted with small French flags.

Girls in their night clothes jumped on the side of trucks and kissed soldiers. A French soldier shouted out of the top of a tank. 'Are the telephones working?'

The woman downstairs, who had the only telephone in the building, shouted back, 'Yes!'

'Call my mother on o-nine-eight-one. Tell her I'll be dropping in for breakfast!'

The single church bell became a chorus from all directions and someone placed a gramophone at an upstairs window and began playing *La Marseillaise*.

Henderson came down with his last bottle of champagne, to smiles and pats on the back from neighbours who'd been avoiding him all the previous day. After taking a couple of swigs Henderson passed the bottle into a truck, with no expectation of getting it back.

'I called your mother,' the woman downstairs cried, as the backed-up convoy started moving again. 'She said she's waiting for you and she loves you!'

Marc had tears streaking down his face as Edith jumped on to a tank and had her slender frame lifted into the turret.

'Where do you think you're going?' Henderson shouted cheerfully.

'Berlin or bust!' Edith shouted back, though she changed her mind and jumped down as her ride neared the bridge.

PT danced around with Laure's younger son balanced on his shoulders as the next line of trucks lit up the top of the hill.

'I can't believe they're finally here,' Paul said, looking at Marc. 'I wish Rosie could see this.'

'She *can*,' Marc said, as he gave Paul an almighty slap on the back. 'She's up there watching, and I bet she's bloody loving it!'

Aftermath

All facts correct as of December 2012.

PARIS

Allied planners wanted to divert troops around Paris, but the resistance uprising and pressure from the Free French led to a change of heart. In the event, American and French troops met little German resistance as they entered the western suburbs of Paris in the early hours of 24 August 1944. A lack of resources and a transport network crippled by bombing and sabotage meant that large-scale German reinforcements never reached the city.

Within two days, most of the troops who swept jubilantly through Paris had exited the city to the east. They were soon engaged in much bloodier battles as the Allies launched their final push towards Berlin.

Explosives had been placed around many of Paris' most important buildings, including the Louvre, the parliament building and the Eiffel Tower. Hitler gave orders that Paris be destroyed. However, the city's commander, General von Choltitz, did not pass these final orders on to the demolition teams.

To this day, von Choltitz is sometimes credited as the Nazi who saved Paris. Others claim that he didn't give the final order because he was keen to surrender to the Allies and save his own skin.

The whole of France was liberated by mid-September.

Resistance organisations disbanded, or morphed into new political parties. The Maquis emerged from the woods, while Milice and other German collaborators were subjected to brutal street justice.

As the hot summer of 1944 ended, most people thought that rapid Allied advances would end the war within months. But the fighting got tougher when the Allies reached Germany and another million people would die on European soil before Hitler committed suicide on 30 April 1945.

CHERUB

Charles Henderson's Espionage Research Unit B was one of more than a dozen intelligence organisations set up by the British during World War Two. As soon as the war in Europe ended, the heads of Britain's traditional intelligence services – MI5 and MI6 – moved ruthlessly to shut down their rivals.

CHERUB was officially closed on 1 October 1944. Campus and all facilities were mothballed. All of the organisation's documents were destroyed, including the records of twenty boys and one girl who were trained for duties in occupied France. As a result, there is no official history of the wartime CHERUB organisation and none of its staff or agents ever received medals, pensions or any other recognition for their war service.

A review of CHERUB's successful wartime activities, along with rising tensions between the new global superpowers of the United States and the Soviet Union, led to a decision to begin a new CHERUB organisation in July 1945. Charles Henderson was appointed head of the revived organisation, along with his deputies, Eileen McAfferty and Elizabeth DeVere (known as Boo).

McAfferty took charge of the organisation following the death of Charles Henderson and ran it for the following twenty-one years. Today, CHERUB campus is a one-of-a-kind intelligence facility that is home, school and training camp to more than 200 highly trained child agents.

PT BIVOTT

In the years immediately following World War Two, PT Bivott returned to working on civilian ships in the Mediterranean. In 1949 he was arrested in southern Italy and extradited to the United States on charges of armed robbery and second-degree murder, relating to an incident that took place in December 1938[3].

As PT was only thirteen at the time of the robbery, a judge agreed to give PT a suspended prison sentence, provided he report immediately to a recruiting office

---

[3] See *Henderson's Boys: Eagle Day*

and sign up for three years' military service.

PT's career in the US Navy was a chequered one, marked by a number of brawls and courts martial for running illegal gambling operations. This naval service was forcibly extended until 1953, due to the Korean War. He saw action on small boats in harassment and demolition operations along the Korean peninsula. PT was decorated for gallant service, but never promoted due to his poor disciplinary record.

Upon release from the US Navy, PT was approached by Eileen McAfferty with a view to joining the expanding post-war CHERUB organisation. PT joined the new CHERUB in early 1954. He served the organisation in various roles, including physical training instructor, and rose to become Deputy Chairman before taking retirement in 1985.

PT was twice married and had a daughter and two sons. He died in 2002 at the age of seventy-seven.

PAUL CLARKE

Paul Clarke returned to Great Britain shortly after the liberation of Paris. He had inherited a reasonable sum of money from his late parents and was enrolled in boarding school, spending school holidays with a maternal cousin whom he had not previously met.

Paul continued to excel in art and drawing. He

studied Art History at Cambridge University, and obtained a first-class degree. After university, Paul did two years' national service in the RAF and his drawing skills saw him assigned to a cartography department.

Throughout this period, Paul dated his long-term friend Edith Mercier, and they married when his national service ended in the summer of 1951. Edith gave birth to twin girls the following year and they went on to have three further children before divorcing in 1978.

Following his national service, Paul tried to make a career as an artist, without much success. A growing young family forced him to take a job in a small London art gallery and, with a keen business brain, he soon made enough money from buying and selling artwork to buy out his boss.

Over the following decades, Paul became a well-known figure in the art world. He was a pioneer of the contemporary art scene, with two galleries in London and additional spaces in Paris, New York and Los Angeles. He was appointed to museum boards in the UK and the United States and wrote two books on modern art.

Paul was a collector as well as a gallery owner and the explosion in contemporary art prices from the 1980s onwards meant that his wealth ballooned to a level in excess of £650 million at the time of his death.

Paul Clarke returned to Beauvais every summer to

visit his lifelong friend Marc Kilgour and the grave of his sister Rosie. He died in November 2011 at the age of eighty-three and was survived by his ex-wife Edith, three daughters, two sons and eleven grandchildren.

CHARLES HENDERSON

Henderson remained a controversial figure, both inside the Royal Navy and the intelligence service. His post-war career was overshadowed by an investigation into the illegal use of chemical weapons during a raid on an underground bunker used to design navigation systems for the V1 Rocket[4].

This investigation was never concluded. Facing a possible military tribunal and a wife who was in and out of mental institutions, Henderson had increasing problems with alcohol addiction and delegated most of the responsibility for setting up the post-war CHERUB organisation to his deputy, Eileen McAfferty.

A drunken row led to an incident in mid-1946 in which Henderson was fatally shot by his wife. She committed suicide two years later, while still awaiting trial for his murder.

Apart from his young son, Henderson had no family at the time of his death and his in-laws showed no

---

[4] See *Henderson's Boys: One Shot Kill*

interest in five-year-old Terence. The boy was adopted by Henderson's assistant, Eileen McAfferty, and became Terence McAfferty.

Terence McAfferty, more commonly known as *Mac*, became a CHERUB agent in 1950. After a career in business he returned to campus as a member of staff in 1983 and was the organisation's chairman from 1993 until his retirement in 2006.

LUC MAYEFSKI

Eileen McAfferty worked hard to find a suitable place for Luc after the wartime CHERUB organisation disbanded. He eventually scraped through the entrance exam for a British boarding school, but was expelled after several incidents of vicious bullying and the head-butting of a PE master.

Luc wound up homeless on the streets of London, but soon found work as a collection agent for a group of loan sharks. After heavy bombings, post-war London was desperately short of housing and shady landlords wanted to evict tenants paying low rents which were fixed by law. Luc thrived, first working as an enforcer for slum landlords and then by building his own property empire.

As Luc's success grew, he tried to position himself as a respectable property owner. This façade collapsed when a newspaper exposé described him as 'Britain's

Nastiest Landlord'. Following this, Luc was charged with several offences and served three years of a five-year prison sentence for aggravated assault, insurance fraud and conspiracy to commit arson. While in prison, Luc's property company was run by an accountant who stole large sums of money. Luc was released from prison in 1968 and declared bankrupt two months later.

Penniless and with his reputation in tatters, Luc moved to Spain and began a new property business. By the early 1980s Luc was enjoying life in a seafront villa with a girlfriend and two young daughters.

In June 1984, neighbours overheard screaming at the villa. Police found Luc's girlfriend bloody and battered after a violent row. Officers chased Luc's car as he tried to get away, but he lost control and died in a collision with an oncoming truck.

Luc was fifty-five years old and was survived by two young daughters and a son from a previous relationship.

MARC KILGOUR

Two days after Paris was liberated, Marc rode a bike to Morel's farm, north of Beauvais, and was reunited with his girlfriend. Both aged sixteen, Marc and Jae were married on Christmas Day 1944, and their first child was born three months later.

Jae's older brothers returned from four years as

prisoners of war in Germany, but both men had serious health problems, so it fell to Marc and Jae to put Morel's farm back into shape. As he was married with a young child and held responsibility for the farm, Marc received exemption from military service.

Marc and Jae waited six years for their second child and had five more over the decade that followed. They doubled the area of Morel's farm by buying up smaller neighbouring farms and led the lifestyle of a wealthy rural family with their seven children.

Marc remained troubled by many of the things he did during the war, and always refused to speak about them. His boyhood wanderlust never returned. He rarely left the Beauvais area and established himself as a pillar of the community. He became a patron of the orphanage where he'd been raised and made generous donations.

Marc also served a single term as Regional Mayor. He remained popular throughout his term of office but did not stand for re-election. Many people said he was simply too nice for the cut and thrust of politics.

Jae Kilgour died in 2009, two weeks after their sixty-fifth wedding anniversary. At the time of writing, Marc Kilgour is eighty-five years old and in good health. He is retired and the family farm is now run by his eldest daughter, Rosie.

OTHER CHARACTERS FEATURED IN THE HENDERSON'S BOYS SERIES

Instructors *Kindhe Boyamour* and *Rufus Kadiri* returned to their pre-war careers working on ships plying cargo between northern Africa and the Middle East.

Campus assistant *Elizabeth DeVere* (Boo) worked on CHERUB campus until she retired in 1987. She died in February 2012 and was survived by three children.

Maxine Clere married a French politician and had two children. She wrote a successful autobiography about her work with the Ghost Circuit, which omitted all references to Charles Henderson and his team. The book was made into a French-language film and a BBC television drama. She received medals from France, Britain and Israel for her wartime service and died in 2006, aged ninety-one.

Mason LeConte was the only one of Henderson's wartime agents to become an agent in the post-war CHERUB. He retired after several successful missions and engaged in a brief career as a racing driver, before retiring to run a garage near to CHERUB campus.

For many years Mason prepared and maintained

vehicles used on CHERUB missions. He still lives close to campus and although he is seventy-eight years old, he still occasionally lends a hand when the CHERUB vehicle shop is short-staffed.

Troy LeConte studied architecture and worked as a manager in Paul Clarke's London gallery. He is currently the trustee of a project to build a permanent gallery to house Paul Clarke's art collection.

The captured German E-Boat known as *Madeline II* was one of the few examples of the type to survive the war. She was used as a support ship by the British Navy until it became impossible to get spare parts. She has now been restored to her original wartime specification and is on display at the Royal Navy museum in Portsmouth. All records of her capture and role with CHERUB were destroyed.

Eileen McAfferty was chairwoman of CHERUB for twenty-one years. She married in her sixties and died following a short illness in 1985.

Campus assistant *Joyce Slater* worked on CHERUB campus for more than twenty years. She was forced to leave the secret organisation when she became a well-known figure in the disability rights movement. Joyce went on to become head of an international aid organisation and was a government advisor on disability issues throughout the 1970s and 80s. She has been a member of the House of Lords since 1988 and still regularly attends debates.

Combat instructor *Takada* worked at CHERUB campus until his retirement in the 1970s. His daughter still works on campus in the same role.

Brothers *Joel* and *Sam Voclain* stayed in France and worked as butcher and heating engineer respectively. Joel died in 2004. Sam is retired and lives in Portugal.

The bodies of the last two orphans kidnapped by the 108th Heavy Tank Battalion were never found. The Beauvais orphanage near Morel's farm is now a modern day-care facility and primary school. A monument on the site commemorates the lives of the five orphans and the nun who was killed while trying to stop them being taken away.

THE ESCAPE
Robert Muchamore

Hitler's army is advancing towards Paris, and amidst the chaos, two British children are being hunted by German agents. British spy Charles Henderson tries to reach them first, but he can only do it with the help of a twelve-year-old French orphan.

The British secret service is about to discover that kids working undercover will help to win the war.

Book 1 – OUT NOW

www.hendersonsboys.com

Hodder
Children's
Books

SECRET ARMY
Robert Muchamore

The government is building a secret army of intelligence agents to work undercover. Henderson's boys are part of that network: kids cut adrift by the war, training for the fight of their lives. They'll have to parachute into unknown territory, travel cross-country and outsmart a bunch of adults in a daredevil exercise.

In wartime Britain, anything goes.

Book 3 – OUT NOW

GREY WOLVES
Robert Muchamore

German submarines are prowling the North Atlantic, sinking ships filled with the food, fuel and weapons that Britain needs to survive.

With the Royal Navy losing the war at sea, six young agents must sneak into Nazi-occupied Europe and sabotage a submarine base on France's western coast.

If the submarines aren't stopped, the British people will starve.

Book 4 — OUT NOW

www.hendersonsboys.com

h
Hodder
Children's
Books

THE PRISONER
Robert Muchamore

One of Henderson's best agents is being held captive in Frankfurt. A set of forged record cards could be his ticket to freedom, but might just as easily become his death warrant.

A vital mission awaits him in France - if he can find a way to escape.

Book 5 – OUT NOW

www.hendersonsboys.com

ONE SHOT KILL
Robert Muchamore

Spring, 1943. The war is turning against Germany, but Hitler isn't giving up. In a secret bunker deep in occupied France, scientists are hard at work on Hitler's latest deadly weapon: code name FZG-76.

Back in England Henderson's boys will need to undergo advanced sniper training if they've any chance of infiltrating the bunker. Parachuting into occupied France, they track down a secret dossier filled with invaluable material - and uncover the meaning of the enigmatic code.

Book 6 – OUT NOW

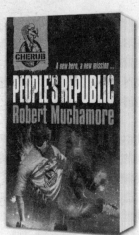